KILLER IN PARADISE

John Leslie

Prologue

December 22, 1988

"Listen, I don't give a damn if you're Hopalong Cassidy," the man said. "Move the fuckin' car so I can get out of here."

Lieutenant Patrick Bowman watched it all from the steps of an appliance store on Chicago's South Side. Bowman, a Chicago cop for nearly twenty years and a homicide detective for the past fifteen, had been investigating a murder in the area when the fracas began.

The guy standing between two cars, a double-parked Nissan Sentra and a Chrysler LeBaron, was screaming through the open window at the driver of the LeBaron. "Let me tell you who the fuck I am," the Nissan owner shouted. He was young, no more than thirty, while the guy in the LeBaron was probably in his fifties. He looked like Ricardo Montalban, sleek, slick, and silver, doing an ad for Chrysler.

"I already told you I don't give a shit who you are," the Montalban type said. "And I don't have time to fuck around here all day."

"No, but you got all the time you want to fuck my wife."

Patrick couldn't believe it. He looked around for the cameras, thinking somebody had to be filming. Lee was in Key West, where he would join her tomorrow. He'd tell her this, and he could picture the funny thing she did with her mouth, the way her front teeth with the space between them would nibble at her lower lip just before she started to laugh.

3

He'd been thinking about her earlier, too, because it was here on the South Side where they'd met fifteen years ago. Two blocks from where he stood. He couldn't believe the way the place had changed, from a working-class neighborhood to Yuppieville.

Montalban, leaning across the front seat, just looked at the guy standing beside the Nissan, then sat up in the seat, cool now, and said, "What do you want?"

"I want you, bozo," the guy said. "And I got you right where I want you."

Montalban opened the door of the LeBaron. He stepped out of the car. "I'm going to call the cops," he said.

Patrick knew he was too late, knew he'd waited too long to step into this even as he began to move. He could see the whole thing coming down as he skipped down the steps of the appliance store, his wallet out, showing his badge and ID, while the guy beside the Nissan lifted a gun out of his coat pocket, saying, "You're going nowhere but dead, bozo."

"Police," Patrick shouted, while at the same time reaching with his free hand beneath his overcoat for his Browning nine-millimeter automatic.

The guy between the Nissan and the LeBaron fired what looked like a small-caliber handgun, and Montalban fell to the sidewalk.

Patrick was beside the driver's door of the LeBaron, his body turned sideways, his own weapon held steady against the car top, pointing at the Nissan owner.

"Police," Patrick repeated. "Drop the gun."

The guy swiveled toward Patrick. Patrick could no longer see the guy's gun, but he heard it go off and felt a sensation like someone had pinched the flesh just above his hip. Patrick fired once and watched the guy between the Nissan and the LeBaron drop.

Jesus. It had just occurred to him that Lee wasn't going to find any of this funny, when his legs gave out and he was on the sidewalk, too.

1

She was standing with her back against the old Civil War fortress, the West Martello Tower, one foot propped against the brick facade, her tight black skirt hiked up to reveal bare leg. It was a classic pose, designed to stop a man in his tracks.

Darling stopped her perambulation of the beach and watched the girl who leaned against the wall of the fort. The moon was high and full. Its light seemed to fall like a heavenly spotlight, flooding the girl in the black skirt. Darling thought of the full moon as her time of month.

She looked around the beach. A couple of guys were walking hand in hand close to the wall that joined the one against which the girl leaned. They were walking in the opposite direction, away from the girl. There was no one else on the beach. A few cars passed by on the road in the distance but didn't stop.

It was a perfect night. A light breeze out of the east, about seventy-two degrees, and two days before Christmas. Darling sighed; the tropics.

She wondered about the girl. She'd seen her out here two or three nights in a row. If the girl knew that this was a gay hangout, she didn't seem to care. Darling had watched her get picked up once or twice, not really enough to make any money. The girl took her tricks into the alcove at the front of the fort which was in shadows, partially hidden from the street, where she probably gave blowjobs for five, maybe ten dollars. Pin money; drug money.

As she walked toward the girl, wondering if she was from out of town, Darling nervously fiddled with the clasp on the purse that hung from her right shoulder.

When she reached the girl, Darling said, "Hey, slow night."

The girl nodded, and put her leg down so that both feet were now on the ground. She was twenty, twenty-one. Maybe not even that.

"Guys are doing the same thing you're doing around the corner, and they're doing it for free. You know that, don't you, honey?"

The girl shrugged. "I do okay," she said.

"I've got some smoke," Darling said. "You wanna do a number?"

"Sure," the girl said.

Darling walked with her around to the front of the fort and into the alcove where the girl gave her five-dollar blowjobs. "Where you from?" Darling asked.

"Montreal," the girl said.

Darling took a hand-rolled joint from her purse and a cheap Bic lighter. She held the joint lightly between her lips and lit it with the Bic. She inhaled deeply and passed the joint to the girl. "It's cold up there. I can see why you'd want to come to Key West."

The girl sucked on the joint.

"You come all the way down here by yourself?"

The girl nodded, holding the smoke in, then said, no, she'd come down with a guy who had run off and left her stranded here.

"What's your name?" Darling asked.

"Francine," the girl said, exhaling. She took another hit, and Darling moved around beside her, her hand in her purse. Francine exhaled. She turned toward Darling. "What's yours?"

Darling put her arm around the girl's shoulders and smiled. In the same motion she removed her right hand from the purse. She was holding a six-inch filleting knife. Francine didn't see the knife; she was holding the joint out to Darling, looking toward the street, beginning to move away from Darling's grasp.

Darling gripped the girl's shoulders tightly and brought the knife up, the thin steel blade splitting the skin of her throat. Blood ran down her neck and clothing. Francine dropped to the ground. Darling watched her there, blood spreading on the cement floor of the fort. She listened, entranced, to the strange sounds that came from the girl's throat.

"Darling," Darling said, in answer to Francine's question. And walked out into the street.

In the early morning light the Marquesas looked like a giant jigsaw puzzle, Patrick Bowman thought. Everything was so startlingly clear, each detail of the isolated chain of mangrove islands that lay some thirty miles west of Key West, the nearest inhabited land.

Patrick stood on the bow of the nineteen-foot fishing skiff, blind casting for barracuda, while his guide, Bill Peachy, poled them across the shallow water of the flats from his poling platform built above the skiff's outboard. Except for an occasional fishing boat in the distance, and, a couple of times a day, the seaplane when it flew round-trip to the Tortugas from Key West, they were alone.

It was just what the doctor ordered, literally. Take some time off, he'd told Patrick. Relax, take it easy for a while. For a man who'd walked away from a gunshot wound with nothing more serious than some trauma and a case of damaged pride, it was not bad advice, Patrick had decided.

He arrived in Key West with the Browning nine-millimeter he had used to wound the crazed and jealous husband in Chicago. He had also brought a fax machine so that he could keep up with the precinct report work that he'd fallen behind on.

Now he watched as a cormorant took flight, skimming across the surface, the black, heavy tail feathers dripping water as its swept-back wings beat against the air, trying to get airborne; cormorants rose off the water around here with the regularity of fighter jets from an aircraft carrier.

Shoreward, a lone white heron and, nearby, an egret, stood one-legged in the shallows, casting motionless eyes into the still water that had the clarity of a mountain stream.

You could almost hate yourself for the idea of being anywhere else but here, Patrick thought. He thought about all the years in Chicago, the early years when he'd walked a beat in the cold, numbing winters before he moved up the ranks and off the streets, to finally become a detective.

For more than ten years he'd been coming here on vacations with Lee. And every time he came he wondered why he didn't just stay.

Deep down he knew why; sitting out here day after day without anything else to do might make the whole scene lose its impact. Also, he was a cop first, then a fisherman.

" 'Cuda at eleven o'clock!" Bill Peachy said quietly, urgently.

Patrick had been casting blind back into the sun on the opposite side of the boat, where it was impossible to spot fish against the glare on the water.

Patrick reeled in the green tube lure and turned, opening the baler, looking to the left of the boat where Peachy pointed, ready to cast as soon as he saw the barracuda.

"He's twenty yards out in the nearside of that white patch," Peachy said. "Facing to the north. He's big. Twenty, maybe twenty-five pounds."

Patrick scanned the light patches of water above several sandy bottoms and saw the fish. Motionless, hovering, a long dark shape at the edge of the sandbar. It would be an easy cast, downwind. Patrick eased the rod back and flicked it overhead, arcing the green tube out thirty-five yards, ten yards beyond the fish, and closed the baler just before the tube splashed the water. He reeled fast, the rod tip down, keeping the tube straight; it was going to pass within five or six yards of the barracuda's nose.

"Good cast," Peachy said. "He's seen it. He's coming."

Patrick continued to reel steadily. He saw the splash of water as the 'cuda turned to follow the lure; coming straight for the boat now, like a goddamn torpedo. Patrick concentrated on keeping the lure in the water, waiting for the strike. The fish was twenty feet from the boat, closing rapidly on the bow. Patrick could see the teeth bared against grinning jaws.

Seconds before he would have rammed the boat, the 'cuda struck, took the lure and ran like a stampeding bull elephant back and forth, crisscrossing in front of the bow of the boat then heading out toward deeper water and finally rocketing from the sea, arching in the sunlight, a mottled bar of silver that fell back to the water in one quivering assault which shook the hook from its mouth.

"Jesus Christ," Patrick said.

"Amen," Bill Peachy said.

When there was a lull, they paused for lunch. It was after one o'clock. Patrick ate a Cuban Mix sandwich which he'd had made up early that morning at the Sunbeam on White Street, a twenty-four-hour convenience store.

While they ate, Patrick told Peachy about the shooting in Chicago ten days ago.

"You been a cop for twenty years," Bill Peachy said, "and that's the first time you were ever shot?" Patrick watched while Peachy took the shells off three hardboiled eggs, salted them, and ate them one after the other.

"And I hope the last," Patrick said.

"What's it like?"

Peachy, always restless, walked around the boat checking the fishing gear before climbing up on the poling platform to begin looking for fish again. He was slender, with a slight build and a careless, almost feminine grace. He reminded Patrick of a dancer.

"It doesn't feel like anything. The hurt comes later."

Bill Peachy shook his head. "Lucky," he said. "I guess you heard about the kid on the beach got killed a couple weeks ago."

It was all he had heard about. He had spent Christmas in the hospital in Chicago, and for a week Lee, who had come to Key West after Thanksgiving to open up the house, had called him every day. She gave him the news about the girl who'd had her throat cut on the beach. When he got here yesterday, people were still talking about it, even though a week had gone by since the murder; but it was the second murder in Key West in little more than a month.

Patrick finished his sandwich and stuffed the wrapper inside the ice chest in front of the console. "Yeah, I heard," he said.

"You going to get involved?"

When the chief of detectives had called on Patrick in the hospital, the third day after he'd been shot, to tell him that the department was granting a six-week leave of absence along with two weeks accrued vacation time, Patrick's first thought was of the backcountry fishing he'd be able to do. The day he came out of surgery, he wasn't even sure he'd ever walk again, and two days later he was not only walking, but had a two-month unexpected vacation.

"I'm here to fish," Patrick said. In the past ten years he had gained some notoriety among national law-enforcement officials, a reputation that had briefly extended into the public sector when he'd appeared on interviews for national TV a couple of times to discuss crime and his success in solving some of Chicago's more heinous murder cases, many of them cases that had been still open after years of unfruitful investigation by other detectives. He had achieved some fame as an expert in the detection of serial killers, and had been called on more than once by police agencies in other cities when they were stymied.

Patrick gave up the TV appearances shortly before they threatened to turn him into a public celebrity.

"The talk around town is that Raul Jiminez isn't up to this," Bill Peachy said. Patrick had heard of Jiminez, Key West's chief of police. He'd come in under a cloud when the former chief was indicted. Jiminez, who'd been the second-in-command—and who many thought should have been indicted, too—was promoted to the top job.

"Give him a chance," Patrick said.

"All right," Peachy said. "But it's like that 'cuda you let get away. How many chances do you get to land a fish like that?"

"You're too competitive." Patrick smiled. "This is supposed to be fun."

Bill Peachy laughed. "Well, Happy New Year," he said, and started the engine.

Patrick remembered that he and Lee were going to a formal New Year's Eve party tonight. Here, in the Marquesas, it was easy to forget that social world. Violent death was less forgettable.

2

Patrick Bowman winced as pain shot across his lower back. He was stretched out naked on the bed in the upstairs bedroom, lying on his stomach while Lee massaged him.

The house, like others of a similar design in Key West, was known as an eyebrow house because of the way the roof slanted across the second-story windows. From where he lay, looking out one of those windows, Patrick could count the stars in the sky. The beauty of the night was bruised only by a breeze that carried the acrid smell of cat piss.

Patrick turned his head away from the window and saw his tuxedo hanging from a hook on the door to the bathroom. He was indifferent to clothes, but wearing a tux for the evening was no problem. It pleased Lee. She liked to see him, all six feet four of him, gussied up. He was much less at ease at the island's various literary cocktail parties than he was in a tuxedo.

Lee's hands kneaded his shoulders, then worked their way down to his lower back, where his muscles automatically tensed. "Hurt?" she asked.

"Only when I laugh."

Lee laughed and nudged his waist with her hands. He turned over. She said, "Don't laugh," and bent forward, taking him in her mouth.

He couldn't laugh. It was too goddamn depressing.

It was crazy. The day he was shot he'd been distracted, thinking about Lee. One of the rare times; he had always discussed his cases with Lee, but he didn't take his home to work. It was guys sitting around talking about their wives, families, or their girlfriends, who were always the most vulnerable.

Patrick didn't do it—except on the day he was shot back in the neighborhood where he and Lee had first met, two blocks from the bar where he was having a beer fifteen years ago and she had come in. Tall, auburn-haired, green eyes, a quirky smile. Pretty, he thought. Too pretty, and he had ignored her, not wanting to risk rejection.

She spoke to him, though mostly small talk. She was from Wisconsin, lived in New York, where she worked as a model. She was in Chicago on a magazine assignment (he remembered being glad she didn't call it a shoot), and with an afternoon free, she was trying to get away from some of the glitz and glitter of studios and fancy hotels. She was walking around the city and had wandered into this neighborhood, where she decided to stop for a drink.

In other words, she was out slumming, he thought.

He didn't tell her right away that he was a cop. It was 1973, and cops—especially Chicago cops, like the military—weren't much in favor. He'd been called pig and spat upon before, but it was a day off and he'd looked forward to enjoying it, not having to defend himself.

She talked about Wisconsin, growing up there, what she missed about the Midwest while in New York. When he finally did answer her directly and tell her what he did, she was interested. She asked questions, good questions, and they talked for a couple of hours.

Then she stood up to leave. Patrick got up, too. Thinking perhaps they could go on, he could take her to dinner, the risk of rejection seemed more worth taking now. She couldn't, she said. There was work waiting for her; she was late now. They stood facing each other. She put her finger on his chest and then kissed him on the cheek.

"I like you," she said. And was gone.

Patrick had another beer.

A couple of weeks later he got a note from New York. It came care of the precinct, handwritten from Lee. "We met in an offbeat bar in Chicago two weeks ago," she said. "I was in a red dress, dark hair, green eyes, and a Wisconsin frame of mind. And I honestly would like to see you again."

At the end of the letter was a portion of a poem: "Lord, let me not wander in barren dreams, yet when I am consumed by the fire... grant me new Phoenix wings to fly at my desire."

Patrick was inflamed. He went out and looked up the poem with the help of a librarian, found that it was by Keats and that Lee hadn't gotten it exactly right. Which he liked. He called her and told her so. And she flew to Chicago, not on Phoenix wings, but a nerve-rackingly late Delta flight.

Fifteen years later he got himself shot near that bar, one he'd often gone back to over the years.

Now, with her mouth on him, caressing him with her tongue, he felt no response. Jesus.

She lifted her head. "Don't worry." She smiled. "We'll keep

16

working at it."

He did worry, but was glad that she wasn't giving up.

He had tried to explain to Lee what had happened. The bullet, from a .25-caliber handgun, had struck him just above the pelvic bone and was deflected off a vertebra before lodging in the lumbar region of his lower back. Luckily, it had missed any organs, but it did cause a hematoma, which put pressure on the sac containing the spinal cord. He had lost all sensation in his lower extremities. A little more luck kept him conscious, and neurosurgeons got to work within an hour after he was shot.

When he came out of surgery it was two of three hours before the feeling was back in his legs. That was the good news; the bad news was that after a week in the hospital he hadn't had one erection, not even in the morning, when he woke.

The doctor told him not to worry about it. It was trauma-related and everything would soon be normal. Just take it easy; don't rush things.

Lee was understanding; Patrick worried.

"Let's stay home from the party and work on it," he said.

Lee got up from the bed. "Not so fast, buster," she said. "The doctor said not to rush things."

"What did he say about going to formal literary cocktail parties?"

"He said it's good for you. Makes you a more well- rounded cop."

"I just want to be a hard cop." Patrick smiled. "Who's going to be at the party?"

"Everybody, including the chief of police, Raul Jiminez."

"Jesus. Thank God, I can still fish."

"Would you rather fish or fuck?"

He picked a pillow off the bed and threw it at her. "I love it when you talk dirty."

Patrick took his time dressing. Lee was ready. After years of quick-change modeling assignments, she could be made-up and dressed to the teeth in a matter of minutes. She took no pleasure in spending hours primping in the bathroom. Patrick shaved and showered and went downstairs to the kitchen and fixed himself a light rum and tonic.

He was clipping on the black bow tie when Lee, half reading while seated in the bedroom in a wicker chair plumped with cushions, said, "You're going to get pumped about these murders. It's all people are talking about."

"I just got here. I'm just a cop, not a magician."

"Your reputation got here before you. You know how people are."

He reached for his cummerbund on the bed, wrapped it around his waist, then adjusted the strap so that it was loose, slightly drooping like a pouch. "They've got their own police force here."

"Apparently there's not much confidence in the chief of police."

"So I've already heard."

"So be prepared."

"And I'm not a Boy Scout either."

"No, but you're a good cop." She stood up, came over and held

18

his jacket out for him to slip into. Then kissed him.

"A disabled cop," he said, still clowning. But Lee didn't hear him, or pretended not to hear. She had already turned and started down the stairs.

3

It was a perfect night, cool, clear, under a full moon. Lee drove. The car, a '63 Buick Riviera, powder-blue, the first of the Buick sports cars, was the car her father—Wisconsin's leading dairy farmer—had given her the year she graduated from high school, the same year she was crowned the state's Miss Dairy Maid.

Patrick understood her attachment to old cars in the same way that he understood her love of elegant parties and fancy clothes—which was to say, not very much at all. But he got some pleasure in indulging her whims. She loved him for that.

She loved him for other things, too. She had her independence. Yet, Patrick was always there for her, and for the most part predictable. She had had to rely upon him more than once to get her out of some jams she seemed to get into from some fault in character. Inherited, she always said, from her father. But Patrick was always understanding; he had never judged or criticized her.

If she had any complaint, it was that he was too involved in his work. But at least she was interested in what he did, and he never excluded her. She even had to admit that she got a certain pleasure out of being married to a famous cop.

A sort of reverse snobbery, Lee thought. The debutante, the society girl, married to a cop. She had come to like it even though she'd had other feelings earlier in their marriage.

Cars were piled up along Washington Street in front of Hamilton Wade's colonnaded home. She had to park two blocks away. They walked back along the street as other cars arrived, and searched for a parking place.

"You look great, Lee," Patrick said. She was wearing a black strapless evening gown from the fifties that she'd found in a fashionable used-clothing store in New York, where she liked to shop. She seldom wore anything new.

She squeezed Patrick's hand. "And you're stunning, Lieutenant."

"Let's try to forget I'm a cop for the next couple of months," Patrick said. "I'm on leave of absence."

A two-month leave of absence. It had been in the back of her mind since Patrick had announced that the force was giving him the time off. She was unaccustomed to having him in Key West for that length of time. It was going to be interesting. As they walked up the brick steps to the wide porch of Wade's colonial mansion, she wondered how she was going to get herself out of the little jam she was in now. And just how understanding Patrick was going to be.

"Baby, you are gorgeous." Hamilton Wade was at the front door as they came in. He hugged Lee, then kissed her on the lips.

Patrick had always assumed that Wade was gay. The excessive emotional displays, the extravagance of the huge house occupied by a single man, the foppish dress—billowing silk shirts and expensive soft leather shoes all contributed to the stereotype of a wealthy gay male, of whom so many resided in Key West.

"And you're not bad yourself," Wade said, taking Patrick's hand, then releasing it and embracing him. Patrick wasn't uncomfortable with Wade; all the repetitious pomp just became boring after a while.

Wade was a novelist, although it had been ten years since he'd last published anything. Royalties, along with a couple of successful movies based on earlier books, and some good investments, kept him financially secure.

As far as Patrick could tell, all the guy did was give fancy parties. And while one would have lasted Patrick a long time, Lee loved them. And so for the next two months he could expect to be entertained by Hamilton Wade at least once a week, while seeing him at similar gatherings two or three other times a week. It was a party town.

"Baby, just everybody's here," Wade said, taking Lee's arm and leading her through the house and into the open garden, where there was an Olympic-sized swimming pool. Patrick followed, his eye on the bar. It was the price he paid for marrying a beautiful woman. At least he went to bed with her at night, not that that counted for much these days.

There was a pig roasting on an open spit in one corner by the pool. A small combo played at the other end, where a patio had been set with large Cuban tiles, offering enough space to accommodate dancers. Several couples swayed to a tropical beat. More people were congregated around the bar, where two young men in white shirts and bow ties tried to keep up with the drink orders.

Patrick decided to stop at the self-service bar that had been set up inside the house and where he could free-pour his own. He caught Lee's eye, winked, and trailed off to the bar.

He stood with his back to the wall, sipping expensive imported rum, and surveyed the crowd. There were several familiar faces from previous years, people with whom he would soon be having meals every other night, but the vast majority of the crowd he didn't recognize, although he did see Key West's gay mayor wander by, and a few city commissioners whose faces he knew from the local paper. He guessed there were over a hundred people here already, and more coming in all the time.

He looked at his watch, poured a second drink. It was only ten-thirty. He couldn't hope to escape this madness before midnight, and by then he'd be lucky to find Lee at all. Another two hours of drinking.

A man in a formal white *guyaberra* shirt stopped at the service bar and poured from the same bottle of rum that Patrick had. The man was short but handsome, with finely-chiseled features and mocha skin. Patrick guessed he was Cuban, the guess confirmed when the little guy offered a bejeweled hand and said, "Raul Jiminez."

"Patrick Bowman," Patrick said. Key West's chief of police. Great. Here he was after only five minutes, about to talk shop with another cop.

"I saw you come in with Lee," Raul said. "You're the lucky husband."

"That's me," Patrick said.

"And the famous cop?"

Patrick smiled. "On a medical leave of absence." "Anything serious?"

23

"The usual occupational hazard. I was shot."

Raul raised his pencil-thin eyebrows. "I didn't think famous cops got shot."

Patrick heard the sarcasm in the chief's voice. Or was he just imagining it?

"Somebody forgot to put it in the manual."

Raul held up his glass and said, "To your recovery." Patrick raised his own glass and drank.

"You hear about our troubles here?"

"The girl on the beach?"

Jiminez nodded.

There was a certain amount of relief in professional talk. Patrick was sure that the Cuban was as uncomfortable here as he was.

"You having any luck?" Patrick asked. The band was on a break. People were lining up for the roast pig which was being served with black beans, yellow rice, and Cuban bread.

"She was a street hustler, twenty years old," Jiminez said. "Turning tricks out on the beach. She'd been around here for a week, according to some guys who had seen her hanging out."

Patrick saw Lee come into the house from the patio and go upstairs. When she came back down, he'd use her as an excuse to slip away from Jiminez.

"She live here?"

Jiminez shook his head. "Canadian. From Montreal. You want to hear something strange? If she hadn't been killed, she would have been dead in six months."

Patrick felt his interest rise. It had happened before when a case went from the routine to the unusual. He had an uncanny ability to pick out some piece of information that was seemingly irrelevant but could often wind up turning things around.

"You did an autopsy?"

Jiminez nodded again. "The chick had AIDS."

"Jesus." Patrick poured himself another drink. The mayor walked over and began talking with Jiminez. Patrick went to find Lee.

She was looking for Hamilton. He had pulled her onto the dance floor when she and Patrick first arrived and was practically humping her right there in front of everybody. Patrick, thankfully, was inside the house. Despite Wade's reputation for this sort of thing, she knew Patrick would have been more embarrassed than hurt if he'd witnessed it.

She wanted to tell Hamilton now, privately, before it got out of hand. She had made a mistake in going to bed with the guy when she came down this year just after Thanksgiving. That had to stop now.

Lee had had a few affairs over the years (she wasn't sure if Patrick had), but she never let them interfere with her life with him. The first sign of trouble and she'd always gotten out. (Someone had once told her that she had a taste for the low life, and she said no, she just had a taste for life.) But she could see trouble with Hamilton; it was time to get out before it escalated.

When she'd broken away from him after the dance, he'd told her to come up. Then she'd seen him go upstairs.

She went, passing Patrick, who was talking to Raul Jiminez. In the back bedroom half a dozen people were standing around a dresser where there was a silver platter containing a fist-size mound of cocaine. Some were snorting straight from the pile; Hamilton wasn't among them.

She backed out and went down the hall to the bathroom. She opened the door. Hamilton Wade was standing in front of the wall mirror above the sink. A young woman was pressed up against him, both of them facing the mirror as she ground herself against him. The top of her dress was down, and Hamilton's arms encircled her, his hands lingering over her nipples as they both watched in the mirror.

When Lee opened the door, they turned to look at her, smiling. She closed the door and walked back down the hall.

"Rather like Jack the Ripper, isn't it?" Wystan Lewis said. Lewis was English. Patrick always felt ill at ease around him, as he did around all short people, because Lewis, no more than five five, had to crane his neck to maintain eye contact with Patrick. He also had a prominent Adam's apple which bobbed up and down when he talked, reminding Patrick of a newborn bird at feeding time.

Lewis, however, had the self-confidence that was the product of a superior attitude, which, Patrick thought, many upper-class Brits seemed to like to affect around their American cousins.

The mayor, Eric Sheldon, said, "Two women killed in a month's time I don't think is cause to make a case for a Jack the Ripper on the loose."

The band had taken another break. Some people were still eating. Others drifted in and out of group conversations.

"They never caught Jack the Ripper, did they?" someone said.

"No," Wystan Lewis said, "they didn't." He turned to the mayor. "But how many dead women does it take before you accept that we have a serial killer on the island?"

The mayor shrugged. "There's no reason to alarm people with those kind of scare tactics." The mayor was protecting the tourist economy, Patrick thought.

"How about another Ted Bundy, then?"

Bundy was scheduled to be executed in three weeks.

Wystan Lewis looked up at Patrick. "We've got an expert on serial killers right here. Why not ask him?"

Patrick smiled. "Give me a chance. I just got here," he said. "I don't know that much about the case."

"Two women killed on the beach about a month apart. They were homeless and probably hustling. Random violence, or the product of one sick man?"

Patrick saw Raul Jiminez join the group just as Lewis was asking his question. Party chatter. Last year they were talking about politics, this year it was murder. Whatever was hot.

Patrick said, "With no more details, I couldn't answer that. No one could. There's no way of knowing."

Jiminez smiled at him.

A woman stepped up, put her hand on Patrick's arm and said,

"Doesn't he look like pictures of Hemingway when he first came to Key West?"

Patrick smiled and stepped out of the group. He poured himself another drink and went to look for Lee.

At midnight she kissed Patrick to the sound of plastic noisemakers, popping balloons, and a calypso version of "Auld Lang Syne." Patrick was high but not drunk, pressing her close to him, kissing her longer than most women married for fifteen years would have expected.

She said, "Let me say good night to Hamilton and we'll go home."

"Guess what," he said.

"What?"

"One of your women literary friends told me I look like Hemingway. Was that supposed to be a compliment?"

Lee laughed. "I hope you told her your name was Jake Barnes."

"Don't be cruel."

She went to find Hamilton Wade for the second time that evening. He seemed to have disappeared again, but this time she wasn't going to open any bathroom doors looking for him. Patrick was waiting at the front door for her. They said good-bye and walked out, toward their car, with a few people who were also leaving.

Other people were out, and as a car came around the corner, she thought she saw Hamilton Wade walking a block away, going toward the beach.

The digital clock on the bedside table read two a.m. Lee heard the phone ring once, twice, felt Patrick's foot rub gently against her ankle. Half asleep, she reached out to answer it.

It was Hamilton Wade.

"Baby, you won't believe this." He sounded high, distraught.

When she and Patrick had left the party shortly after midnight, they had driven along the beach front, looking at the sea, the moon, talking about the party, the people they'd seen and talked to, then gone home, had a nightcap and gone to bed. Tomorrow, she had promised herself before going to sleep, she would call Hamilton Wade and talk to him.

He called her first.

"Please, it's two o'clock in the morning," Lee whispered.

"Baby, I know what time it is. This is important."

She was awake now. She felt Patrick turn over in the bed.

"What's wrong?" she asked.

"Another girl was killed."

"When?"

"An hour ago. The police called here for Jiminez. They sent a squad car over here for him."

Lee felt numb. She wanted to hang up and cling to Patrick. Why had Hamilton singled her out to call about this at this hour of the morning?

"She had her throat cut, just like the other two," Hamilton said. "Jiminez has got a problem on his hands."

Hamilton was still high, but there was something in his tone of

29

voice that bothered her. He sounded elated.

4

Patrick was up at five. A mild hangover tormented the edges of his brain. Had he been able to sleep, he knew he could have slept it off, but he was an insomniac. For the past fifteen years, and beginning a few years after he'd returned from Vietnam, he'd slept only five, sometimes six hours a night. Rather than fight it, however, he'd learned to make use of the early mornings, the one time of day when he would be totally alone, without interruptions, when he could give all his attention to whatever case he was on at the time.

It was times like these, however, when he wasn't working, that he missed the luxury of being able to sleep in—only an insomniac could understand sleep as a luxury.

He had slept fitfully through what was left of the night when they returned from Hamilton Wade's New Year's Eve bash. Awakened when Wade had called, he had talked briefly to Lee, then tried to get back to sleep, only to wake up every hour, stare at the luminous dial on his wristwatch and listen enviously to Lee's regular breathing. His mind had begun to chew on the killing spree, his mental process not unlike the slow, invisible assault of termites on Key West's frame houses.

Now he sat at the kitchen table with a mug of coffee and the Browning stripped down on a back issue of the *Key West Citizen.* While he cleaned the gun he thought about the three dead girls in Key West. However annoying his inability to keep his mind free of work, he had always taken some pleasure in trying to find the early links that invariably helped solve these cases.

When he finished cleaning the gun, he poured more coffee, got a yellow legal pad, and began to make some notes. He was on vacation; he did not have to be involved with this case. And his initial impression of Raul Jiminez was that the chief wouldn't want him to be involved with the case, either. Small-town police chiefs were usually little inclined to accept help from their cousins in the city. Which was just fine with Patrick; he wasn't going to offer his help. But if it was requested, it wouldn't hurt to have a head start.

Lee, knowing his habits, had saved some back issues of the *Citizen* and the *Miami Herald* detailing the two murders. On his legal pad Patrick wrote down the dead girls' names, their ages, and the date, time, place, and manner of death.

The first victim had been discovered in the dense shrubbery and mangroves near the bridal path across the road from Smathers Beach along South Roosevelt Boulevard, her throat cut. The second victim was the girl from Montreal who had had AIDS and whose throat was cut at the West Martello Tower, also near a beach, Patrick observed. Both girls were killed at night. The most recent victim, according to Wade's early morning phone call to Lee, had died in the same manner and at about the same time as the other two girls, and on the beach.

The first two victims were street people, girls who were runaways, prostitutes, or both, victims even before they became the ultimate victim, Patrick thought.

The paper did not mention that the Montreal girl had had AIDS, Patrick noticed, nor was there mention of an autopsy report on either girl, even though Jiminez had confirmed that an autopsy had been performed on the girl from Montreal. Patrick made a note to check for autopsy reports, if Jiminez should ask for his help.

The first girl was killed a week before Thanksgiving, the second a few days before Christmas—just a day, Patrick noted, after he had been shot in Chicago. And the third girl was killed on New Year's Eve, or more precisely, early morning of New Year's Day. Was there a connection with holidays?

He turned to the inside section of the paper and read the weather. The night of the first killing was clear, warm, typical south Florida weather in November. The *Herald* weather almanac showed a full moon occurring four days after the murder. The Montreal girl died two nights before a full moon; and the third victim within a week of that same full moon.

Was the full moon the key? Violent crime, it was documented, was always up during periods of the full moon, and Key West was well-known for its unparalleled madness during these lunar cycles. "Blame it on the moon" was a common refrain here during the week when it was full.

If so, the killer was severely limited in his time frame for committing murder.

Patrick put his pen down and took a sip of coffee, realizing he'd made a couple of unfortunate assumptions. He was already thinking in terms of a serial killer, just like the rest of the community—except for those, like the mayor, who wanted to avoid any publicity that might frighten away tourists.

All the earmarks were there to suggest a serial killer, but they could never know for sure—the second and third killings could be the work of copycats—until there was some communication from the killer, or he was caught.

The other assumption, so difficult to avoid in the thinking process, was his choice of gender-identifying pronouns—he, him, and his, in relation to the killer.

True, most serial killers were white and male, but it was always best to avoid psychological barriers imposed by those limitations. For now, in his imagination, the killer's sex and race were undetermined.

Patrick picked up the pen and drew two circles—moon symbols, he thought—but then completed the female symbol by adding a cross beneath it, and smiled sadly as he added a limp arrow to the male symbol.

Lee said, "What are you doing?" She stood on the back deck in a light cotton robe, which the breeze occasionally fluttered open to reveal her smooth, bare legs.

"Trying to get rid of the smell of cat piss," Patrick said. "And maybe the cats." He poured ammonia around the foundation of the house.

"Which is worse, ammonia or cat piss?" Lee asked.

"Cat piss," Patrick replied definitively. "The smell of ammonia doesn't hang around forever. Good morning and Happy New Year."

He looked up at Lee, admired the way she stood there, one hand smoothing down the cotton robe over one thigh. He winked.

"Same to you," she said, and walked back into the kitchen. "How long you been up?" she called through the open window.

"Since five."

"I see you've been making some notes. Are you getting involved?"

"No, just trying to get it straight in my head for some idle chatter at the next cocktail party."

"That's at four o'clock at Wystan's on the beach."

He knew. Wystan, the English poet who, in the role of devil's advocate, had annoyed the mayor last night, spent a couple months in Key West each winter, and gave a party each year on New Year's Day, on the dock that extended from his home overlooking the ocean, where he served punch and nothing else. Patrick thought of taking a flask of rum with him this afternoon.

The phone rang. Patrick looked at his watch. Nine o'clock. He heard Lee answer it and come back into the kitchen, where she called to him through the window. "Pat, it's for you. Bill Peachy."

Good. Maybe they would go fishing today, and he could avoid the poet's punch.

Patrick went into the house. Bill Peachy said, "Hey, how about a drink and some lunch at the Full Moon Saloon?"

"No fishing?"

"The wind's picking up all the time. A front's moving through."

"Too bad. The Moon at noon, then."

He went back into the kitchen, where Lee was making fresh coffee, and told her his plans.

She came over and put her arms around him. "Fine," she said. "When you get back, maybe we can work on our secret project."

"Our joint problem?"

Lee smiled.

Lee waited until Patrick had left to meet Bill Peachy before calling Hamilton Wade.

"We have to talk," she said when he answered.

"You're going to Wystan's, aren't you?"

"Yes. But I want to talk to you alone, privately." Silence.

"Baby, you sound unhappy," Wade said. "You upset with me over the business in the bathroom last night?"

"The business was young enough to be your granddaughter," Lee said. "And that's not why I'm upset."

"What else?"

"I can't go on like this. I'm going to stop seeing you." Silence

"Look baby, I'm kind of tied up right now. Let's talk tomorrow."

Lee felt a surge of irritation, mostly with herself for being in this mess. Still, Hamilton Wade had no right to call her at two o'clock in the morning. He had no right to dance with her the way he did last night, and the "business," as he called it, in the bathroom had nothing to do with her. She had no claims on Hamilton Wade, didn't want any, but it had left her feeling uneasy.

"We looked for you when we left last night. You weren't

around." Later she would wonder what instinct had prompted her to mention this to Wade, but now she just blurted it out.

Another silence.

"You sure you looked everywhere?" Wade said defensively.

"Looked and asked," Lee replied. "Someone said they'd seen you go out."

"Really?" Wade said. Pause. "Look, the girl in the bathroom was out of it, and you're right, she was young. I thought it was best to take her home."

"Hamilton," Lee said, "I'm ending this affair. It was a mistake. I'm getting out. I hope there will be no hard feelings."

Again, there was a long silence. Then Hamilton Wade said, "You'll change your mind. Everyone's a little uptight right now."

She could picture him grinning confidently. She said, "I don't think so." And hung up.

The second or third year she and Patrick were married, about the same year that she'd bought the Key West house, their marriage was temporarily grounded.

Those were the days when she'd been trying to get Patrick to leave the force and go to law school. Now she couldn't imagine him as a lawyer, or anything else except a cop, but she had thought then that she knew what was best for him. Just like her mother, she thought. Her mother who always knew best, who always knew what one should do, "should" combining with almost every active verb Lee ever heard her mother utter.

Her mother, who kept her father's fortune together, who

entertained lavishly, selectively, and constantly at usually dull and formal dinner parties—the brightest and most powerful of the Wisconsin society elite—while Lee and her older brother were growing up.

Her mother never missed an opportunity to criticize Lee's father for the freewheeling life he lived—at the age of forty (the year her mother died, when Lee was fifteen) he was still a skilled calf roper, competing in rodeos around the state. He also wrote poetry that seldom got published, and had affairs, which did.

Lee loved him; tall, romantic, a spoiler of every woman he ever came into contact with, including her. Yes, her mother saved the family fortune, but her father knew how to live.

When he died ten years ago, Lee's brother—who had married a woman a lot like their mother—took over the dairy farm; Lee heard from them only once a year, at Christmas, when she received a computerized form letter telling them all about the family and what the kids had done the past year.

Lee took after her father. Except on rare occasions when her mother's controlling voice with its "should do's" overwhelmed her—such as when she was trying to get Patrick to go to law school.

Patrick had told her he had no interest in becoming a lawyer. For nearly a year they fought about it. Until a modeling assignment took her to Europe for six months where she traveled and appeared on a variety of magazine covers. After five years in the business, she woke up one morning famous. Just like that.

People wanted to know about her as much as they wanted to see her pictures. The press followed her—they loved the story of her being married to a cop back in Chicago—and recorded her every movement. She was photographed skiing in Switzerland, interviewed at a sidewalk cafe in St. Mark's Square in Venice, and gossiped about on the island of Skiathos in Greece, where she was briefly a guest aboard the yacht of a rich Greek journalist.

Lee Bowman. Tall, auburn-haired, made famous for her unconventional beauty, highlighted by the gap between her front teeth, and an active personality. Like her father, she was always doing things, physical things. Getting publicity for it.

And sometimes trouble.

Two weeks after the affair with the Greek, she found herself pregnant. By that time she was in London preparing to return to the U.S. She delayed her trip back, got an abortion, which she managed to keep secret, and three weeks later went home to Patrick, wondering what she would tell him.

He greeted her at the airport, and she was happy to see him. He said he'd been reading all about her. He said of all the places she'd been, he most wanted to go to Greece. She looked at him, unable to tell if he was being sarcastic, and so said maybe they'd go together sometime.

He said he'd been promoted. He was now in the detective division, homicide.

She said she had missed him. She never mentioned the abortion. And they never again talked about law school. They substituted the Florida Keys and Key West for the Greek islands.

Where she met Hamilton Wade.

5

Patrick sat beside Bill Peachy, his elbows on the bolstered bar of the Full Moon. There was still some revelry in the saloon, while only a minority of the clientele seemed to be fighting a losing battle with hangover despair; it was a bar for professional drinkers.

"How was the night?" Patrick asked. Peachy looked tired, his face drawn, and he seemed worried. A lanky blonde with wide-set eyes put their drinks in front of them. Patrick, who seldom drank during the day, had an Amstel Light.

"I stayed home," Bill Peachy said. "New Year's Eve is always a letdown. I gave it up years ago."

Peachy lived alone in a small house he owned on Baker's Lane, three blocks from Patrick and Lee's. Apart from their fishing trips, Patrick would see him for a drink once or twice a week if Peachy didn't have a charter, but always only the two of them. Peachy wasn't social, although he had some reputation as a ladies' man. He also kept current with what was going on politically in Key West. He was an outspoken environmentalist.

"So why the hangdog look?"

"Jiminez," Bill Peachy said.

Patrick shook his head. "You've got some kind of obsession with the chief, don't you?"

"Listen." Peachy lowered his voice, leaned toward Patrick; conspiratorial, Patrick thought. Key West was a small town. Rumors were as thick as a weed line in the Gulf stream.

"I'm listening," Patrick said.

"Raul Jiminez has got problems."

"Three of them," Patrick said. "All dead."

Peachy shook his head. "Those are professional problems. There's personal stuff, too."

"You know somebody who doesn't have personal stuff?" Patrick said. "You want to hear mine?"

Again Peachy shook his head. "Raul's different. The guy's in a bind, and sooner or later he's going to get pinched. When he does, anything can happen." Peachy drank from his bottle of St. Pauli Girl, then, putting the bottle back on the bar, he absentmindedly caressed the Dutch maiden on the label with his thumb. Patrick waited.

"There's an internal-affairs investigation going on in the department, with Jiminez as its focus. It's supposed to be a hush-hush thing, but everybody on the force knows about it— including Jiminez."

"And you," Patrick said.

Peachy smiled. "I've got my ear to the ground."

"And the upshot?"

Peachy's thumb paused in its circular motion around the Dutch maiden. "A suspicion that Raul's got his hand in the till. They're trying to find enough evidence to convince a grand jury to look into it."

"Is it a witch hunt?"

"Except for a few of the old-timers on the force from before the previous chief was arrested, Raul doesn't have a lot of friends. But the word's out that they've got some strong evidence against him."

Patrick tilted the bottle of Amstel to his lips. "What's Jiminez doing?"

"Just what you'd expect him to do. Trying to take some of the heat off. If he can solve these murders, they might forget the other stuff. Or so Jiminez reasons."

"Has he got something?"

Peachy shrugged. "My ear's not that big. But I can tell you why his hand was in the till."

Patrick sensed Peachy had called him here just for this moment. He waited.

Bill Peachy said, "Three kids, two of them in college."

"Higher education's expensive, but I'd guess Jiminez makes pretty good money."

"Right. But the third kid's in Miami, seeing a shrink."

"Jesus," Patrick said. "What's wrong with him?"

Peachy smiled. "You'd never guess."

Patrick said, "I won't even try."

"He's a transvestite," Peachy said, reaching for the Dutch maiden.

Lee thought about the first time she saw Hamilton Wade's face. It was on the dust jacket of one of his early books, and she thought he was beautiful. Not attractive; not handsome. Beautiful. Boyish and feminine, sensitive and sensuous, a face with guile and not a little meanness in the dark, brooding eyes and the full lips that contained the hint of a pout. She was attracted.

She'd read the book, a novel, and later a review that told her the book was largely autobiographical. She was attracted even more to Hamilton Wade, whose bio on the inside of the dust jacket mentioned that the author had a home: in Key West, Florida.

Less than a year after reading Wade's early novel, she made her first trip to Key West, and a year after that, she bought her home here—a winter residence, she explained to Patrick.

She didn't explain to him that in some wild fantasy she wanted to meet Hamilton Wade. Seduction was probably in the back of her mind, but by the time she met Wade and got to know him, the boyish and sensitive looks had coarsened, and the brooding eyes were meaner than she had found them a few years earlier. Still, there was the guile and the sensuousness. As well as a memory of an old photo on the back of a dust jacket. They had all gone through changes.

She'd been having an affair with the memory of a man she didn't even know; someone she'd invented for herself from his books and a youthful dust-jacket photograph.

Now she wanted it to end. Lee knew that Wade was going to want to know why. Her guilt over Patrick would not satisfy Hamilton. Nor would the fact that she was no longer comfortable around him. He would want something more concrete. But how did you tell a guy you knew intimately that you thought he was a killer?

Staring now across Wystan Lewis's crowded deck, she watched Hamilton, who stood alone, looking at the water. Like he was waiting for her, she thought. Although she knew better. Hamilton was a man who took what he wanted when he wanted it. If anything, it was she who had done the waiting.

She wasn't sure when the idea came to her that Wade might have been linked to the deaths of the three women. But the sight of him walking away from his own party, heading in the direction of the beach, lingered in her mind.

Then there was his obsession with sex. He had a drive to accumulate women, to overlap them as if they were cords of wood to be taken out and burned whenever he chose. And an almost demonic compulsion for each to know about the other, daring them to resist him, as though he wanted to be caught the way she had caught him with the young girl in the bathroom. He could, after all, have locked the door.

"Truce?" she said to Wade.

"Why are you doing this?" he asked. He was smiling, still leaning on the deck rail, looking out to sea.

"I'm uncomfortable," Lee said. It was true. Wade didn't scare her so much as he made her feel that she was just a prop, there for his own amusement. Hamilton Wade used people. He was a manipulator, and she could tolerate that in the interests of his profession, but wouldn't tolerate intentional cruelty—or violence. She had the feeling that she might appear in one of his autobiographical novels one
day, if he ever published another one; but though her vanity at one time might have required that sort of stroking, it no longer did.

"That's no reason," Wade said.

"It's reason enough for me, and it will have to be for you, too."

"It won't be," he said.

It was dusk. Patrick stood talking to a group of people near the bar, where Wystan poured the drink concoctions that Patrick avoided. Lee told herself she could call Patrick and ask him to come over, to avoid Hamilton's probing. She didn't. She knew that she had to resolve this herself.

"We had our fun," she said. "It's over. That's all. You've got plenty of other women."

Wade grinned. "You're jealous of the kid in the bathroom."

Lee shook her head. "The male ego," she said. "I'm not jealous of anyone. I'm just ending this affair."

"Suppose I won't let you?"

"You can't stop me." He was playing with her, she knew.

"Have you told Patrick?"

Lee looked at him, the face that had so interested her at one time, now aged, dissolute. She knew what he was getting at, couldn't believe that he would play emotional blackmail with her. She smiled. "No," she said, "but I will."

Patrick accepted the champagne punch, then carried it to the deck, where he spilled it into the ocean. He refilled the stem glass with rum from his flask and turned back to the party.

Lee was talking to Hamilton Wade. Again. They seemed to seek each other out at these social events and spend time in rapt conversation together. He had often wondered what they continued

46

to find to talk about, since he and Hamilton seemed to have little to say to one another.

"Books," Lee said. "We talk about books and writers."

Looking at them now, their serious expressions, Patrick thought they must be talking about books they didn't like. He wasn't jealous, and Lee, whatever she did when they were not together, was not the type to flirt with other men when he was around.

The party, minus perhaps a hundred people, was a replica of the New Year's Eve bash the night before. People waved, blew kisses, smiled and toasted one another as if it had been a year since they'd last been together, instead of only twelve hours.

Wystan Lewis appeared at the deck rail with a tall woman in tow and stood dwarfed between her and Patrick. "The mayor wasn't too keen last night on hearing theories about a serial killer."

"Maybe this morning's news changed his mind," Patrick said.

"Isn't it awful?" the tall woman said. "Is there anything you can do?" she asked Patrick.

"Probably not, and I haven't been asked," he replied.

"I think you will be," Wystan Lewis said. "Several of us took Raul Jiminez aside last night and asked him to consider bringing you in."

"I doubt that he was receptive to the idea."

"But, like the mayor, this morning he may have changed his mind."

The moon was like a half-closed eyelid. Surrounded by the brilliance of the stars, however, its remaining dark circumference was illuminated; almost like an eclipse, Patrick thought.

He sat on the cement abutment at the water's edge behind the fort and looked at his watch. Eleven-thirty. He had walked around the fort a couple of times, and up and down the beach, stopping occasionally in the shadows of the fort or by one of the bandstands, where he could watch the few people who passed. Very few. And no women. The guys who wandered by were mostly together, only one or two strays.

Patrick had tried to talk to one of the loners, but when he approached and began to ask a question, the guy took off. Just turned and walked away. Less than a week after a murder, it seemed that no one was willing to take a chance with a stranger. And he had no authority here.

Patrick thought he would sit for a while, then make one more pass along the beach before heading home. He was aware of two guys making out at one corner of the fort. Other than that, he wasn't aware of anyone else in the area.

And was surprised when he heard footsteps in the sand near where he sat. Patrick turned away from the water. A young man, more a kid, in his early twenties, shoeless, wearing shorts and no shirt, stood ten feet from him.

"Looking for action?" the kid said. His hair was thick and disheveled. He didn't seem to be high.

Patrick shook his head. "Information," he said.

"Cop?"

"Off-duty."

"Look, I talked to the cops already, a couple times. Check it out." The kid began to back away.

"I have," Patrick said calmly. "But we're investigating a murder here. New questions come up."

"Man, I told them, I didn't see anything that night."

"But you were here," Patrick said.

"Sure, I told you guys. I walked through on my way to a party."

"Cruising."

"Naw, walking. On my way to a party. P-A-R-T-Y."

Patrick ignored the sarcasm. "But you hang out here."

"I've been here before," the kid said.

"Hustling."

"Jesus." The kid shook his head and dusted the surface of the sand with a bare foot.

Patrick stood up. "I'm not here to bust you," he said. "Just give me some straight answers and you can be on your way. I don't want to see anybody else getting killed out here. You can understand that."

The kid looked up from the sand. "Look, people cruise here at night. It's no secret, it's what happens here."

"Girls?" Patrick asked.

"Sometimes, but not many. Most of the action goes the other way here."

"You ever see any of the girls, talk to them, maybe smoke a joint together?"

49

The kid began running his foot across the sand again. "Yeah, once or twice," he mumbled.

"What about the girl? Listen, what's your name?" Patrick asked.

"Paul."

"Lieutenant Bowman, Paul." Patrick extended his hand. The kid shook it. "What about the girl who was killed? You ever run into her?"

"Look, I've already answered these questions."

"Answer them again for me, Paul, because I may get to one you didn't answer."

"Yeah, I seen her, not often and not the night she got killed. I didn't see her then."

"When you saw her, where was she?"

"The other side of the fort," Paul said.

"Show me. Let's walk over there."

Paul led him to the west side of the fort, the brick wall in the shadows behind the swings and the monkey bars. "She hung out here?"

Paul nodded.

"How many times did you see her?"

"A couple, three maybe. Not many."

"But you talked to her?"

"Yeah, nothing heavy. Passed the time once."

"Share a joint?"

"Oh, man. Yeah. Once."

"Mess around?"

"No."

"What'd you talk about?"

"Nothin' really. She said she was from Montreal. She was trying to make a few bucks. I told her about the place. She said she was doing all right."

"How'd she seem? Frightened? Unhappy?"

Paul shook his head. "Naw, she was just a typical chick trying to get by."

"You ever see her go with anybody?"

"Nope."

Patrick looked across at the swings and monkey bars. Kid stuff. Just a typical chick trying to get by. Except she had AIDS and she was a long way from home.

"How long you been cruising this beach?" Patrick asked.

"I been in Key West a couple years. I started coming here maybe a year ago. I used to sleep on the beach, but I got a room now."

"A job?"

"Yeah, I bus tables."

"You must get to know the people who come here and hang out, then."

"Some of 'em."

"In the last few weeks, you see any that are different, strange?"

"They're all strange."

"No, I mean different, somebody new you haven't seen around before, maybe who dresses differently, or hangs out by himself. Anybody out of the ordinary—ordinary for you, I mean."

Paul thought about it. "Only one guy I can think of who's kind of different. He's not around often."

"Can you describe him?"

"He dresses funny. Always got on expensive clothes, fancy shirts that look more like blouses, and leather shoes. Nobody comes out here in shoes. Sandals, sneakers. But not leather shoes." He looked down at his own feet as if to prove it.

"The guy tall, short? What's he look like?"

"Tall, maybe older than you. I don't know. I never paid that much attention."

"How long's he been coming here?"

"I don't know. A month, maybe two."

"And what does he do?"

"Nothin'. Walks around. Sits. Kinda like you were doing."

"Never bothers anyone? Nobody tries to hustle him?"

"I don't know. I always see him alone," Paul said.

"You tell the cops about him?"

"They never asked."

Patrick smiled. "You see? You answered a different question."

Paul shrugged.

"Tell me one more thing," Patrick said. "You're not scared hanging out here after what's been going on?"

"Why?" Paul said. "I'm not a chick."

6

Raul Jiminez sat in the small, windowless office behind his paper-cluttered desk. Someday, he thought, he was going to get himself an office where he could take a couple of steps and look out a window instead of being surrounded by cinder blocks painted the color of puke. Someday.

At one time getting a more comfortable office would have occupied a good part of his daily ritual. Now as he sat reading the coroner's report from the latest murder, the size of his office seemed only a moderate inconvenience compared to everything else that was happening.

Someday this whole goddamn pile of cinder blocks was going to tumble right down on him if he didn't get control of things. Three murders in Key West in less than two months! In the past, if all of Monroe County had three murders a year, it would be considered unusual.

Murder here was normally confined to locals doing in each other: a drug deal gone sour, a domestic who got carried away by island fever fueled by too much sun, too much boredom, too much booze, and a jealous spouse. It went with the territory.

Seldom, though, did murder carry into the tourist or transient community. In the winter season tourists got the predictable; they were mugged, raped, had their cars and their rooms broken and entered. That went with the territory, too, in a poor town with a twenty-five-million-dollar industry. Tourists. They could be a pain in the ass, but up to now they weren't getting killed, and a chiefs biggest headache was squeezing the last drops from a tight budget while figuring ways to get some of the drops to land in his own lap.

Jiminez had inherited a system that had pretty much worked for previous administrations—until the last chief was caught and jailed—and Raul had seen no reason to break with tradition, although he'd tried to be a little more careful in his dealings.

Key West, however, was growing up fast, faster maybe than it could comfortably manage without busting some seams. In recent years the town had filled up with transplanted Yankees who were bent on changing the system. They talked about honest government, law and order, competence, and then worked to push out the old-line conchs, people born and raised here. And it worked. The Yankees had built the place up to the point where, if you walked downtown, you couldn't tell Key West from Connecticut. Prices were driven up, and the conchs left—driven out because they couldn't afford it. Just the way the Yankees wanted it.

It didn't take any doctor of philosophy, Raul reasoned, to figure out that his own time here was numbered. The first excuse they could find for replacing him with one of their own, and Raul Jiminez would be history.

Jiminez didn't intend to make history by giving them that first chance. But the fifty grand a year the city was paying him didn't go far with two kids in college and another seeing a shrink in Miami because he couldn't figure out if he wanted to be a boy or a girl.

At the end of the year, even with his perks, Raul Jiminez was having a hard time making it.

So he had made a few unauthorized requisitions in the past few months, minor stuff in comparison with what had gone on in the past, but unauthorized nonetheless. He was aware that internal affairs was looking into those requisitions, but he was sure he was covered. They'd have a hard time finding anything other than some minor oversight which was hardly going to warrant a grand jury investigation. He wasn't worried about that.

What he was worried about were three dead women, girls really. The coroner's report on the latest victim read much the same as the other two. From all appearances, he had a serial killer on his hands.

And a nationally recognized expert on serial killings on vacation in Key West. Mother of God.

The pressure to call in Patrick Bowman was building. The mayor had called Raul twice in the past twenty-four hours, as well as some commissioners and a number of the winter social crowd with whom Bowman and his wife hung out.

Jiminez figured he had less than a week to close this case before he was forced to admit defeat and bring in Bowman. Raul wasn't ready to admit defeat.

Maybe, on the other hand, there was another way to skin this cat. If he went to Bowman now, picked his brains, used him as a kind of consultant without acknowledging that the Chicago cop was in any way an active part of the case, Raul wouldn't have to worry about admitting defeat if this case dragged on. That would be showing some Yankee ingenuity.

Raul reached for the phone.

Sexual fidelity, Patrick Bowman thought, was one of those mysteries like the Virgin birth. Who the hell believed in it, and if it was true, if it existed, who the hell cared except for a few scholars and moralists?

When he married Lee it was understood that this was no conventional marriage. He didn't go into it with great expectations, and perhaps because of that, he felt he'd been rewarded with a good marriage. There had been, of course, infidelity (such a high-toned ridiculous expression, he thought) on both sides during the six months when she had been in Europe and he had been uncertain if she were coming back.

And, he was certain, she had continued to have intermittent affairs during her career. But for fifteen years, sometimes even struggling to beat the odds, they had managed to survive.

It was true that he loved Lee. But more than that, he liked her, liked who she was, what she did—and that, he thought, counted for a good part of their success.

When she told him she'd had an affair here and that it was over, he wanted to know if she was hurt, had been hurt in any way; and she said, no, are you?

Patrick thought about it. Yeah, he was hurt, but he wasn't dying. He wanted to know if it had anything to do with his own inabilities. Lee said no. It was just some damned infatuation she'd had from years ago that had finally run its course.

He didn't ask who it was; she didn't tell him. It was over, just in case he heard anything.

Well, no crime had been committed, had it?

No, no crime had been committed, she didn't think.

Well, then, they would both get through it. They had gotten through worse.

They were in the upstairs bedroom. Lee reached out and put her arms around him. She didn't say anything. They held each other.

The phone rang four times before Lee pulled away and picked up the receiver on her side of the bed. She listened, then held the phone receiver out to Patrick.

"Who is it?" he whispered.

"The police chief," Lee whispered back.

"Patrick Bowman?"

"Speaking."

"Raul Jiminez, Key West police chief."

"Sure," Patrick said. "I remember. We drink the same brand of rum."

"I'd like to talk to you, pick your brain about these murders. Unofficially, of course."

Of course. Jiminez had been distinctly defensive on New Year's Eve. What had changed? Patrick wondered.

"When?" Patrick asked.

"How about tomorrow morning? Ten o'clock. My office at City Hall."

"Fine, I'll come down," Patrick said.

"Appreciate it," Jiminez said. "And like I said, it's unofficial. Let's keep it on the q.t."

"No problem." Patrick handed the phone receiver back to Lee to hang up.

"Well," she said.

"He says he wants to pick my brain. Unofficially."

"You worried?"

"Worried, no. Wary, yes."

Lee came over, snuggled against him with her arms around him. "We're going to be all right," she said softly against his ear.

I hope so, Patrick Bowman thought. I hope so.

After eight years in a business not known for its pension plans, Lee had stepped back while she was still in demand. It was a calculated risk that paid off. She retired when she was twenty-nine and went back to work when she was forty, to discover that her face hadn't been forgotten; there was a ready market for the fashion model who had more than just a pretty, blank face for the public to look at, the public that had grown older with her. She went back to work and called her own shots. She turned down more assignments than she accepted, unheard of when she was starting out.

For the eleven years she was out of the modeling business, she had combined a career as a wife, fixed up the Key West house, and spent time learning photography from the other side of the camera.

Except for Hamilton Wade, she no longer had affairs.

And by the time she went to bed with him, she did so more out of

58

curiosity than desire.

Sex with Hamilton Wade was exactly that, curious. He was consumed by the erotic, driven by prurient fantasies, a need to experiment. There was nothing outside the bounds of his imagination for sexual manipulation.

There were no gymnastics in her lovemaking with Patrick, who tended to be more sensual and tender, even though, after fifteen years, predictable.

The first few times she had gone to bed with Wade were interesting; later, they became ridiculous, until finally she found herself utterly depressed.

The last time they'd been together was just before Christmas, a few days before Patrick was due to arrive. Hamilton liked to think that he was irresistible, that once he'd fucked you, you would automatically be back for more. Lee had vowed that would be her last time.

She had made up her mind that she would get out of Wade's trap, although she didn't want to have to just drop him, because they had too many friends in common; in a small, social town like Key West, he would be unavoidable. But she wasn't about to continue to be manhandled on the dance floor and treated as if she were a piece of his property.

Her curiosity about Hamilton Wade was over.

Although there was still the lingering apprehension: Hamilton Wade staggering in the direction of the beach sometime after midnight on New Year's Eve.

She had a key to Hamilton's that he'd once given her, with permission to use the pool whenever she wanted. Tomorrow she would return the key. Tomorrow, the day he had told her at Wystan's he was going to be in New York on business.

Tomorrow she would go to Hamilton's house and take a look around. Look for what? She didn't know.

She was thinking about that when the phone rang. It was her modeling agent in New York. *Vanity Fair* would like to feature her on the cover. Was she interested?

She said she was, and her agent said she would get back to her with a schedule of shooting dates.

Later, she would think: the timing couldn't have been more perfect.

7

"Here's what we've got," Raul Jiminez said. Patrick sat on a folding chair in the cramped office and in front of the cluttered desk. Jiminez shuffled papers on the desk, then leaned back in his chair and looked at the ceiling. "We've got a partial footprint, looks like a sneaker, in the dirt just outside the West Martello where the Montreal girl was killed. There's some dried blood mixed with the dirt. My guess is the killer stepped in the girl's blood as he was leaving the scene."

Jiminez paused and lit a cigarette with a great deal of elegance and exaggeration. Then he leaned back and continued to stare at the ceiling while he talked.

"Then we got a joint, actually a roach, that's got some partials of the dead girl's prints and no one else's." Jiminez inhaled from the cigarette, held the smoke, then released twin jet spirals through his nose. He closed his eyes, seemed to be in thought.

Patrick uncrossed his legs and banged his knee against the front of the desk. Jiminez opened his eyes and looked at Patrick for the first time. "I been trying to get a bigger office for the last year," Jiminez said. Then leaned back in his chair and smoked some more.

Finally, he leaned forward and said, like he'd just made some big decision, "The only thing we've got that ties these three murders together is the manner of death."

Jesus, Patrick thought, what am I doing here? He said, "They had their throats cut."

Jiminez nodded, looking at Patrick. "It looks like with the same instrument."

Instrument. Patrick remembered the Pulitzer divorce case a few years back. Newspaper headlines about the wife having sex with a trumpet. He said, "What instrument?"

"A knife," Jiminez said. Then drew on the cigarette, exhaling while he spoke. "Forensic says it was something very thin-bladed, razor sharp. Not a pocketknife, probably not even an ordinary kitchen knife. More like a boning knife, the kind they use down here for cutting up fish." Jiminez leaned back in his chair again and finished the cigarette. He stubbed it out in a glass ashtray filled with butts. "You got any ideas?" he asked Patrick.

Patrick shook his head. "You've been on the beach, asking questions, and nobody saw any of these girls before they were killed?"

"I got two detectives on this. They're still asking questions, but so far nobody's seen anything."

"You run a check through the computer network for any similar murders?" Patrick thought of Wayne Higgs, a man he'd conferred with often who worked at the FBI's VICAP— the Violent Criminal Apprehension Program.

"They've got a strangler in California and an ax murderer up in Michigan. That's it with serial killers right now. We've got the only slasher around."

"Any connection among the victims?"

"All girls, young and white and street people. Healthy, except for the girl with AIDS."

"How about your mental health people? Anybody running around the streets who shouldn't be?"

Jiminez laughed. "In Key West? Probably about every third person you meet on the street." He paused. "I've covered those bases. Nothing."

Patrick studied his sneakers. He was in jeans and a tropical shirt, clothes he kept here and only wore here. Vacation clothes.

"There may be another link," Patrick said. "The full moon. All these girls were killed within a week of a full moon."

Jiminez smiled. "This town's wacky enough to buy that, but I wouldn't care for letting that theory get out. We've got enough problems with the weirdos."

"Just a thought," Patrick said.

"You willing to make yourself available?" Jiminez leaned back in the chair, eyes to the ceiling. "A sort of unofficial consultant?"

"Look," Patrick said, "I'm down here on vacation—"

Jiminez looked down and smiled. "Medical leave."

"Yeah, medical leave. That doesn't mean I can't enjoy myself. I don't know what I can do"

"Give the benefit of your experience," Jiminez replied.

Patrick nodded, still uncertain what Jiminez was trying to achieve here, but knowing it went beyond a question of help. "However, I can help," he said.

Jiminez stood up. "Unofficially."

Patrick nodded again.

"Good," Jiminez said. "Come upstairs, I'd like you to meet a couple people."

Patrick followed Jiminez up the drab stairs of City Hall and into a conference room where half a dozen people were seated around a table with portable tape recorders in front of them.

When he saw how he'd been set up, Patrick considered walking out. Jiminez was cunning. He'd pulled the separate pieces together by calling a press conference, then leading in the prize story without a hint of what was about to happen. What was about to happen, Patrick decided, was that the chief was going to get some good headlines.

Patrick took the seat Jiminez was offering, deciding since he'd gone this far he might as well let Jiminez play out his hand.

Jiminez walked to the head of the table as the reporters clicked on their tape recorders.

"I want to bring you up to date on the investigation of the recent killings here," Jiminez said. "I've got a couple of things that are new. One, we've pretty well established that the same weapon was used to kill all three victims, and after a little more lab work, we should be able to identify precisely what that weapon was. Two, I've got some evidence found at one of the crime scenes that will help in identifying the killer. Obviously, I'm not able to tell you what that evidence is."

"Any suspects yet?" one reporter asked.

"We're questioning a number of people," Jiminez said.

"You said that one murder weapon was used in all three

killings," a female reporter said. "Do you now regard these as the definite work of a serial killer?"

"Yes," Jiminez said. He looked at Patrick. "And I'd like to introduce you now to Patrick Bowman. Lieutenant Bowman is a homicide detective with the Chicago Police Department. He is well known around the country for his work in the area of serial killings. I have asked my friend, Lieutenant Bowman, to act as a kind of consultant in our investigation."

Patrick wanted to smile at the way Jiminez handled his introduction—without embarrassment, as though he, Jiminez, was personally responsible for bringing "his friend" to Key West to help solve these murders.

"Lieutenant Bowman is not acting in any official capacity, but more as a favor, I hope, to me."

Jesus.

The reporters turned to Patrick and began to question him about his background. Jiminez, smiling, watched happily.

Once they were satisfied with his credentials, someone asked him about the Key West case. "I know little more than you do right now," Patrick said. "I wasn't really prepared for a press conference." He glanced at Jiminez, who hadn't stopped smiling.

"What are the chances he'll kill again?"

Patrick lifted his hands. "I'd say the chances are good, unless the killer is caught soon."

The chief frowned, then interrupted. "I'd like to give the lieutenant a chance to familiarize himself with this case before you ask him to speculate further. I promise to keep you up to date on our progress, and I'd appreciate your directing any further questions to my office rather than Lieutenant Bowman. Also, I think from the evidence we're putting together, w e should be making an arrest within the week."

A stunned silence. Jiminez knew how to handle the press, Patrick thought, but he was putting himself on a limb with that sort of grandstanding. Unless Jiminez knew something he hadn't told Patrick.

The female reporter broke the silence. "Just one more," she said, looking at Patrick. "How do you think this investigation has been conducted up to this point?"

"The chief seems to have a good grip on it." He smiled.

"That's all the questions," Jiminez said.

The reporters began to pack away their equipment, talking among themselves. A flash went off as someone snapped a picture of Patrick and Chief Jiminez, who had come over and stood beside him.

When the press was gone, Patrick said, "That was quite a show. You running for office?"

"You get hired to this job, not elected," Jiminez said. "And by the way, you want to be careful down here talking about more killings. It freaks the Chamber of Commerce. You saw the mayor's reaction the other night. This is a tourist town."

Patrick walked home to William Street from City Hall. Jiminez was a piece of work, a guy with a minimum of self-confidence and a full head of arrogance. It was a deadly combination. When Jiminez erupted—which he would, Patrick reasoned, if he lost control of this investigation—it wasn't going to be a pretty sight.

But despite the chief's arrogance and the theatrics of his calculated performance, he did have a good grip on the case. He seemed to be doing all that he could, Patrick thought, and for the moment, at least, Jiminez was nothing to worry about.

Lee was another matter. He hadn't pressed her about the affair she said she was ending, accepting her reason for why she was telling him about it now. Yeah, he would have been upset if he'd heard about it from someone else first. Lee knew that. He didn't have to wonder why she was ending it, either. They had talked about this sort of thing before they got married.

"Look," she had said, "I don't know if I can promise I'll never sleep with somebody else. It seems like an unreasonable expectation to have of people over a long period of time."

"I suppose there are more important things to expect of someone you live with," Patrick had said.

"Let's list them," Lee replied.

"How about honesty?"

"Okay."

"And consistency."

"Okay."

"And being good, trying to be the best at what you do, even if it's only making beds."

"Or unmaking them?" She had gotten that look in her eye then, and begun to bite her lower lip.

Laughter. "Okay, but we're not talking debauchery, are we?"

"No, we're not talking debauchery."

So they'd come through fifteen years of living together with several minor skirmishes, but only a couple of major battles, and most of the debauchery now occurred between them in the privacy of their own bedroom. Or had until a couple weeks ago. Their past affairs had been conveniently forgotten, so he had been taken by surprise by her recent announcement.

Now he found himself wondering who she'd slept with and why she'd decided to end it. He couldn't recall seeing her hanging around anyone much except Hamilton Wade, and he'd always thought Wade was gay. He'd have to ask Lee about it.

He turned off Windsor Lane onto William Street. All his life he'd been honest, and, he thought, consistent. He knew he was a good cop. But right now he felt like a failure. Jesus, lunk head, some inner voice said, three weeks ago you were shot, you could be dead. Just because your dick won't get hard doesn't make you a failure.

Yeah, but it makes you think you are, and that's the same thing, isn't it? Patrick's own voice questioned.

The inner voice didn't answer.

8

Standing on the deck of Hamilton Wade's swimming pool, Lee Bowman surveyed the house. The sliding tinted-glass doors that opened onto the pool area were closed, as were the windows. She had waited until mid-afternoon to come over, since Wade had indicated he was leaving for New York at noon. He would be gone for one, possibly two days, he had said, for a meeting with his publisher.

The key he had once given her opened not only the back gate to the pool area, but also the sliding glass doors to the house.

She was nervous. She had been here several times before, but never to snoop. Her suspicions of Wade had calmed some after Wystan's party. He wasn't so drunk, and therefore did not seem so evil to her or as capable of murder as he had at his own New Year's party. In fact, he was almost pitiable the way he begged her not to do anything until he got back from New York.

Still, she carried a mental image of him lurching toward the beach on New Year's Eve. And needed somehow to satisfy herself that Hamilton wasn't capable of murder. She walked over to the house, turned the key in the lock, and slid the glass door open, walking barefoot across the cool Cuban-tiled floor and through the living room with its fireplace and simple but elegant furnishings.

Down a hall beyond the stairway leading to the second floor was Hamilton's study. Feeling an edge of panic, she paused, looking over her shoulder before entering the studio. The house was dead quiet.

There was a large, old-fashioned metal desk in the center of the room, a computer and printer on its scarred surface. An IBM Selectric was on a metal typing table at a right angle to the desk. There were three filing cabinets along one wall, two four-tier bookcases along the wall behind the desk. The other walls were covered with paintings, a Japanese drawing on silk cloth, and several framed photographs, mostly of Hamilton Wade—among them the photo used for the book jacket that had first stirred her interest in him. She studied it, then looked at the other photos and observed the progressive decline in the innocent, good looks.

She walked behind the desk and sat down in the cane chair padded with thick cushions. She tried to pull open a side drawer; it was locked. The center drawer was the only one open, and she rummaged through the usual mess of pens, pencils, paper clips, and scraps of paper and stamps until, by running her hand around the underside of the desk itself (she wasn't a cop's wife for nothing), she found a set of keys in a magnetic container.

She opened the other drawers to the desk. There were business files and yellow legal pads scrawled with notes, characters, and story ideas in Hamilton's handwriting.

There were diaries; last year's lay on top of a stack of five in one drawer. She picked it up, thumbed through it. More notes, story ideas, and dialogue. She read a page, thumbed a few more pages, read some more. And stopped. She was reading a conversation she'd had with Wade in February, a year ago. Verbatim. Dialogue. She thumbed through more pages and found more of their conversations written down, word for word, as they'd had them.

Jesus. It was spooky. There were other bits of dialogue, obviously taken from people he'd been talking to. She turned to November, trying to remember when the first murder had taken place, sometime around Thanksgiving. Nothing. Three days, in fact, of blank pages.

December. There was the conversation they'd had when she told Wade Patrick had been shot. The second girl was murdered a day later, she remembered: another blank page. The thirty-first was also blank. Of course, he would have recorded the party on the first, presumably, in a new diary.

She walked over to the filing cabinets and tried a drawer. Locked. One of the keys opened the cabinet. Inside were more files, and magazines. Pornography. Hardcore pornography and videotapes.

She opened another drawer. More files, one labeled "Novel Ideas." She pulled out the folder and found newspaper clippings from each of the three Key West murders. There were loose-leaf notes in Wade's hand, outlining a novel based on the recent killings.

Lee read the notes, found references to Patrick, the famous cop brought in to solve the murders.

The murderer, it turned out, was a famous novelist. According to Hamilton's notes, the plot hinged on a competitive spirit between the novelist/murderer and the famous cop. Also in the outline were more conversations between Hamiliton and the famous cop's wife. Again, real conversations that she remembered having with Hamiliton, as well as made-up dialogue. Fiction.

This was no longer spooky. It was very damned frightening.

Patrick established his routine. It was the same routine that had kept him going in countless murder investigations that had always appeared hopeless in the beginning. The routine was quite simple. He returned during the day, and night, to the scene of the crime, and he talked to people.

Each day he would stake out a different section of the beach to comb, and wander around it, picking up odds and ends of lost and discarded junk—sometimes even valuables—that he recorded in a notebook he carried, along with the time, place, and date that he found it, before pocketing the item in a sack he carried for that purpose. He became a beachcomber. Wearing shorts, a T-shirt, and sandals, a mesh-bill cap that advertised Key West, and sunglasses, he was indistinguishable from the hordes of tourists who flocked to the beach during the day. At night he came out in jeans and a sport shirt imprinted with various faded hibiscus, the tail of which he wore loose over his jeans to conceal his holstered nine-millimeter, which he carried strapped to his belt and wore in the hollow of his lower back.

From the beaches he picked up buttons, coins, sometimes pieces of clothing—torn T-shirts, caps, the bottom half of a bikini, panties, some soiled Hanes underwear, and once, one sneaker in which holes had been deliberately cut in the tops and sides. He found a half-eaten Snickers candy bar that showed a clear imprint of teeth, Styrofoam cups that had lipstick on them, and more than a few used condoms.

Band-Aids with blood on them and discarded Tampax he handled with care and regarded as treasure.

At the end of the day he would carry the stuff that he'd gathered over to the police lab and leave it with a clerk, along with his attached notes, where it could all be checked for fingerprints and other identifying marks along with stuff that the KWPD detectives were bringing in; together, labeled and stored, all this was a potential gold mine of evidence, if they ever got a suspect they could relate it to.

If. It was all chance, trying to lower the odds, trying to build some reserve, and in doing so, raise new questions and, ultimately, new hope.

For Patrick it was routine.

Along the beach he stopped to talk to people, and within two or three days he knew many faces by sight, knew who were locals, who had been staying for a couple of weeks, people who were down for the winter, and new arrivals.

He was careful not to ask questions as a cop, but rather to chat, just another friendly tourist talking about the weather, the town, other people on the beach. Strangely, few people talked about the murders. And unless he had a particular reason to do so, Patrick didn't either.

He was getting the lay of the land.

He was also in pain.

As the day progressed he began to favor one leg, until by the end of the day he was walking with a noticeable limp. All because he was doing the very work that he was supposedly down here *not* to do. He could have stayed in Chicago, he told himself, and taken this kind of punishment.

It was cold in Chicago.

And there was not, as far as he knew, a serial killer on the loose there who was preying on young street hustlers.

He paused at a concession stand to buy a bottle of Gatorade, which he used to wash down a couple of extra strength Tylenol before continuing on his rounds.

Lee looked at her watch. She'd been in here an hour and a half already. Just reading, finding out more about Hamilton Wade, the man, the novelist, than she was sure she wanted to know. None of this, of course, proved him a killer, but she couldn't help thinking of the reviews from that first novel she'd read nearly twenty years ago, pointing out that it was largely autobiographical.

How far was Hamilton Wade willing to go for his material? And how much did she know about this man with whom she'd been intimate a few brief times during the months she was in residence here the past couple of years? It made you wonder. How much did anyone know about anyone else? Really know. Yes, it was frightening.

She wanted to stay here and read this stuff. No, she'd like to take it with her, she realized, at least copies of it. Why? Evidence? She was thinking it without thinking it, without wanting to admit it. But there it was. Hamilton would be back tomorrow or the next day.

There wasn't much time.

Lee put the stuff back in the filing cabinets and the desk, relocking the drawers and depositing the keys in their container, which she replaced beneath the desk.

Then she went upstairs. There was a room there that she wanted to see, a room that Hamilton kept locked, telling her it was another study where he kept his private papers. What had she just seen if not private papers?

She went into the bedroom where they'd made love. The door to Wade's private room was opposite the foot of the bed. She tried the knob; it was still locked. Well, she'd found the keys to the desk and filing cabinets. She'd damned well find them to this door, still the famous cop's wife.

She searched through the bedside tables, under the base of lamps, in the closets. And found another magnetic container attached to the bedframe. The key was inside.

She noticed that her hand trembled slightly as she inserted the key in the lock. To hell with it. She was hardly going to be shocked more than she already had been.

She was wrong. She entered a small room and stared at some weird furnishings. And herself. On the walls were photographic blowups of Lee and other women. No, Lee and girls—in their teens.

Somehow Wade had photographed them—separately, since she'd never seen these girls before—in moments when they were all in some active sexual activity. Then he'd combined the photos in a collage so that it appeared that they were together, or at least the

75

photos in which Lee appeared. Perhaps the girls were actually photographed together. But whether they were or not, they were all pictured together.

Naked. On the bed. On the floor. Touching themselves. *Appearing* to touch each other. He was sick, Lee thought. And mad. She examined all of them and wanted to tear them down. She imagined Patrick seeing this. Debauchery. This was debauchery, and in a sense, she was a participant.

She moved back instinctively, away from what she was looking at, and bumped against something. Startled, she turned and stared at a table filled with the plastic and rubber accoutrements sold in sex shops and by mail order, advertised to enhance sexual pleasure. She looked around her.

In the center of the room was a contraption that she at first thought was an exercise bike, except that it was equipped with a motor. When she examined it more closely, she saw that a hole had been bored through the center of its hard leather seat. The seat was mounted to a frame, a toggle switch just below it. She flicked the switch. The motor began to hum quietly as a plastic dildo surged piston fashion in and out of the opening in the seat.

Jesus.

Lee walked home. What had begun as a harmless affair had now, as it ended, turned into a nightmare. Hamilton Wade. Twisted. Tortured. Sick. And obsessed. It was the obsession that bothered her, the blown-up photographs of her taken, she had discovered, by a hidden camera mounted above the door in the locked room and focused on the bed.

Yes, the first time she was at his house she had gone along with the kinky sex—she wondered why he'd never brought her into the locked room—and there had been times when she was aware of doing things alone on the bed while Wade watched, directed even (out of camera range), and she should have guessed then that something was wrong. But it was erotic, kinky, and apparently harmless. They were tantalizing each other, fulfilling fantasies, she had told herself, which was, after all, the whole point of an affair. Wasn't it?

She tried to imagine Patrick's reaction if he were to walk into that room, see the blowups; what he would do.

Steady, stable Patrick. The good cop, the famous cop. The cop who had never been on the take, who had never used undue force in restraining anyone. Patrick, whose integrity was his word, who, if he'd ever been with another woman, it was only because she, Lee, had had to split temporarily. Like the time she went to Europe.

Come on, stop it! Why was she doing this? He wasn't that good. No, goddamn it, he was that good. And she felt, come on, say it. All right. Guilty. She had walked into that room, that den, whatever it was, saw everything, and felt the guilt pour out. It took a blown-up photo of her masturbating on a bed to bring it out. But it was there. Now how did she get rid of it?

Patrick would take one look in that room, and he would turn and walk out. Where other guys would turn into rage and want to kill, Patrick would turn inward. He would go home, work around the house, spend days, maybe weeks, doing things like dealing with the problem of cat piss. He would work, keep himself in check. Then he would come to her and ask if she wanted to talk about it.

He wouldn't leave her, he was too stoic. She thought back to the time they'd first met. One of the things he told her—and he hadn't told her much about himself—was that he had a kid sister who was in college. She didn't pay much attention to it then, just conversation about family. It was two years before she learned that he had put the kid sister through college on a rookie cop's pay when their mother, who had been the sole support of the family since they were kids, died.

Lee probably wouldn't have found out about it then except his sister was killed in a car accident two years out of college. A year after she and Patrick married.

She was going to have to figure out on her own a way to deal with this mess with Hamilton Wade, to cleanse herself, and to protect Patrick.

What she wanted most of all right now was to save herself, and save her marriage.

That night he walked across the same stretches of beach, empty of people now except for the occasional pairs who wandered out to look at the water, or stare at the dark sky seeded with stars and its cuticle-like moon, while they held hands or embraced, oblivious to anyone except themselves and the natural setting which seemed to have been put there like a backdrop to enhance the couple's already romantic mood.

Paradise.

Patrick would watch, thinking they were newcomers who had not yet heard that there was a killer loose in Paradise, wondering if he should suggest that it might not be safe out here at night. Sometimes he nodded when they passed, and watched as they went back to their cars or hotel. But they seldom noticed him, or if they did, they chose to ignore him; a habit of people who were in love, Patrick reflected, caught up as they were in their own happiness, or wanting to avoid the loneliness of strangers.

He walked along the deserted Rest Beach bounded by condos that had sprouted like weeds in the last decade. The latest was still under construction, its support columns up, some of the floors poured, but open to anyone who cared to sneak in and enjoy a free night's rest before the rent went up with the walls.

It offered, Patrick thought, a perfect haven for the kind of people who got by in life by selling sex on the beach.

He climbed the open, outside stairway and examined each of the floors of the three-story structure with the help of a flashlight. The empty beer and soda cans on the floor, the discarded sandwich wrappers and cigarette butts, could have been dropped there by the construction crew.

He found no sign of anyone sleeping here. Of course, on a clear night, the ground would offer more comfort than concrete.

Patrick walked down the stairs and back out onto the beach. He looked at his watch. It was nearly ten o'clock. He'd been working for the better part of twelve hours. He'd had three doses of Tylenol during the day, but the ache from the gunshot wound was persistent, telling him it was time, past time, to call it quits.

He would have liked to talk to more people like Paul the busboy. Although he'd gotten little of value, he thought, it was people like Paul who were always, and frequently unknowingly, most helpful in solving these kinds of cases. In Chicago he relied on an entire network of individuals, street people of all backgrounds, who he could depend upon to give him useful information when he needed it.

Some were informants, some just people who carelessly answered his questions, thinking they were telling him nothing. Many were friends, people whom he saw daily on the streets, part of the fabric, the network of the city. He looked out for them, and they in turn—some of them— trusted him. Without them his job would have been impossible.

He needed to build that network in Key West, he thought. But it took time, and time wasn't something he had much of right now.

Walking up the beach back toward Lee's car, he passed two gays making love on a blanket thrown on a hollowed-out area of weeds. They didn't pause as he passed by them.

Paradise. As he passed, Patrick wondered if one of the participants was Paul, hustling, making some extra money and finding excitement after a dull day of washing dishes.

He thought about going back, interrupting them to ask some questions and begin building his network. But he couldn't bring himself to turn around. Because he was too tired, or out of deference to the lovers? He couldn't tell which—certainly it wasn't embarrassment. After fifteen years as a cop, he'd seen everything. Probably he was just feeling sorry for himself, he thought, and his own inadequacy.

9

CHIEF CALLS IN CHI COP was the headline in the *Key West Citizen* the day after Jiminez had sprung the surprise press conference on Patrick Bowman. The subhead announced Jiminez's intentions to have the beach killer behind bars within the week.

The main article read the way Patrick had expected it to, the way Jiminez had it planned. There was a lot of emphasis placed on the chief's opinions and pronouncements, which were many. There was some background bio on Patrick, most of it gathered, he guessed, from AP wire files, but there was no question that Patrick Bowman was there merely as a consultant to Chief Jiminez, to do the chiefs bidding.

A photo in the center of the article showed Jiminez smiling contentedly, not a worry in the world. Patrick appeared startled, somewhat wide-eyed, as if he'd been caught by surprise. Which, in a sense, he had been.

Lee had brought home two copies of the paper. They sat in the kitchen. Lee, head down, arms on the table, the paper spread flat, read every word. Patrick held the paper in both hands and, after getting the gist of the front-page article, turned inside to the *Citizen's* more interesting crime report before turning to an article on fishing.

When he finished, he got up to get a glass of rum. Lee was still reading the front page. She had been subdued, distant the past couple days, and he attributed it to the end of her affair. He had left her alone, forgetting to ask even whether Hamilton Wade was gay or not.

In time he knew this would pass. He put one ice cube in a glass, covered it with rum and added a couple drops of fresh-squeezed lime. When he turned back to the table, Lee was staring at him.

"Do you ever regret that we never had kids?" she asked.

Patrick took a sip of the rum. "Want a drink?"

She shook her head.

They had talked about having children the first years of their marriage. The tough years. And decided neither one was ready for that kind of responsibility. Lee because she was too independent; Patrick because he'd had the financial burden of his sister for nearly five years. They said there would always be time. They didn't have to rush into anything. They were still children themselves. He remembered hearing someone say: You never really grow up until you have kids of your own. Patrick knew enough people who had kids who were still kids themselves to refute that belief.

"I don't much think about it," he said. "You either do or you don't, and we didn't. No regrets." He was a believer in what was done was done. There was no point in fighting the past.

"Sometimes I think . . ." She shook her head. Moisture glistened in her eyes.

"Think what?"

"It doesn't matter." She wiped her eyes. "How would you feel if you read a book, a novel, and found yourself a character in it?"

He laughed. "You thinking of taking up a literary career?"

"I'm serious."

He took another drink, tasting the near perfect combination of sour and sweet. "I don't know. Am I the good guy, or the bad guy?"

"You're the cop, always the good guy."

"That's not always true."

"In your case it is."

He shrugged and drank more rum, uneasy, though flattered as always by her unwavering belief in his moral judgment. "Look," he said, "you're trying to get at something. You want to share it?"

"Hamilton Wade's writing a book. We're in it."

He thought about that for a minute, and for some reason it irritated him. He'd never read a Hamilton Wade novel, mostly because he didn't read novels, but also to some extent because he didn't care much for Wade. Nothing concrete that he could put his finger on, he just didn't much like him. And because of that, he guessed, he didn't much like the idea of Wade writing a book about him. What could Wade know about him? Patrick wondered.

"It doesn't sound like a very entertaining idea," Patrick said.

"I didn't think you'd care for it."

"How do you know about it?"

Lee looked down at her paper. "He's writing about these murders, using them as the basis for a novel." She looked up from the paper. "He told me," she said.

The thought crossed his mind that Lee was lying, just some instinct that came with living with a person for fifteen years. But why was she lying? He wouldn't ask her that. But more than anything now, he wanted to know what her attachment to Wade was.

"Something I've always wanted to know about Hamilton Wade," Patrick said.

"What?"

"Is he gay?"

Lee stared at him, the way she'd been staring when he'd turned from the counter after mixing his drink. "He's perverted," she said. He knew she wasn't lying.

It was the beginning of a network, Patrick thought. Sort of ragtag, but it was there. It had possibility. He was walking along Duval Street at nine o'clock in the evening, trying to get a handle on the street life in this town. It had all but disappeared from the beaches, at least the girls. And it was girls, young girls, the street hustlers, that he was interested in.

Kids hanging out around the arcades across from Sloppy Joe's were wearing skintight Spandex shorts and extra-large cotton pullover shirts with the arms cut out and seemingly random holes designed and cut into the cloth, their hair spiked and sometimes dyed green, or pink, or blue; they looked to Patrick like an adolescent street gang that might exist more naturally in the New York subway system than here in the tropics.

They were so androgynous he couldn't tell boys from girls. Some had skateboards that they careened through traffic on and up and over the curbs around the arcade. Others stood in packs talking, chewing gum and smoking cigarettes with the self-awareness of beginners. They passed a joint back and forth with expertise, however, and had a wary eye out for cops.

Patrick paused and watched. They didn't appear to be on the make, or interested in anyone outside their own group. He tried to guess their ages. They could have been between twelve and twenty, and probably were. He thought about approaching them, then decided they would only ignore someone so obviously from the straight world unless he presented his credentials. He didn't want to do that yet, and so he walked on.

A block later he found what he was looking for.

She was sitting alone on the wall of the church outside St. Paul's Episcopal on the comer of Duval and Eaton. Young, with a round, childish face that was punctuated with the eyes of a viper. Back a block the kids were still kids, Patrick thought, despite the smoke and the weird garb. Here, though their ages were similar—he guessed her to be seventeen, maybe eighteen—the kids in front of the arcade and this one on the wall was the difference between day and night.

She looked at him as he passed, her eyes just a breath away from dead, her lips formed into a slight but unmistakable pout.

He stopped, leaned against the wall as people strolled by without taking notice of them. He said, "I'd like to talk."

She said, "I bet!"

Her name was Carol, and she took him around to the back of the church to a secluded grassy area fenced in from the street, dark, and surrounded by trees and thick shrubbery so that they were hidden from the street traffic. They sat on a park bench.

Where Paul the busboy had been diffident, Carol was insolent. He neither denied nor confirmed her accusations that he was a cop. He wanted to talk; she thought he wanted to get into something kinky. He said no, he really just wanted to talk, spend some time— and money. Ten minutes of her time was worth ten dollars, Carol said.

He took a bill from his wallet, and after showing it to her, clenched it in his fist.

She said, "What do you want to talk about?"

"You," he said. "I want to know about you."

"You writing a book?"

"Maybe."

"Well, ask me something, then."

"Where are you from?"

"Key West," Carol said. "I'm a Conch."

"You go to school?"

Carol sulked, crossed one leg over the other and swung her foot furiously. "Look, I'm over eighteen, okay?"

"Okay," Patrick said.

"I know all the cops in town, so you must be new." Patrick had wanted to play this differently, see if he couldn't gain her confidence before revealing himself. He hadn't counted on her being local.

"I'm from Chicago," he said. "I'm helping investigate these murders."

"Dinks," she said.

"What?"

"Dinks. The three girls got killed were all dinks."

"Why?"

"All three of them were from out of town. And they let themselves walk into something."

"What about you? You never walk into anything?" Thinking she'd walked back here with him without any hesitation.

"Never," she said. And added, as if she'd read his mind, "I knew you were a cop."

Patrick let that go. He said, "Did you know those girls?"

"I seen one of them around, but I didn't hang out with her."

"Which one?"

"The first one. She got killed sometime around Thanksgiving."

"You talk to her?"

"Not much. Just pass the time once in a while."

"Can you think of any reason why anybody would want to kill her?"

Carol thought a few seconds and shook her head.

Patrick let the silence hang over them for a moment. Carol didn't seem edgy or uncomfortable. She was getting paid a dollar a minute, more than most cops made, even though she only worked for brief periods of time.

"Carol," he said softly, "you know a lot of people in Key West. Guys."

"Yeah, I suppose so," she said.

"And some of them you've been with."

"So?" Defensive.

"I'm not blaming you for anything," Patrick said. "But maybe you can help us."

"I've already talked to a couple of cops," she said. "What did you tell them?"

"That I didn't know anything."

"But you may know more than you think you do."

"Like what?"

"Guys who are rough, for example."

"I'm not into that."

"No, but you may know people who are."

"What do you want, a list of names?"

"Anyone who's really weird."

"I don't fink on my friends." She stood up.

Patrick looked at his watch. He'd been here for ten minutes. He handed her the ten-dollar bill in his hand. "I'm not asking you to fink on your friends. Somebody out there is killing girls. I don't think you want that to go on."

"I'll think about it," Carol said, and walked away.

Patrick watched her go, then stood up. He hoped he'd scared her enough to get some cooperation but not so much that she would disappear. Despite her own confidence, he was aware that she could be a future victim. He walked home remembering what a good source of help potential victims made.

Lee liked taking pictures at night, working with fast film and a flash, and sometimes capturing some detail that was bathed in just enough street light, or in a couple of rare instances, moonlight, to get a picture that was so disconnected it seemed to belong only in the realm of night shadows.

She had photographed people on Duval Street at night who wandered aimlessly, lost beneath the neon lights of bars and boutiques. For a while she shot only plants, especially night-blooming ones like the cereus cactus, and water lilies set against odd backdrops.

And houses. She had taken pictures of writers' houses all over the island, the living and the dead. From the top of the lighthouse on Whitehead Street, with a telephoto attached to her Nikon, she had been able to look into the bedroom window of the Hemingway House one afternoon. A tour was in progress. She waited for them to pass, but a couple of stragglers stayed behind, two guys, who climbed onto the writer's bed and mugged for a friend's camera, and unknowingly, Lee's.

Lately she'd started shooting houses at night, things that she'd see when she was walking during the day that she thought would make unusual night shots.

Like the house on Elizabeth Street. Over the years she'd been drawn to it, fascinated by its size, its gray, weathered exterior, the way it sat right on the edge of the sidewalk, absolutely stark, without a tree or bush to give it relief. She couldn't count the number of times she'd been by that house, paused to look at it; and today, for the first time, she saw something she'd never seen before.

A door on the side of the house that led nowhere. There was no step, no threshold, no lintel. But there was a round, old-fashioned porcelain knob. And at ten o'clock that night, while Patrick had gone over to the beach area to ask questions, she walked three blocks and shot the door with the Nikon and a flash.

Shortly after she got back home, Hamilton Wade called.

"They bought the book," Wade told her. His voice was dull, his speech slurred. He was drunk.

"Congratulations," she said, equally without enthusiasm. "What's it called?"

"*Moonkill*," he replied. "And it's got best-seller written all over it."

"Interesting title," she said. Wondering how long she could keep up this pretense. "What's it about?"

Wade laughed. "You don't know?"

"How would I know?"

Silence.

Then, his tone of voice belligerent, "Because someone was snooping around in here while I was gone."

"You had a break-in?"

"I didn't say that."

"Then what are you getting at?" she asked, trying to control the tremor that had crept into her voice.

"You're the only one who has a key."

Lee felt her heartbeat quicken as momentary panic overcame her. She hesitated. But what did it matter now? What could Wade do to her that she hadn't already done to herself?

91

"What was taken?" she asked.

Wade laughed again, harsh, without humor. "Come on, Lee. You went through my desk, my files. What were you looking for?"

She thought about admitting it, confronting him with the pictures she'd found plastered over the walls in that room. The thought of that room provoked her anger, but not sufficiently to overcome the fear that Hamilton Wade provoked. She decided on caution, denial.

"I don't know what you're talking about," she said.

Another silence. Then Wade snickered, and she could hear the sneer in his voice. "I could bring charges against you for trespassing, baby."

"Not when you gave me a key." She was trying to keep control.

"I want the key back," he said, his voice even now, without the threatening edge to it. His personality could change so quickly. The thought occurred to her that he was truly crazy.

"You'll get it back," she said.

"Tomorrow."

"All right. Tomorrow."

When she hung up she was trembling. She knew she had to settle things with Wade. She wanted those pictures off the walls. Then suddenly she began to doubt her own response to Wade: perhaps she was wrong, overreacting. He wasn't really as monstrous as she had convinced herself he was; maybe she'd jumped to too many conclusions. He was just drinking too much, wound up by the excitement, the tension of beginning a new book.

"If you want to know the writer, read his books," Hamilton

Wade had once said.

She had read his books. And notes from one that he hadn't even written yet. It occurred to her that she did not know Hamilton Wade at all.

10

Darling walked. She walked slowly along the sand at the edge of the water. As the water eddied it sucked the sand from under her bare feet. She carried her sandals dangling from one hand, her purse hung from her shoulder. She felt the rhythm of the sinking sand, the pull of the water. And she felt her naked thighs brush together beneath the short denim skirt she wore. The moon was a bare slit in the sky. She was alone. It was exciting. These were interesting times, she thought.

Lt. Patrick Bowman, a Chicago cop. *The* Chicago cop. In Key West because of *her*. Darling sighed, her expelled breath mingling with the sound of the water, the light breeze coming off the water. She had read the paper, clipped the article and read it over and over. She felt like she knew Patrick Bowman. There was something pulling them together, as unavoidable as the shifting sands beneath her feet. But she would beat the lieutenant. She had no doubt about that. And she looked forward to the game they would play together. She liked games.

"Ma'am."

Darling stopped, her hand tightening over the clasp on her purse. She'd thought she was alone. She had seen no one walking toward her, and, absorbed in her thoughts, had heard nothing. Some scuzzball had creeped up behind her. She would have to be more careful. She turned, undoing the clasp on her purse.

A uniformed cop stood there, his carefully trimmed moustache

94

covering his upper lip. She smiled. "You startled me," she said, her voice carefully modulated, soft, husky, sexy.

The cop, very young, grinned. "Sorry about that," he said. She looked toward the road. His cruiser was parked there. He had walked across the beach, followed her. "We're patrolling more around the beaches since these murders. It's not a good idea to be out here alone."

"I couldn't sleep," Darling said. Smiled. "The water's so soothing. I'll be all right."

"You intend to be here long?"

"Not long."

"I'll be in the car, then," the young cop said. "I'll keep an eye on you."

She smiled again. He nodded, said good night, turned and walked back toward his cruiser.

So they had pinpointed the beaches. They had a killer who killed young girls on the beaches, and now that was their target area. Fools.

Darling looked at the moon, as though she could will it to grow. They had no idea who they were dealing with; she would show them. And Patrick Bowman.

11

In their fifteen years together, Patrick had never once contemplated life without Lee. They had always worked through their problems, and he was prepared to work through this latest one. And you started by putting the past behind you; what was done, was done, he told Lee. Now she seemed unreasonably troubled. He wondered if there was something more than just the end of an affair.

While he and Bill Peachy fished, Patrick worried about Lee.

With the unseasonably warm weather, Peachy had seen some tarpon in the harbor yesterday. The front that had passed through earlier in the week was mild, temperatures only dropping into the mid-seventies, and it had warmed up again quickly with the steady breezes out of the east.

Bill Peachy had wanted to fish the flats and see if they could scare up a tarpon on a plug. It would be a couple months before they could begin fly casting for tarpon, but it was always fun to anticipate the big fish, and if they couldn't scare up a tarpon, there was always barracuda, or they could fish for something to eat.

Patrick was happy just to fish. And to think.

As things turned out, the only tarpon were the ones Peachy had seen in the harbor, and the barracuda were scarce. There had been a lot of moving from one place to another, and by the end of the day they had wound up catching only yellowtail and a couple of good-sized mutton snapper.

Which was fine with Patrick. He was tired, and irritated because he wasn't in better shape—the lingering effects of being shot at the age of forty-two. He was beginning to look at his life from a different perspective. Was it going to be downhill from here to the finish?

It was after one in the morning when he'd come in from the beach last night. Lee was still awake, waiting for him, worried, she said.

He had smiled. She had always worried. It was something you didn't get used to, living with a cop's hours and not knowing if he would come home that night. She lived in dread whenever a siren went off.

"I'm fine," he said. "Tired."

"Find out anything?"

She was in bed, a book across her sheeted stomach.

"I don't know," Patrick said. "But the other night I was talking to a kid who hangs out on the beach. A hustler. Something he said rang a bell."

"What was it?"

"He described a guy who occasionally showed up there wearing shoes and fancy clothes. Strange attire for beachcombing, isn't it?"

Lee yawned and said, "Probably, but so what?"

Patrick shrugged. "I don't know. Something about the kid's description made me think of Hamilton Wade."

He was unbuttoning his island shirt, the one with tropical birds and bright colors, the one he never wore in Chicago. He tossed it on the back of a chair and turned back to the bed. She was staring at him, the way she'd looked at him at the table that afternoon after she'd read the article. And told him Hamilton Wade was writing a book about the murders, about them.

"You're sure."

Patrick shrugged. "The description fit, fancy shoes, blousy shirts. You know the way he dresses. You know anybody else who goes to the beach in leather shoes?"

He slipped off his pants and went into the bathroom. And heard her say, "Hamilton."

With a toothbrush full of toothpaste in his mouth, he said, "What do you think he's doing? Gathering information for his book?"

She said, "I don't know."

That was last night.

Before heading back to the dock, Patrick watched Peachy, who had been unusually quiet all day, sharpen his boning knife against a whetstone before fileting the yellowtail and snapper. Reminded of Jiminez's suggestion that the killings may have been done with such a knife, Patrick mentioned the fact to Peachy, who without a pause worked the knife under the thin skin of one of the yellowtail without tearing the flesh.

"How'd he come up with that?"

"Forensics."

Peachy flipped the skin overboard. "He really going to have someone in jail in a week?"

Patrick grinned. "Some poor damned fisherman," he said.

When they got to the dock, Peachy said, "You want a beer? My treat."

They walked up to the floating houseboat restaurant in Garrison Bight, just down from where Peachy tied up. Patrick stopped to put a quarter in the machine for a *Key West Citizen.* The headline that greeted him said: LOCAL WRITER MURDERED. A picture of a younger Hamilton Wade stared at him from the front page.

Lee had risen earlier than usual, but Patrick was already up and out of the house. She made herself some breakfast, then sat at the kitchen table drinking coffee, which made her more nervous than she already was.

She was going to see Hamilton today and return his key. Most of the night she had been awake, thinking about what Patrick had said about Wade's eccentric behavior. If Patrick suspected anything more than eccentricity, he wasn't saying.

And Lee didn't want to mention her suspicions and have to make explanations she was unprepared to make. She had to somehow get those photos off the walls at Hamilton's. She should have done it while she was there the other day, she thought, just ripped them off the walls. As it turned out, she had nothing to lose, since Wade suspected she had been in the house.

Now the fear had returned. There was no predicting Hamilton's mood. The drinking, the anger, the accusations she'd made. Anything could happen.

She thought about her life. How she'd always been unconcerned by convention. Bored by it, in fact, so that she had always seemed to live life for the moment, without thought of the consequences. At one time she had even been considered a radical. She wasn't one of those airhead models chomping gum between photo sessions. Demonstrations, marches, equal rights, equal opportunities. For a time in the seventies she was involved, committed.

Then she'd married a cop, though he was a good cop, and other things took her time and attention.

She finished her coffee and went upstairs. In her white robe, she stood in front of the bathroom mirror and applied makeup to her face. The half-moons beneath her eyes seemed darker, the lines across her forehead more deeply furrowed. The deadly combination of stress, worry, and age.

When she had finished with her makeup, she walked back into the bedroom, shedding her dressing gown, which she dropped on the bed. Naked, she stood in front of the mirror that hung over the dresser. She was proud of her body, comfortable with it. She enjoyed looking at it, touching it. She ran a hand over her flat stomach and up her long waist, feeling the smooth softness of skin, touching the underside of her left breast. Her breasts were still high and firm, the nipples large and erect, and it gave her pleasure to look at them. The only sign of age was the freckles that were darkening across her shoulders.

She opened a drawer and took out clean pants and a pair of shorts which she put on. She took out a knit pullover that she slipped on without a bra, then decided it was cool enough for a light sweater and opened Patrick's drawer to take one of his that she liked wearing. It was cotton with long sleeves she wore bunched up above her elbows, the collar of her shirt dimpled above the crew neck of Patrick's sweater.

She was about to close the drawer when something protruding from beneath another sweater caught her eye. She lifted the shirt. Patrick's service pistol lay in its holster. She picked the automatic up, took it out of its holster. She could smell the oil from the recent cleaning.

She had fired this gun a few times when she'd gone with him to the practice range. He had taught her how to fire it, to hold it to get the best possible aim. And she had proved to be a reasonably skilled marksman.

She removed the clip, saw that it was full. She put the gun back in its holster and dropped it on the bed. Then went back to the bathroom to comb her hair.

By the time she finished, she had made a decision. Hamilton Wade was not only frightening, but unpredictable. She went back to the bedroom and dropped the gun into her bag.

Lee used her key to open the gate that led to the pool and the back of Hamilton Wade's home. The sliding glass doors were open to the house, but no one appeared to be around. She carried a large open straw bag suspended from leather straps over her right shoulder. She said, "Hamilton."

There was no answer. She stood by the edge of the pool, reluctant to enter the house, sure that Wade was inside, yet hopeful that he wouldn't be. She saw herself going in now, straight to the upstairs room, removing the pictures and leaving without confronting him.

She walked to the back of the house and said in a conversational tone of voice, "Anybody home?"

Again no answer. She stepped across the threshold and walked quietly across the open living area toward the front of the house and looked in the kitchen. Empty. She walked around to his study, where she'd rifled his desk a few days ago. Also empty. If he was inside, then he had to be upstairs. She walked to the staircase and looked up, waiting, listening. Again she said, "Hamilton," and without getting a reply, started up the stairs.

The thought crossed her mind that he might have seen her coming, was up there lying in wait. There had once been a playful, teasing side to him. She didn't want to be teased, and she didn't want to be scared; she was already frightened enough.

She realized her hand was inside the bag, wrapped around the metal grip of the gun. At the top of the stairs she started down the hall to the bedrooms, pausing once to listen. She thought she heard a noise but couldn't be sure.

The door to his bedroom was closed. She put her ear to the door but heard nothing. She turned the doorknob. Another empty room. It looked as unchanged as when she'd been here before. She stepped inside, looked up over the closed door leading to the other room as she remembered the camera and purposely stayed out of its range, away from his bed.

She went to the closed door, listened, and now heard an

intermittent light scraping sound like a chair being pushed across the floor. She smelled the tangy residue of marijuana in the air. She put her hand on the doorknob. She should have called, telling him she was coming. But at some instinctive level she knew she had planned this. She wanted to surprise him.

She twisted the knob, and the door opened.

Hamilton Wade was on his knees beside the exercise bike with its customized vibrator. He was naked, making it with a young girl who was also on her knees, but Wade seemed to be supporting her, his hands on her hips, pulling her onto him while she clung to one leg of the bike stand, which grated against the floor to the rhythm of Wade's movements.

When the door opened, Wade slowly turned to face her, releasing the girl, who dropped to the floor. Lee thought the girl was dead until she saw her body move, her head turning toward the door. The girl's eyes were blank, drugged. They seemed to stare unfocused, and then close. She was out of it.

"Don't you ever knock?" Wade said. His voice was thick, and he also seemed to be drugged, or drunk. He stood up, looking ridiculous, still half erect, his hands outstretched.

"Take the pictures down," Lee said.

Wade looked around the room like he didn't know what she was talking about. "Listen, baby—"

"I don't want to listen. Take them down."

Wade walked toward her. He was grinning. A jaded imitation of the dust-jacket smile.

"I'm celebrating," Wade said.

Lee walked into the room and began pulling the photos from the wall. Ripping them, and shoving them into her bag. Wade followed her. Screamed at her. "What the hell's gotten into you? Are you crazy?"

Yes. She moved around the room, tearing and ripping the slick paper with her face and body blown up. Yes, crazy. "But not as crazy as you are," she said. And stepped over the girl who still hadn't moved.

She held the torn photos down in her bag with one hand, and held Wade's key out to him in the other.

She moved back to the door. Wade took the key from her. "Listen, baby, what was that all about?"

"I get paid to have my picture taken," she said. Looking at the disgusting scene she had walked into, her anger was back, the fear momentarily forgotten.

Wade held his hands out. The key clattered on the wooden floor. He ignored it. "What is this? Why are you doing this to me? What the hell did you expect, a saint, a boring middle-class cop like your husband?"

Lee turned and walked out of the room. Wade followed, grabbing her roughly by the shoulder before she reached the bedroom door. "Listen, who did you think you were getting involved with?" he demanded.

"A writer," Lee said. "A good writer."

Wade snorted. "Is that a judgment on my morals, or my fiction?"

"It no longer matters. Look around you, look at what you've become." She tried unsuccessfully to free herself from his grasp.

"You were here while I was gone. And you went through my papers, didn't you? Admit it!"

She didn't say anything.

He put both hands on her shoulders now, squeezing the tendons, hurting her.

She squirmed and hit at his hands with her fist.

He began to massage her neck. "Why? What did you think when you read that stuff? That I killed those girls?" He was grinning at her, tormenting her.

"Let me go," she said. She tried to back out of the room, kicking, fighting to get free.

His hands closed around her neck and began to squeeze.

"Please."

"Please what? Please don't kill me? You want to know something?" he said. "A writer is always learning about himself, learning what he's capable of."

He was leering at her. His breath smelled of stale alcohol.

"You think I write about what I know, but it isn't that. I write to find out what I do know. Can you understand that?"

His hands were tightening their grip on her throat. She struggled to breathe. And looked into his eyes, eyes that didn't seem to see her at all. He pushed her up against a wall. She thought: he's going to kill me. And with her back against the wall, she got some power behind her when she kicked him. He paid no attention, just kept grinning, squeezing her throat.

Lee dropped her hand into the bag and found the gun beneath the crinkled photos. She wanted to scream at him to stop, beg him to please stop, but the words wouldn't come when she tried to speak; she choked, barely able to breathe now.

She lifted the gun from the bag and fired once, blindly.

His eyes changed, then clouded; the grin disappeared and his hands loosened from around her neck.

"Baby—"

Whatever he was going to say was left unsaid. Wade crumpled to the floor and lay in a ragged pool of blood at her feet.

Lee took several deep breaths, held her hand to her throat, then turned and fled from the bedroom.

She thought of her father. Who, when she was fifteen, had instructed her so she would know as much as she needed to know to make her own choices in life. She could decide what time she went to bed, when she got up, whether she went to school or not. It was up to her. She was in charge of her life. She made the decisions. If she had doubts, needed advice, he was there. But the final decision was hers to make.

The thing to remember was that she probably wouldn't make the right decision every time. She was going to make mistakes, because everybody did. It was unavoidable. But she had to learn to live with her decisions, to learn to live with the mistakes as well as the easy choices that wouldn't present any conflict.

Although she had no choice, she knew she'd just made one of the biggest decisions of her life. And she also knew she'd never learn to live with it, right or wrong.

And worst of all, there was no one who was going to help her, who could find a way around her decision.

Not her father.

Not Patrick.

This was final.

12

Bill Peachy sat at the table, his feet tucked around the legs of his chair as though to keep it from being yanked out from under him. He had the shy, cautious nature of men who spent their lives on the sea, Patrick thought. He had read the *Citizen* article while drinking a beer, and wondered how Lee was going to react to Wade's death.

The death of a friend. This was going to be hard on her.

Bill Peachy looked up from his own paper. "You knew this guy?"

"He was a friend of Lee's," Patrick said.

Peachy shook his head. "You think this has anything to do with the others?"

His mind jumped to Paul the busboy, who had described a guy much like Hamilton Wade on the beach at night. And Lee, who said: How would you feel if you read a book and found yourself a character in it?

"Anything's possible," Patrick said, and finished his beer.

They'd had dinner at home. Patrick had prepared the snapper he'd caught that day along with a garden salad, baked potato, and a bottle of white wine. They'd each had a drink before dinner while Patrick cooked, the phone interrupting whatever conversation they started. Lee had seemed hesitant, as though she were stalled somewhere out of reach, just as she had been the past day or two, and reluctant to talk about Wade's death.

All of the phone calls were for her, the literary social set calling in to pass on rumors and start new ones. Finally, in the middle of dinner, she had unplugged the phone.

Patrick had tried to draw her out. "Any interesting theories on Wade, who killed him?"

"No," she said. She was still distant, visibly distressed. He poured her more wine.

"You don't want to talk about it," he said.

"I don't know what to say."

"Did you really like the guy, Lee?" Because of his own incompatibility with Wade, Patrick had always strived to try to understand his appeal to others.

She ate tentatively, drinking more wine than usual. "I thought he was a good writer," she said. "I respected that. He was interesting, not likable, perhaps even sick."

"Perverted, you said." She nodded. "But a good writer."

"I thought so."

She refused to talk any more about Wade. They finished eating, and while Lee cleaned up the kitchen, Patrick read. He picked up a book, an early novel by Hamilton Wade, and began it. When Lee came in she didn't say anything, and they both read until ten o'clock, when she turned on the tube and got the late-night news from Miami.

The lead story was the death of Hamilton Wade. Two Pulitzer prize-winning authors from Key West were interviewed, both of whom repeated essentially what Lee had said at dinner. He was a good writer, though none of them said that he was sick, or unlikable, although Patrick was sure they probably thought so.

The news anchor said that according to Chief of Police Raul Jiminez, there was no apparent motive for the killing, and no suspects were being questioned at this time. The anchor ended by saying that Key West had been plagued by several unsolved murders recently and mentioned the brutal deaths of three women who were thought to have been slain by a serial killer.

Lee had been relieved to hear no mention on the news of the drugged girl who was at Wade's. Either she had gotten out—perhaps calling the police herself, Lee thought—or they were keeping her identity quiet for some reason.

After the shooting she had been extremely calm. There was blood on the sweater she had worn. She had taken it off and put it in her bag along with the gun. She wiped the doorknobs of any fingerprints she might have left, and went into his study, where she unlocked the desk and got his diary for the past year. The one in which he'd recorded their word-for-word conversations. On the desk was his diary for this year, which she also took.

The other stuff, the novel ideas, she left, reasoning that the police would go through it and find the evidence they needed to identify Wade as the killer they were looking for.

And if he wasn't? Well, there was still nothing that could link her to his death—she couldn't bring herself to even think the word "murder"—but the thing that did keep going through her mind was that Wade was evil, that he had gotten what he deserved.

She wiped clean what she had touched, then went home.

She washed Patrick's sweater in cold water, dried it in the drier while she burned the photos and the diaries in a metal garbage container in the backyard—which made her feel more criminal. Damn it, Wade was bad. He had come at her. She hadn't known what he was going to do.

So what was she going to plead, self-defense?

She had put Patrick's sweater along with his gun—which she cleaned, replacing the bullet—back in the chest of drawers. Then she went crazy. She got the shakes, began crying, wanted to call someone and talk about what she'd done— wanted to talk to Patrick and knew she couldn't, knew that she never would be able to. She drank some rum, which seemed to help a little, careful not to overdo it.

By the time Patrick came in, she thought she had control— she'd stopped shaking and was able to keep back the tears.

She was terrified of having to talk about it, and when he came in, he had the paper. He held it up and said, "You see this?"

She nodded and started to cry. So much for control. He held her. "Jesus," he said, "this is some town. I'll fix us a drink and make dinner. You feel like talking?"

She shook her head. Then the phone had started ringing.

Now she was glad to be in bed, escaping reality under cover of darkness. Tomorrow, she thought, she could pull herself together, get back to normal. Or would she ever feel normal again? She wished Patrick would fall asleep.

He said, "There will probably be a connection made between Wade's death and the three women who were killed."

"What makes you think so?" She continued to look at her book, which she hadn't read a word of since they got into bed.

"A hunch," Patrick said. "Wade's presence on the beach at night."

She didn't say anything.

"The other day you said he was perverted. What made you say that?"

"You're reading his book," she said. "Can't you tell? It's autobiographical."

"You want to know what I think of this book?"

Really, she didn't. She said, "What?"

"He's too cute. Everything's a joke. He comes across as a show-off."

She restrained herself from defending Hamilton; a strange position to be in now, she thought.

"Did it ever occur to you that Wade might have killed those girls?"

Lee thought of Hamilton's camera trained on his own bed. "Yes," she said. "It did."

"That's why you've been so upset, isn't it? So distant." He moved toward her, and held her.

13

Raul Jiminez sat in his cramped office with his chief of detectives, Lt. Neil Maloney. Maloney kept him apprised of what the internal affairs division was up to in their investigation. Raul had always had a good rapport with Neil, whom he had promoted to his present rank. The lieutenant was fair, but more important, he was loyal. Despite his ambitious nature he would never go against the chief, even if he had eyes for the job himself, should a replacement for Jiminez ever be sought.

Raul was doing his best to see that never happened. And with the documents that lay on his desk now, he felt confident that it wasn't going to happen anytime soon. Although he should know better than to use a word like never.

The documents piled on his desk weighting down all the other loose papers were the notebooks, diaries, and personal papers of Hamilton Wade. According to Maloney, who had spent most of a night and day in Wade's home conducting the investigation, the papers revealed a novel in progress paralleling the three recent homicides in Key West.

"He was writing a novel about it, huh?" Jiminez said. "You read through all of this?"

"Some of it," Maloney said. "There's a lot of stuff here."

Jiminez put on his reading glasses and thumbed through the top notebook, pausing to read a few pages, then closed the book and removed his glasses. "A lot of familiar names," he said. "A little unusual for a novel, isn't it?"

"Truman Capote," Maloney said.

"Who?"

"He wrote a book, *In Cold Blood,* about a family murdered in Kansas, I think it was. Maybe twenty-five, thirty years ago."

Jiminez wasn't much of a reader. He read a book and forgot it a day after he put it down. "A novel?"

"No, it was the real thing. As I recall, he wrote it just the way it happened, interviewed everybody in the town, including the killers when they were caught."

"You think that's what Wade was doing?"

Maloney stood up, walked about three steps to the door and back, which was about as far as you could pace in this room. "I don't know," he said. "Somehow this is different. Everybody's there. You're in it, that guy Bowman, his wife, the girls who were killed. He had files on them, everything that's been written, stuff I haven't even seen from out-of-town papers. It's weird."

Jiminez leaned back in his chair. The idea of being a character in a book appealed to him, provided he was portrayed in a flattering manner. Good press was always useful. But Maloney seemed to be trying to get at something. "Weird how? Wade had a big ego," Jiminez said.

Maloney shook his head. "I don't know. It's like Wade was writing himself into the story, too." He paused. "I don't know much about books, but the thing is, it was being told by the writer, but it was like it was being written by the killer."

Jiminez lit a cigarette and said matter-of-factly, "You think Wade killed them?"

Maloney swept his hand through the smoke from Raul's cigarette. "The thought crossed my mind."

"It would be goddamn convenient if it was true," Jiminez said. "You get any prints in the house?"

"All over the place," Maloney replied. He sat down. "Didn't he have a New Year's party?"

Jiminez nodded. "I was there," he said, as an afterthought.

"You knew him pretty well?"

"One big party a year when everybody in town was invited. Other than that I never saw him," Jiminez said. He didn't mention that Wade had called him twice, urging him to get Bowman's help on the homicide investigation.

"Wade was into some heavy stuff." Maloney smiled. "You ought to take a look. There's one room in his house, looks like a sex shop on Duval Street."

Jiminez seemed to recall that Wade had a reputation for sleeping around. He also had the coroner's report on his desk: Wade had had sex moments before he was killed.

"I'd say it was bordering on the kinky," Maloney said. "Even for this town."

Jiminez stubbed out his cigarette. "I'll read through this," he said. He sensed Neil wanted to get chatty.

Maloney stood up. "A couple things," he said. "There are several diaries in there, going back a few years, but last year's is missing. Also a bunch of pictures or something were recently removed from the walls in that room with the sex stuff."

Jiminez nodded. "Anything else?"

"Yeah. There was a camera in that room. Mounted on the wall above the door. A hole was cut through the wall so that it focused on Wade's bed in the next room."

Jiminez shook his head. "I see what you mean, the kinky bit. Film in it?"

"We're getting it processed now."

"And you're checking the neighborhood, right? Maybe somebody saw something."

"We're doing that, too," Maloney replied.

"Any break yet on the woman who called in and reported the death?"

"No," the lieutenant said.

"Keep me informed," he said. "Also, you're checking around the fish houses, aren't you?" He saw Maloney nod before going out, closing the door behind him.

Raul picked up one of Hamilton Wade's notebooks and started to read.

"What I'm trying to find here is a motive," Jiminez said. "Why anybody'd want to kill the guy."

Patrick felt good, like a kid looking forward to things again instead of an old man on the downhill slide. Amazing. All because his dick had gotten hard the other night. Lee had put him off, saying she was too upset, but they had made love in the morning and a couple of times in the afternoon. He'd even slept for seven hours last night. Jiminez now seemed less threatening. Amazing.

Patrick said, "I knew a guy in Chicago got killed over twenty-five cents. It doesn't take much these days. People out there are on a hair trigger." He'd called Jiminez to tell him what he'd found out from the kid on the beach the other night, and the chief had asked him to come in. Wade's murder dominated their talk. Wade was society, the girls simply street people.

"Nobody's called in with a tip? Somebody who might have seen something unusual that didn't mean anything at the time, but now that he's dead—"

Jiminez glared at him with those arrogant eyes, as if to say he didn't need any hotshot cop from Chicago telling him how murders were solved. "We're talking to people," the chief said.

"I talked to a kid myself on the beach the other night."

"You don't have jurisdiction down here to set up your own personal investigation," Jiminez said. "I called you in on an advisory basis. I thought we were agreed on that."

Patrick checked his growing anger. "I haven't set up a personal investigation. I identified myself and asked a few questions and came here to tell you about it."

"Who'd you talk to?"

Patrick decided to refrain from mentioning Carol, the girl he'd talked to in the churchyard the other night. He said, "Paul, a busboy.

He's a hustler on the beach, around the fort."

"I know. We already questioned him."

Patrick smiled. "Your questioner missed something. It happens. Which is why it sometimes works to follow up with a different set of questions and a fresh face."

Jiminez stared hard but didn't say anything.

"Paul gave a pretty good description of Wade, who apparently had started hanging out on the beach at night."

Now Jiminez smiled as though relieved. "I know," he said. "We think Wade was researching material for a book he was writing."

On instinct Patrick decided to withhold from Jiminez his own awareness of Wade's literary venture.

"You won't believe it," Jiminez continued, "but the guy had quite an interest in you. You're a main character in the book, along with a serial killer stalking young women on Key West beaches." Jiminez sat back, grinning like he'd scored a knockdown.

"You read the book?"

"The first three chapters, for which he got a contract from his publisher just before he was killed. Hamilton Wade was going to make you famous. More famous," Jiminez added, still grinning.

"No kidding."

"No kidding. In fact, Wade was setting up a little competition between you and the killer. He was going to turn you into quite a hero. At the expense of the Key West Police Department, no doubt."

"Well, you don't have to worry about that now, do you?" Patrick said.

"I don't know. Do I?" Jiminez smiled. "By the way, I photocopied those chapters. I was going to give them to you, let you or your wife read them. We're not that literary around here and there's something we don't understand."

"What's that?"

"Well, you take a look." Jiminez passed a manila folder across the desk to Patrick. "The way I read it, a case could be made for thinking Wade killed those girls himself. He was a strange guy."

"You might want a little more proof than a manuscript for a novel."

"We're working on that."

The phone rang as Patrick stood up. Jiminez answered it, listened and said, "You're kidding." He listened awhile longer, then hung up and looked up at Patrick. "Listen," he said, "I'd really like your wife to read those chapters, then come in and talk to me about them. Would you ask her to do that?"

"What for?"

"She understands this kind of thing." Jiminez smiled. "Maybe she can shed some light on it."

Patrick returned the smile. "Of course," he said. And went out.

He sensed that Jiminez knew something, or suspected something about Wade and Lee that he was not sharing, a thought that troubled Patrick more than he wanted to admit.

Confession was cathartic, good for the soul; through it guilt could be relieved. In everything that she'd ever read, confession resulted in forgiveness. Lee longed for forgiveness.

In the morning when she awoke, she was in tears or on the verge of them. At night, now that she and Patrick were making love again, she went to sleep in tears. The tears did nothing to wash away her guilt. The cruel irony was that the time when she most needed to be alone, to think—was a time that should have been joyous, which she and Patrick could have shared as they once had. It now seemed like cruel and unusual punishment. She wondered what Patrick thought when she refused him and then cried herself to sleep.

Up to now he had been sympathetic. He would understand that Wade had been her friend, his death had shocked her. But how long could she expect him to go on being understanding before he started to ask questions? And what if he were to join in the investigation of Hamilton's death?

All along she had only been trying to protect Patrick. Wade was evil, he might even have been a killer, but Patrick would never understand her becoming the man's judge and executioner. Her mind had resisted acknowledging that she was a criminal now. A murderer. And in Patrick's mind she knew there could be no justification for that unless her life were threatened. Was her life threatened? Wade had choked her, his hands squeezing her throat. He was drunk. But would he have killed her, or was it just more of his dramatic, drunken posturing? Would he have killed her because of what she knew about him? Yes, she wanted to scream—but couldn't because she didn't know.

A crime of passion? There was little defense for that sort of thing in this country. You got away with that in France, in South America, not here. She was confused. She wanted to be rid of the guilt, to be forgiven.

When Patrick came in and handed her the manila folder containing three chapters of Wade's novel, she said, "I slept with Hamilton." It was a partial confession, and like all partial confessions, still left her feeling terrible. She knew that all she had to do was change her confession and it would all be over, at least out in the open.

She also knew that by changing that confession, Patrick could never forgive her.

14

Bill Peachy sat in the Monday-night city commission meeting, his mind a million miles away from the discussion.

You could keep your ear to the ground forever, he thought, but sometimes the herd was just quiet. The way it was now. There was talk about the Wade murder, abundant gossip and speculation, but Key Westers would take far less interest in a society homicide than they would in three dead girls knifed on the beach. The reason, Peachy thought, was because Wade was only a winter resident, rich, spoiled, and jaded, beyond the reach and understanding of the average citizen. Fundamentally, they couldn't care less about a guy who contributed little more to the community than the occasional national attention he brought to Key West as the result of some boozy, embarrassing personal episode. And of course an annual New Year's party in which a few select locals were invited to rub shoulders with the great man. Or something.

Wade's murder was probably even predictable, given his lifestyle. And finding out who done it would be routine.

On the other hand, there was nothing predictable about three victims of a crazy killer with a fascination for slashing throats. Someone was out of control. If he wasn't caught, the entire community would be terrorized.

Jiminez had managed to stem that terror temporarily by announcing that he expected to make an arrest within a week. And introducing Patrick Bowman to the case. It had the calming effect of a tranquilizer. At the end of the week, however, the drug would wear off. Peachy didn't believe Jiminez could deliver in that short a time—even with the help of the expert, Patrick Bowman. He only had a couple days before the end of the week.

Peachy knew the source of his antagonism for Raul Jiminez. The chief—then, he had simply been a cop on the beat—had once made a mistake.

Sam Purdy, a commercial fisherman and a man Peachy had grown up with—even though they were never close friends—had found more profitability in smuggling dope than fishing back in the early seventies, when it was still a relatively secure way to make a living. Purdy was rumored to have had a cop in his corner who added to his margin of security.

On the last enterprise of his career, Purdy had been offloading several bales of marijuana from his boat into the back of his pickup camper parked at the dock near the fish house. It was four in the morning.

Raul Jiminez was on duty when the still night was suddenly pierced with the noise of squealing sirens from two cop cruisers that pulled into the fish house. Before they got to the dock, there was a gunshot, and by the time the cruisers pulled up to Purdy's boat, Sam was dead on the back deck.

Raul Jiminez came walking out of the shadows, holstering his gun. He told the arriving cops from the squad cars that Purdy had been armed. There was an inquiry. A rifle was found on the deck of the boat, and Jiminez explained that he'd been on routine patrol when he noticed some activity around the dock and had gone to investigate. He was about to call in for backup when the squad cars arrived unexpectedly.

Jiminez was vindicated, but few of Purdy's friends believed that the cop, Purdy's corner man, hadn't shot him in order to protect himself. No one ever satisfactorily explained why Jiminez left his beat to come to the fish house that night, nearly half a mile away.

The party, the first since Hamilton's death, was festive. Nothing was likely to interfere for long with the interminable Key West social scene, Patrick thought, offering a canape to a Danish woman who had come with Wystan Lewis. She was reportedly linked to Denmark's royal family so Patrick referred to her privately as the princess.

He watched the woman eat her canape, and decided she ate it like everyone else, so she couldn't be too special.

He had tried to talk Lee out of giving this soiree, arguing that she was still depressed. Without adding: over Wade. Lee fumed. "I'm not depressed," she said. "You're depressed." And they had the fight that had been building since she told him she had slept with Hamilton Wade.

It was true, he was depressed. His lack of judgment about Wade, whom he'd always thought was gay, was one thing; the fact that Lee was having an affair with Wade practically in front of his eyes, was another. Despite the fact that they had talked about this sort of thing, he was so mystified by it that his composure was shaken.

And so they battled it out, a rare stand-up shouting match in which Lee hurled a plate to counter his accusations, but neither of them won. Instead, two days passed without them speaking to each other at all. Until this afternoon, when they'd called a truce, both apologizing, for the sake of an amicable evening.

"I'm going to New York in a couple of days," Lee said. "On assignment."

He refrained from suggesting that it might be an assignation rather than an assignment, and adding another battle to their private war. He said instead: "When will you be back?"

"I don't know. But we'll get this party out of the way and you won't feel any social obligations."

The social scene: my place tonight, yours tomorrow night.

He carried the canapes through once more, passing the princess who was standing with Raul Jiminez beside the stairway. Patrick overheard her asking Raul to explain the American criminal-justice system.

People spilled out onto the deck in back, flowed through the house and talked in small groups; and as one person left one group, someone new came in to take his place, keeping the conversation alive and varied. Moving from one group to another, Lee soon found that it was not all that varied. Dead, Hamilton Wade was as much the focus of attention as he had been alive.

Lee avoided pausing for long in any one group. She smiled, sipped a drink, and putting her hand lightly on the person's forearm to whom she was talking, excused herself by saying she had to see about the bar, or bring out more hors d'oeuvres.

She found herself unable to talk about Hamilton Wade. Patrick probably was right—she shouldn't have given this party—but she wanted to keep busy before she left, to have people around her, hopefully to hurry the time until she could get herself back together.

Fool, she thought. I've killed someone. How will I ever get back together?

Coming from the kitchen, she nearly bumped into Patrick, who was returning with an empty serving plate.

"They're eating like a pack of wolves," he said. "You having a good time yet?"

Lee smiled. "Any time now," she replied, and brushed past him. She was having a miserable time, and decided to go upstairs to get a moment alone before she broke.

Raul Jiminez opened the drawers in the two bedside tables, but found nothing of interest. He got down on his hands and knees and looked under the bed. In his experience, guns were usually kept in bedrooms; also, without children around, most people didn't bother to lock up a gun. There was nothing under the bed.

The downstairs bathroom had been busy, and people stood in the hallway outside, waiting to get in. He had taken a chance and come upstairs, where he found a bathroom, and alone in the Bowman's bedroom. It had presented an ideal opportunity to make a quick survey. He opened the closet and ran his hand over the top shelf. No weapons.

There was a chest of drawers, and he opened one drawer, then

126

another, and saw, protruding from beneath a sweater, the butt of a holstered handgun. He was about to reach for it when he heard someone on the stairs and quickly closed the drawer.

He stood leaning against the dresser, looking at a framed black Madonna and child on the wall above it, when Lee came in.

He turned. She was obviously startled to find him here. "The bathroom downstairs was busy," he explained. And smiled.

Lee stood in the doorway. She looked from Raul to the painting.

"I'm not much on Haitian art," he added.

"Too primitive for your tastes?"

Jiminez continued to smile. "I like things to look the way they're supposed to."

"And you know how everything's supposed to look?"

"I've got a pretty good idea," Jiminez said.

They stood staring at each other. Lee said, "Were you coming or going?"

"Going," the chief said. And walked past her and down the stairs.

She went to the dresser and, holding her breath, opened the drawer. The gun was there. She pulled Patrick's sweater over it, then went in the bathroom and cried.

It was after midnight, closer to twelve-thirty, when the city commission meeting broke up inside the chambers at City Hall. Peachy had sat through more than four hours of seemingly endless discussion by the mayor and four commissioners who debated and listened to various local interest groups—Bill was the vocal majority

127

by virtue of his sole membership in a group of one—as they tried to pass ordinances and approve or disapprove of the business on that night's agenda.

Peachy had begun attending these meetings years ago as a spokesman for the fishing industry in their conflicts with the various arms of city government who wanted to levy higher and higher fees against the fishermen who docked and conducted business from the city marina.

Over the years, as development threatened to destroy the Keys environment, Peachy spread his interests. He was an effective and articulate speaker who had built up an intricate network of contacts on which he relied for information.

He had gained a reputation, though not always a good one, even among the people whom he claimed to represent. So eventually he spoke only for himself. He lost many of the battles waged within the chambers of City Hall, but he won a few, too, although never enough to begin to believe that he was winning the war.

When he walked out of the place at odd hours of the night, it was usually more in distress than triumph, and, unless he had an early charter the following morning, his mood would carry him to a bar where he would celebrate or, more likely, cry in his beer.

Tonight he felt like walking. Beer wasn't going to quell the sense of impending disaster that he felt. Of course, nothing was. He wanted some air, a little exercise to calm him down before going home, and he didn't feel like talking to people.

Peachy drove out past the county beach, cruising slowly by the

West Martello without seeing anyone or anything unusual. He drove on down Atlantic Boulevard, passing two huge condos which he had personally lobbied against, one of which was still under construction, but concrete evidence nevertheless of his defeat.

When he got to Smathers Beach, he parked his car and got out. He could walk the beach as far as the airport, a good mile there and back. There was no one out here, hardly any traffic. He walked on the sand, staying inshore, away from the water. It felt and smelled good out here after four hours inside the smoky, incandescent hubbub of City Hall. He let his mind wander, thinking really of nothing at all, trying to rid himself of the dread he felt.

Moments before he would have turned to walk back to his car, he saw her coming toward him, walking slowly across the beach a hundred yards away. As they closed the distance between them, she seemed not to notice him. He watched her, walking with her head down. She would pass between him and the water. Probably some tourist who just arrived today. He thought about stopping her, telling her it wasn't safe to be out here at night alone.

He watched her, trying to make eye contact when they were five yards from each other. She looked up once, smiled, then tucked her head back down. Pretty. Young.

He walked on another five yards, then turned back and started toward her. "Hello," he called. He saw her stop, glance over her shoulder. He said, "Wait a minute." Then she started to run.

And everything went to hell at once. He was running after her, about ready to say to hell with it, when he saw the flashing lights of a police car. And one brief blast of a siren. The car screamed to the curb. Two cops got out and jumped the seawall. "Freeze," one of the cops shouted, his gun drawn. But Peachy had already stopped running; he stood rooted in the sand.

The cop with the gun approached him. The other went after the girl.

"What do you think you're doing?" The cop came up, nervous, excitement showing in his eyes and in the way he moved.

"I was out for a walk, saw the girl, and thought I should warn her about being here. She started to run."

The cop looked at his watch. "It's one in the morning."

Bill Peachy shrugged, aware of the inadequacy of further communication. The other cop brought the girl back. He was smiling. "Guess what?"

Peachy watched the face of the cop with the gun when he turned and looked at the girl. Who wasn't a girl at all. Her wig had slipped while she was running. She was a he. The cop who had stopped Peachy stared, shaking his head. "What the hell is this?" he said. "You two better come downtown. I think we should have a little chat."

Raul Jiminez swore as he picked up the phone receiver in mid-ring, abruptly halting the irritating noise. It was two A.M. Maloney was calling from the office. Raul was still feeling the effects of the rum he'd drunk at the Bowman's.

"The hell's going on?" Jiminez said. Beside him, his wife

continued to snore rhythmically. She could sleep through a hurricane.

"I'm sorry," Maloney said. "I know it's a ridiculous hour. Fred has been covering the beaches at night this week. He called me an hour ago. For the past half hour I've been trying to decide whether to call you. I think you better come in."

Jiminez was fully awake now. He could detect the tension in Maloney's voice. "You going to tell me about it?" Raul said.

"They picked up a couple people on the beach. One's a fisherman."

Jiminez could feel his heart thudding against his chest. It was the end of the week when he'd promised publicly to make an arrest. He had a press conference scheduled for ten this morning and he hadn't decided how to play it. Maybe things were starting to fall into place. Raul smiled. "Excellent," he said. "Who's the other one?"

There was a pause. For a minute he thought Maloney had walked away from the phone.

"Neil?" Jiminez said.

"The other one's your son Rafael," Maloney said.

"Rafe?" He couldn't believe this. "Rafe's in Miami," Jiminez said.

"I think you better come in," Maloney repeated.

"Mother of God," Jiminez said. "I'll be right down."

He thought about waking Mercedes, who continued to snore peacefully. Then thought better of it. He looked at her body, which ballooned beneath the covers, and for some reason thought of Lee

Bowman, of the picture he had of her locked in his desk drawer. The one Neil Maloney had called to tell him about, which had been developed from Hamilton Wade's camera the day Patrick Bowman had been sitting in his office.

They were about the same age, Mercedes maybe five years older than Lee. But Mercedes was Cuban and the mother of three children. Lee was a fashion model. And she didn't have a son that he knew of, and if she did, he'd bet the boy didn't dress up in women's clothes.

Raul got up and put on his own clothes, irritated that life had to be so damned complicated.

Rafe was sitting in Maloney's office when Raul walked in. Sitting there, the makeup on his face smeared, a blond wig held in his hand. The boy was dressed in a short skirt and blouse, a pair of low heels on his feet. His luminous brown eyes showed fear.

Raul wanted to cry, perhaps would have if Maloney hadn't been there. He had witnessed this scene once before and had hoped never to see it again. The first time, Raul had gotten angry. And scared. Scared his boy was a *maricon*—a fairy. In anger, Raul had slapped him. Now he just felt sad and depressed.

The shrink in Miami had explained that not all cross dressers were homosexual. Most were not, and Rafe appeared to be comfortable with women. A relief. If the kid wanted to dress like a woman, Raul decided, he could live with that easier than he could if his son was a *maricon*. And as long as he didn't have to witness it.

Maloney quietly left the office.

"Rafe," Raul said. He held out his hand, forced a smile. Rafe

132

took it, and some of the fear left his eyes. The kid did have a certain feminine beauty. "I thought you were in Miami."

"I wanted to come home," Rafe said, his voice thin.

"How long have you been here?"

"A few days."

"Where you staying? Why didn't you call your mother and me?"

"I got a motel," Rafe said. "I didn't want to bother you."

Raul shook his head. He sat down and put his hand on Rafe's bare knee. He noticed the boy had shaved his legs. "It's no bother. We want you to call when you're going to be here. What about your job in Miami?"

"I took some time off." He worked at Jordan's department store in Cutler Ridge and had a small apartment near the shopping center. Raul paid for the shrink and subsidized part of the rent on the apartment. He guessed Rafe probably spent most of his money on women's clothes. Hopefully, Jordan's was giving him a discount.

"Lieutenant Maloney said they picked you up on the beach."

Rafe's eyes went flat. "I was walking, minding my own business," he said.

"Rafe, we got a killer in Key West. He's murdered three girls on or near the beaches."

"This guy started coming after me."

"Rafe, I gotta ask you this." Raul leaned back in his chair. "You weren't coming on to the guy, were you?"

Tears welled now in Rafe's eyes. Raul tried to imagine being Rafe's age and living under this kind of emotional stress. He wondered where they had gone wrong. Whose fault? His, Mercedes's?

Rafe said, "I've told you I'm not into that." And began to cry.

"Okay, son, it's okay. I'll have somebody drive you home."

"I want to go back to the motel," Rafe said.

"Okay," Raul replied. "Will you call your mother tomorrow?"

Rafe nodded and took a Kleenex from his purse.

Maloney was outside in the hallway. "Where is he?" Jiminez asked. Maloney motioned to a closed door down the hall. "Who is it?"

"Bill Peachy."

"Peachy," Jiminez said. "He's a charter-boat captain." Jiminez knew him as an activist, a pain in the butt if he opposed you, but other than that, they never had contact.

"Says he was at the commission meeting tonight and went for a walk afterward to clear his head. Saw a girl on the beach and thought she was a tourist, that he ought to warn her."

"You search him?"

Maloney grinned. "He had a pocketknife on him."

Jiminez scowled. "You know a fisherman who doesn't?" He was irritated again. "I'll talk to him. Get somebody to drive Rafe to the motel where he's staying."

Jiminez walked down the hall and opened the door to another office. Peachy was sitting beside the desk, reading a Police Benevolent Association newsletter. He looked up when Jiminez came in and said, "Hello, Chief. You bringing charges against me or

134

just providing late-night company for a few bored cops?"

"You think of any charges I might bring?"

"Not unless there's an ordinance against walking on the beach at night."

Jiminez ignored the sarcasm. "Lieutenant Maloney says you were carrying a knife."

"I was, and have most of my life. I'm a fisherman. Knives come in handy in this profession."

"Yeah, three girls have found that out in the last couple months."

"That's it, then?" Peachy said. "You're charging me with murder?"

"I didn't say that, but as long as I'm conducting an investigation, you can cooperate, or not, it doesn't matter. We'll get to the same conclusion one way or the other."

"I'm always happy to cooperate with the law, even though there've been times in this town when it was hard to tell the good guys from the bad guys." Peachy smiled.

Jiminez remembered now that the last time Bill Peachy had opposed him was more than fifteen years ago, when Sam Purdy was killed.

"The knife," Jiminez said. "You won't mind if we hang on to it for a while."

"You can have the damn thing," Peachy said. "It never would hold much of an edge. Am I free to go?"

Jiminez nodded. He really would have liked to hold him overnight, tell the press tomorrow that they had someone in custody.

Peachy stood up. Raul had to open the door and step outside to let him pass. As he walked by him, Peachy said, "Give my regards to your son. I didn't mean to scare him."

15

The young blond street hustler was in the same place where he'd last seen her over a week ago, on the wall in front of St. Paul's. He had walked by here several times the past few nights without seeing her, but she was here tonight with two other girls about her age. She didn't see him when he came up.

He stopped and said, "Carol?"

She looked at him with the same dead eyes, then hopped down from the wall.

"The Chicago cop," she said. The other girls stared at him. "You solved any murders yet?"

"No," he said. "I've been waiting for you to help me."

The two girls with her laughed, while Carol's face seemed to be set in an eternal pout.

"Tell him," one of the girls said, touching Carol's arm.

"Tell me what?" Patrick said. They were like schoolgirls egging each other on, he thought. He was glad she was not alone.

"Nothin'," Carol said.

Patrick ignored her comment. "Somebody been hassling you?" He looked at the other girls. One of them wouldn't hold his eyes and looked at the ground.

He turned back to Carol. "Who is it?"

She sighed. "Look, it's nothin'. A fisherman, he gets drunk he goes a little crazy, but it's not serious."

"What's his name?"

Carol didn't say anything.

The dark-haired girl said, "Paco."

Patrick said, "Paco? That's all?"

Carol swore. "Yeah, that's all."

"What kind of a fisherman?"

Carol wouldn't say any more. She started to walk, taking the others with her.

As they left, the dark-haired girl said over her shoulder, "The kind that likes to play with knives."

He thought about going with them, then decided against it. He wasn't going to get any more from Carol, and probably not from the others as long as they were with her. He could have taken them to the police station and had them officially interrogated, but that would certainly mean losing whatever network he had established.

He let them go and walked home.

Lee was in bed reading when Patrick came in. She had nearly finished the fifty pages of Hamilton Wade's manuscript, the three chapters she hadn't seen in his house the day she went snooping. When Patrick came to bed, he picked up the earlier Wade novel, the one with the author's pretty face on the dust jacket that had so beguiled her years ago.

Patrick read, holding the book propped against his chest with one hand. His other hand rested on her thigh. If she turned to look at him, she saw Patrick in profile and a young Hamilton Wade staring at her from the dust jacket.

She read the last of the loose pages, shuffled them together before putting them back in the file folder. Patrick, who had read the chapters earlier, put his book down and looked at her. "Well?" he said.

Even though she'd seen some of Wade's notes, parts of the outline for this book, she was not prepared for what she'd just read. Because the writing was so remarkable, and, with its implications, frightening.

"It would have been a good book," she said. "Perhaps his best."

Patrick wanted to know why. He had always been awed by her education. To Patrick, a book was either good or bad depending upon his enjoyment of it. It amused him to hear her offer critical opinions of what made a book good or bad. It had become a joke between them that whenever she talked about books, or art, he would end up by asking, "Did you learn to talk like that at Bryn Mawr?" And she would say, no, I learned how to fuck at Bryn Mawr. My mommy taught me how to talk.

Lee said, "It's the point of view and the voice of the narrator. Everything is seen through the eyes of the killer, or the eyes of the detective."

"The detective being me," Patrick said.

"Based on you," she said. "It's like a dance, back and forth, back and forth. In each segment the reader gradually learns more about these two characters as they move around and toward each other."

"Except you never know who the killer is," Patrick said.

"Which is the brilliant part. You're seeing everything through the killer's eyes without knowing who he is. I don't even know if it's a man or a woman. It could be any of us, the dark side of any one of our personalities." She faltered. Her mind pulled back to the day she opened the door to Wade's room and found him copulating with the drugged girl, her face thrust into the floor as Wade drunkenly pounded against her.

"Even Wade?"

"What?" She realized he had repeated the question.

"How far would Wade have been willing to go in his research of this character?"

She shook her head. "If you want me to say from these fifty pages that he might be your serial killer, I can't." She turned to face Patrick. He had turned on his side; his hand had worked beneath her nightgown and was stroking the flesh of her thigh. Her skin tingled, unpleasantly sensitive to his touch. "On the other hand," she added, "I can't say that he wasn't, either."

"Jiminez knows that. He's going to want to know more."

"About me and Wade?"

Patrick shook his head. She could see the pain in his eyes.

"Will you tell him?" he asked.

"No," she said. "It's none of his business." She had the feeling that Patrick was coaching her, making sure that she would protect herself against Jiminez's probing questions.

Patrick didn't say anything. His hand inched up, stroking the fine hair where her thighs met. He said, "Want to show me again what you learned at Bryn Mawr?"

For the first time in her life she used a line she thought she would never be caught dead saying. "Not tonight," she said. "I've got a splitting headache."

Jiminez didn't ask. Not right away, anyway. When Lee came into his office, he appraised her with the familiar leer Latin males could project in the presence of a woman. She handed him the file folder and sat down. Jiminez sat down behind his desk. "How well'd you know Hamilton Wade?" he asked. The leer faded, replaced by a smile of camaraderie.

Lee had steeled herself. When Patrick told her Jiminez wanted to see her, she had felt doomed. The manuscript could only be a pretense. There were a dozen people in Key West, professionals, who could have answered his question about those three chapters with more precise knowledge than she had. So she had come prepared for a confrontation.

"I knew him socially for at least ten years," she said.

Jiminez continued to smile. "You like him?"

Lee returned the smile. "He was a difficult man," she said. And added after a pause, "But a wonderful writer."

Jiminez studied her, and she realized how easy it was to feel intimidated by a cop, despite being married to one.

"You know why anyone would want to kill him?"

"No," she said, straight-faced now. "I don't."

"He was a difficult man, you said."

Lee flicked a curl of auburn hair back from her face with a toss of her head. A model's practiced gesture. And said, timing it

141

perfectly, "Do you know a man who isn't?"

Jiminez sighed and leaned toward her, offering a cigarette from a pack of Marlboros that he picked up from the clutter of his desk. She refused the offer with a wave of her hand. "For a beautiful woman like you," he said, lighting a cigarette, "I can't think why there would be any difficulty." He made a production of exhaling a cloud of smoke. "But I guess sometimes there is." He was like something out of a forties movie, she thought, before the Surgeon General, when the cigarette was still a romantic prop.

She didn't say anything.

He continued to smoke, then motioned with the cigarette to the file folder. "You like Wade's book?"

"The writing is good," she said. She began to relax a little.

"You're not bothered by your husband being a character in it?"

"It's a novel," Lee explained. "Patrick was probably the only detective Hamilton knew. There was bound to be some similarities between his fictional detective and Patrick. It happens all the time."

Jiminez shrugged. "If you say so," he said. "But if I was a writer, I think I'd be a little afraid of putting real people in a book. Some of them might want to kill me." Jiminez smiled again.

"I'm sure once it was finished, Patrick wouldn't have recognized himself."

"So you weren't upset with Wade?" Jiminez twisted a pencil in his hands, talking around the cigarette in the corner of his mouth, smoke swirling up over an arched eyebrow. Macho Cuban.

"No," she said.

"He had a reputation, I hear, as a ladies' man."

Lee stared at Jiminez. "What are you getting at?"

"A motive for murder," Jiminez said. He removed the cigarette and ash spilled on the floor.

Lee felt her stomach cramp and crossed her legs. She was wearing shorts; she pressed her palms against the top of one bare leg. "I'm afraid I can't help you solve Wade's murder," she said, struggling to keep her voice under control.

Jiminez shrugged. "We're just talking," he said. "You never know what information will help."

"I thought you wanted to talk about Wade's book." Jiminez smiled again. "Did the possibility that Wade could have killed those three girls ever occur to you?"

"Because of the way those chapters are written?" Jiminez nodded.

Now Lee smiled. Cool, wanting to turn the tables on the cocky chief of police. "If a few chapters of a novel brought convictions, you'd have half the writers in America in jail," she said.

Jiminez didn't bat an eyelash. "There's more than just the chapters. Didn't your husband tell you? Wade had taken to hanging around the beach at night."

Patrick had told her; she didn't know he'd told Jiminez. She said, "That still doesn't make him a killer."

"I understand that," Jiminez replied. "I'm just trying to get a picture of things, look at the possibilities." He leaned forward and pulled open his desk drawer. He put his hand in the drawer and rummaged around. "Speaking of pictures," he said. He withdrew his hand from the drawer, holding a three-by-five photograph. He looked at it, then held it out to Lee.

Her stomach began to cramp again. Instinctively, she knew what it was. She took the photo and saw herself lying naked on Hamilton Wade's bed.

"He apparently liked taking pictures of his guests," Jiminez said.

Lee held the photo, picture side down, against her leg. It seemed almost hot against her skin.

Jiminez stood up. "I've got a press conference. You were right, Wade was a difficult man. By the way, you can have the photo," he said. And added, "We've got the negatives." He paused while he lit a cigarette. "But if you have any thoughts on who might have killed Wade, or why, I'd appreciate a call." He smiled through the smoke. "We can always talk."

Lee left the office. On her way out she asked at the dispatcher's window for the women's room. Inside a stall she tore up the photo and flushed it down the toilet. She wished she could as easily get rid of the horrible feeling in the pit of her stomach.

Patrick sat with his yellow pad, making notes at the kitchen table. Under the heading of "Knives" he had a list of hardware stores and marinas having shops that sold marine hardware in one column, their addresses and phone numbers in a parallel column.

Below the hardware stores was a list of motels, boardinghouses, and apartments that rented by the day or week. Some of those he had obtained by looking in the classifieds of the *Key West Citizen*; others had come from Bill Peachy. They were part of the few remaining rundown places where street people—those with just enough income to be able to afford a modest night's lodging—might stay. People like Paul, the busboy, for example.

Bill Peachy had called earlier. He told Patrick about the encounter on the beach, and being questioned by Jiminez at police headquarters. He'd said, "If the guy was a magician, he'd be pulling rabbits out of his hat."

"He's frustrated," Patrick replied. "We all are. He's talking to Lee right now."

"What about?"

"The Wade thing. Jiminez is looking for a rabbit."

"He's in deep," Bill said. "Maybe even looking for a lifeline while he's going down. Be careful. The guy's dangerous."

"I'll keep it in mind," Patrick said. "Tell me about Jiminez's son."

He listened while Peachy described Rafael Jiminez. Unbelievable. It was the sort of thing that made you glad you didn't have kids. Patrick asked Peachy for the information on some more motels, then told him not to worry and hung up. He went back to his legal pad.

Half an hour later Lee walked in. She looked gray, drawn and tense. He stood up from the table. "What happened?"

She was trying to hold back tears, clutching her hands. He went to her and took her in his arms. "Tell me," he said.

She held him close, her mouth next to his ear. "Jiminez thinks—" He felt her body tighten against him. "He thinks I killed Hamilton," she said.

Patrick felt anger. Anger at Jiminez, and at Lee for letting herself get mixed up with Hamilton Wade in the first place.

Later, when they were in bed that night, he tried to comfort her, sooth her, coax her to sleep, only to find that once he had succeeded, he was unable to sleep himself. He got up and walked down to the kitchen, where he poured a shot of rum into a glass, then stood staring out the window into the darkness while he drank.

He tried to tell himself that none of this was Lee's fault— that she was simply the victim of excessive curiosity and a passion for life. But no matter how many times he made the excuse, there was always the realization that she had made choices throughout her life; choices that had come to hurt him.

Hamilton Wade was only the latest.

But he would forgive her—he had always forgiven her, and his weakness angered him. Tomorrow, after a sleepless night, he knew that he would take his anger out on Raul Jiminez.

Angry, Patrick called Jiminez the first thing the next morning. "What the hell's going on?" he demanded.

Jiminez said, "What are you talking about?"

"You're harassing my wife," Patrick said.

Jiminez was silent. Patrick tried to calm down. Get a grip, he thought.

Jiminez said, "Bullshit. I'm conducting a murder investigation."

"It's beginning to look like a witch hunt!"

Jiminez blew up. "Look, I don't need some big-city cop coming in here to tell me how to do my job. I'll ask the questions. If you don't like it, you can ride out of here on the same horse you rode in on!"

Patrick said through clenched teeth, "Lee's got nothing to do with this."

"She knew Hamilton Wade. Wade's dead. I've got to talk to the people who knew him."

Patrick began to calm down. He knew that he'd overstepped his bounds, but Jiminez's attitude had been wearing on him. "That doesn't mean harassing her," he said evenly.

Jiminez hesitated, then said, "Like the song says, I'll do it my way."

Patrick decided to withdraw, change the subject, as he felt the anger creep back inside him. He said, "There's a girl on the streets by the name of Carol, a local girl. She knows something about a fisherman called Paco who might be worth looking into."

"Which one?"

"Which one what?"

"Paco. There's probably at least half a dozen of them in the fishing industry."

"Just a suggestion. I wouldn't want to tell you how to do your job," Patrick said. And depressed the disconnect button on the phone with his forefinger, before releasing it and dialing Bill Peachy's number.

Surprisingly, Peachy was in. He had a half-day charter in the afternoon, nothing this morning, he explained.

Patrick said, "Tell me something more about Jiminez." He was still charged with anger after talking to the chief.

"I already told you," Peachy said. "The guy's on the wrong side of the law. He ought to be in jail instead of running the department."

Patrick had assumed that Peachy's animosity for Jiminez had always been personal, derived from the unconfirmed perception that Jiminez had deliberately killed a fisherman years ago to protect himself. Bad cops were like chameleons, constantly changing their color and often equally hard to detect. Yesterday Patrick had been willing to give Jiminez the benefit of the doubt; he was now beginning to question that attitude.

"I thought there was an internal investigation going on."

"There was. Then they got a couple different murder cases, and with the department already ten men shy of what they're budgeted for, my guess is an investigation into a little mismanagement was put on the back burner."

"What would it take to get it revived?"

Peachy laughed. "You having problems with the chief?" Patrick recounted a portion of his conversation with Jiminez.

"Jesus," Peachy said.

"Look," Patrick said, "I'm trying not to let it get personal, but I don't like bad cops, and I get the feeling Jiminez is looking more for scapegoats than running a solid investigation."

"Like I said yesterday, his back's to the wall," Peachy said.

"You have time, see what you can find out about the I.A. investigation."

"I'll ask around, but I wouldn't count on anything solid."

"Whatever you can get. And something else."

"What's that?"

"You know any fishermen by the name of Paco?"

"I know there's some around. I don't know them personally."

"You want to see what you can find out about one who's got a thing for knives and young street hustlers."

"Sounds like a deadly combo," Peachy said.

"It has been."

16

The face of Jack Palance, evil, intense, filled the seventeen-inch black and white television screen. Thin, worn drapes were drawn against the window of her motel room while Darling lay in bed at four o'clock in the afternoon. The air conditioner kept the temperature down to a perfect chill.

She loved these old cable movies. Jack Palance was a bonus. She loved Palance, the quiet menace that he suggested, better than Cagney, who was too stagy. You could believe in Jack Palance.

On the floor next to her clothes was a Domino's Pizza carton. A half slice of pizza and some congealed cheese littered the inside of the carton. The nappy bedspread was covered in newspapers and magazines, all of them opened to feature stories about the wave of killings in Key West.

In the last couple of days something had happened; the spotlight had shifted from Darling and her victims to some rich socialite named Hamilton Wade.

At five the movie ended and Darling got up. She dressed in the clothes that lay on the floor, went into the bathroom and began the daily ritual of applying makeup to her face. When she finished, Darling ran a comb through her short, thick hair, cut in a pixie style, grabbed her purse and left the room, walking toward the motel office.

It was her custom to get a *Key West Citizen* from a vending machine outside the office, then walk down to a local diner where she could sit unbothered and read over several cups of coffee.

The motel office was open-air, covered by a palm thatch roof and open lattice siding. Faded green outdoor carpeting covered the cement floor. Clients did business at a window that opened into one of the motel units where the resident- manager lived.

As Darling came around the corner she saw a man standing at the window talking to the manager. She stopped and walked back in the direction she had come as though she had forgotten something, then stood out of visual range but where she could hear what was being said at the window.

Though she had seen only his profile, Darling had studied his face in newspaper photographs and recognized Patrick Bowman. She stood listening, fumbling in her purse as though looking for whatever she had forgotten.

Lieutenant Bowman was asking for the motel's registration list for the past month. The motel had only fourteen units. Darling had been here less than a week. She made a point of staying in a place for no more than a week, and sometimes for only a few days. She changed names with each change of address and paid her room bill in cash. In a tourist town in the peak of season, there could be nothing suspicious about a woman staying alone in a motel for a week.

Bowman asked if anyone seemed suspicious to the manager. She did not hear the manager's reply.

"Any prostitution that you know about?" Bowman asked.

She heard the manager laugh. "You think I check on what's

going on in these rooms once they're rented?"

Bowman said he was just wondering if he'd noticed anything.

There was a silence, and after a moment, an exchange that Darling could not hear. Then Bowman thanked the manager and left.

Darling walked around to the front of the office and up to the *Citizen* vending machine with a quarter she'd found in her purse. Patrick Bowman was getting into an older-model blue car, it looked like a Buick.

She deposited her quarter and removed a paper from the machine. The headlines jumped out at her. WADE LINK WITH BEACH KILLINGS? She read the first couple of paragraphs, in which the police chief hinted that there might be a link between the Hamilton Wade killing and the other recent murders.

She couldn't believe it. The chief of police had even questioned suspects in both murders. Who? The paper didn't mention names. It was a bluff, Darling thought. Probably by the hotshot lieutenant whose name didn't appear in the article. He was running the entire show now, hoping to flush her out by making her think they knew who the killer was. Then why didn't they make an arrest? Because they were guessing, trying to confuse her.

She stuffed the newspaper into her bag and walked to the corner diner, where she drank several cups of coffee, read the paper, and practically memorized the lead story. Hamilton Wade had been writing a book about the murders on the beach. She had never met Hamilton Wade. How could he write a book without knowing her?

This was Bowman's work. He was the clever dick behind this,

just as she had known he would be. The caffeine triggered thoughts of what she had to do next in order to get Lt. Patrick Bowman's attention, and in her head she began to plan the details.

17

Several hours went into tabulating the information Patrick had gathered from the motels and boardinghouses where he'd asked to look at their registration records for the past couple of months. It had taken him three days to get the information he had. He had even checked the records at the more exclusive resorts.

Everyone had cooperated. He was, after all, investigating a series of murders. He was also, he knew, overstepping his bounds, his agreement with Jiminez. He was no longer serving merely as a consultant. But with another murder case to work, Jiminez's attention was divided between two fronts now. Patrick reasoned this was something he could do quietly and quickly. If something came of it, good; if not, no harm was done other than the waste of time it represented.

It was a long shot, Patrick admitted to himself. The idea that the killer might be one of four million tourists who passed through Key West each year didn't make for very good odds. While Jiminez pursued the local angle, Patrick had set out to reduce those odds.

He sat at the kitchen table, the chart, pages of his legal pad taped together, spread out around him. Under each establishment he had the names, dates, time of arrival, and time of departure of the various guests. He had home addresses, and credit-card numbers for those who charged.

Further, he had the occupants listed according to sex, and

whether they were by themselves, part of a couple, or in a group. He had license-tag numbers for those who had registered their cars.

By discarding those who weren't registered at the time of one or more of the murders, he had managed to winnow the names on the chart down to cover a mere twenty-seven sheets of paper.

He was most interested in the guests who had occupied a room alone. So far he had not been able to find the name of anyone who had been staying here during all three murders. There were several overlapping names, however, during the time two of the killings took place, the one just before Christmas and the other on New Year's Eve.

On the other hand, he had to assume that a killer staying in a motel or a guest house would probably move around, and certainly use different names.

There were 133 names that he had underscored with a red marking pen that he wanted checked. They were all single, 119 were male; women, it seemed, were less inclined to come here alone. All who were marked in red had been here over the holiday period.

Another group, also single occupants, marked in blue, had been staying in Key West at the time of one murder. Two hundred eleven people, most of them men.

He faxed the total 344 names into the detective division in Chicago and asked to have them plugged into the computer to be checked.

The person monitoring the precinct fax machine at that moment was a colleague. He sent back a sarcastic reply about being delighted to receive 344 suspects to run through, since it was cold outside and he could look forward to some inside duty. And signed off with a comment about fun-in-the-sun crime detection.

Patrick used the Buick to drive around to the various marine hardware stores, where he looked at boning knives. They came in different lengths, with different style handles, but by purchasing a half-dozen knives, he found that he had a representative collection. From the hardware stores he drove to Stock Island and began hitting the fish houses, asking questions. Fun in the sun.

Three days ago he had driven Lee to the airport. Her agent had called, she told him, with a week's worth of work in New York if she wanted it. Magazine ads. She had seemed glad to get away from here, Patrick thought, saying that she might even spend a few extra days in the city. The agency would put her up in a hotel while she was shooting.

So Patrick had nothing to do but work. At night he would talk to Lee on the phone, tell her how it was going, what he had done that day. She would talk about her assignments and wonder at how she had found this such a glamorous business twenty years ago. She still seemed distracted, distant. Like she had cut some part of herself away from him, or was hiding something. Whatever it was, it depressed him that he was unable to get through to her anymore. He worried, and he worked.

It took him two days to get the information he wanted from the

156

fish houses—names of each company's crew members who worked on fishing boats. Those names he also phoned into a colleague in Chicago.

Running names through the national crime computer was, he knew, nothing more than a stab in the dark. But it was all he had to go on. A single, simple break, one link with the killer, could make all the difference. So far no one had found that link, and until they did, there was nothing to do except routine police work—the tedious checking and crosschecking that was such a frustrating part of this job.

After more than a week at it, Patrick remembered that he was supposed to be here recuperating. He took a break and went fishing with Bill Peachy.

For the past week Raul Jiminez had established a routine with his chief of detectives, Neil Maloney. Every day at one o'clock they would lunch together. It gave Jiminez the opportunity to keep abreast of the investigation and, in the relaxed setting, to feel Maloney out about the ongoing internal affairs investigation. They usually ate in one of two or three places, chosen for economy and the provision of a certain privacy for their conversations. The Cuban restaurant, El Siboney, on the comer of Catherine and Margaret, was Jiminez's favorite. He'd steered Maloney there twice.

With the limited manpower available to him, Raul had set up a two-pronged investigation. Maloney was to divide his four-man team—including himself—between questioning the sizable fishing fleet in Key West and finding the girl who had reported Hamilton Wade's murder.

Jiminez still believed that Wade and the beach killings were linked. Nothing would have pleased him more, at this point, than wrapping this case up by having a dead man found guilty of the three murders on the beach.

A possible witness to the Wade death was the closest thing he had to a lead.

Sitting at a corner table in El Siboney during the busy lunch hour, Maloney had just told him they had questioned a girl last night who claimed to know the girl they were looking for.

"Where is she?" Jiminez asked. He mixed some black beans with a bit of plantain and put it in his mouth.

"Carol, the girl we talked to, hasn't seen her for over a week. She's pissed." Maloney was working his way through a Cuban Mix sandwich.

"What's our girl's name?"

"Denise."

"She got a last name?"

"Probably, but Carol doesn't know it."

"Mother of God! Who are these people?"

Maloney smiled. "Hustlers, coke whores, street people. You name it. Also, Carol's local."

Jiminez remembered his conversation with Patrick the other day. He'd also mentioned Carol.

Then he thought of Rafe, who Mercedes had convinced to stay at home with them. Just for a few days, Rafe said. He had moved in with a suitcase full of skirts and dresses that were hanging in the closet. Raul sometimes felt like he'd been asleep for a decade and when he woke up the entire world had gone crazy. "Maybe Denise is in jail," he said.

Maloney shook his head. "Carol just got out of jail. She was in for a week for possession before she could come up with bail. Carol had left clothes with her, but now Denise's split and Carol's pissed."

"Carol got any ideas where she might be?"

"You'll love this. Palm Beach. She thinks Denise was from Palm Beach and may have gone back there."

Jiminez shook his head. "Down here slumming?"

"Maybe."

"Could that explain her connection to Wade?" Jiminez still had a hard time connecting Hamilton Wade with tramps.

Palm Beach was Kennedy territory, along with Pulitzer and Trump. Which didn't mean their daughters were incapable of mingling with the common folk on occasion, getting down and dirty.

Maybe Wade knew the girl's family.

"She mentioned Wade," Maloney said. "He had a thing going with most of them, but Denise was his favorite. Carol didn't like him. Said she was afraid of him. 'He'd push you,' she said, 'to see just how far you'd go.' "

"How did Carol know Denise was with Wade before he died?"

"She was with her when Denise called the police."

Jiminez thought about that. "I can't figure why she'd call us, why she'd even get involved in the first place."

Maloney shrugged. "Maybe Palm Beach girls are more civic-minded."

Jiminez drank some iced tea. "Find Denise," he said.

"We've got a BOLO for her in Dade, Broward, and Palm Beach counties," Maloney replied. "With her picture. It's a doozy, taken with Wade's own camera. Carol identified her."

Raul nodded and went on eating, thinking of Lee Bowman, who had gone to New York on business, according to her husband. "We're looking for a nine-millimeter automatic. Carol know if Denise had anything like that?"

"No, she didn't know about any guns."

Raul finished his meal and pushed his plate away from him. One of the fat Cuban waitresses in tight white jeans brought him a *buce*—a shot of pure sweet coffee that was like liquid medicine in a small cup.

"You having any luck on the docks?"

"The usual. At least a quarter of the commercial fishermen have got some kind of record. It's taking time just checking them all out."

"Time's in short supply." Raul drank off the shot of coffee in one gulp. "I'm particularly interested in any guys named Paco."

Maloney took out a notebook and jotted the name in it. "We're getting some help," he said. "Bowman's been around asking questions, too."

Jiminez wiped his mouth with a napkin and lit a cigarette. "Bowman's just here as a consultant. He's got no authority to work this case."

"Better tell him that. He's been hitting the hotels around town, too. I've got three men on this besides myself. We're working ten- and twelve-hour shifts."

Jiminez stood up. They both laid money down, and Maloney slid out from behind the table. "We can use the help," Maloney added as they walked out the door.

They had driven here in separate cars. Maloney walked over to the driver's door of his car and stood there expectantly.

Raul said, "How's the other investigation going, the internal affairs thing?"

Maloney grinned and hunched his shoulders. "Who's got the time?" He got into his car and drove away.

Raul got into his own car, drove back to the office and called Patrick Bowman.

Patrick stopped by the chief's office the following day, expecting to be berated for interfering in a local police investigation. Instead, Jiminez's attitude seemed almost conciliatory.

"You work in your own way," the chief said.

"Quietly," Patrick responded. "I haven't been stepping on anyone's toes, or calling attention to myself, I hope."

"That's good."

"It's still your show."

Jiminez nodded. He looked tired, depleted. The chiseled features of his face seemed puffy, ashen. Patrick, by contrast, was tanned and rested after a day on the water. He knew he would have to pace himself, and knowing when to stand back and look at what they had was as much a part of an investigation as the legwork and note taking he had been doing. The principal thing was not to crack.

"What have you found?"

As the chief listened without expression, Patrick brought him up to date.

"When you get a report back from Chicago, I want to see it," Jiminez said when Patrick had finished.

"You'll be the first."

"How long's your wife away?"

"Another week, I think."

"That's too bad," Jiminez said.

"Why?" Patrick bristled, feeling his pulse beat erratically against his temples. He had to work to keep control.

Jiminez smiled. "I enjoyed our meeting the other day. I've been looking forward to talking to her again."

"I'll let her know the next time we speak."

"Do that," Jiminez replied. "And remember to keep me informed of anything relevant."

Patrick nodded. He had the feeling that if the chief had any information of his own, Patrick would not be on any favored status list.

18

Patrick received the fax report from Chicago two days later. It contained thirty-one names from the original 344 he'd sent in. Of the thirty-one, twenty-two had petty crime records—shoplifting, auto theft, traffic violations—and the other nine were of more than passing interest.

Of the nine, three names came up blank, unknowns. Originally there had been eleven unknowns, but after an initial check by the department, eight of those had proven to be aliases.

Patrick wrote the names out in alphabetical order on his legal pad, along with addresses, when they differed from his original list, and any other relevant information that had been included in the report. What was disturbing were the three names whose addresses were listed as unknown, for it meant that the addresses used on the motel registration forms were probably false.

Clemente, Anthony. Garlind, Ricky. Johnston, Tom. Leigh, Daniel. Power, Virginia. Priest, Mike. Ross, Steve. Thurman, Nancy. Wilcox, Karen

Patrick read through the material on each name several times, absorbing it, looking for the unusual—or even the obvious—to strike him.

Anthony Clemente was a convicted felon, armed robbery, living in Miami. He had spent two years in jail and had been out a month when he came to Key West, where he stayed in one of the more

163

moderate, but not the cheapest of motels, in town. He had been in Key West through Christmas and New Year's.

Ricky Garlind, address and whereabouts unknown.

Tom Johnston, who lived in New York, in Queens, was also in Key West over Christmas and New Year's. Johnston had been convicted of rape in 1985 and did less than a year in jail.

Daniel Leigh, from Detroit, had been arrested several times for assault against his wife, but after each arrest she refused to press charges. They eventually divorced. Leigh was moving around, apparently was six months in the Keys working odd jobs until he arrived in Key West in December and stayed in a cheap motel for two weeks.

Virginia Power, from Cleveland; a warrant out for her arrest on charges of embezzlement. Last known destination was the Florida Keys.

Mike Priest, address and whereabouts unknown.

Steve Ross, charged with child abuse in Wichita, Kansas. Served two years at Leavenworth, 1980-82. Now living in Miami, with a woman who had three kids.

Nancy Thurman, Chicago, convicted of attempted murder of husband's girlfriend. Served one year of a three-year sentence in 1987.

Karen Wilcox, address and whereabouts unknown.

As he read, Patrick tried to get a mental picture of each of the nine people, a sense of who they were, how they lived. With six out of the nine, he could do it at least partially, because over the years he'd dealt with many similar people. It was the unknowns, of course, who he couldn't get a handle on, and they piqued his interest the most. People who just dropped out and disappeared for one reason or another, changed identities, changed their names—they were the hardest to pinpoint.

He would have the FBI and the IRS run checks for him, but it would be a total shot in the dark, as all of his efforts had been to this point. The odds, he knew, were stacked against him.

Patrick put away the papers and called Lee in New York.

They found Denise in Miami. She was hooking on Biscayne Boulevard when she was picked up by Vice and charged with possession of three rocks of crack cocaine. An hour after being busted, the Miami cops linked her to the BOLO issued by the Key West police. It was seven o'clock in the evening when Maloney took the call, then phoned Jiminez at the chiefs home.

Raul flew to Miami the next morning to question the girl. The two of them were left alone in an interrogation room. Denise chewed gum and stared insolently at Jiminez.

"Denise Jacobs," Raul said, studying the report provided by the Miami police.

Denise didn't say anything.

"Three rocks of crack and soliciting. They got you pretty good, Denise. You got a lawyer?"

"I can get one if I need one."

Raul studied her closely. Dark hair, angry eyes. Her facial skin was dry, wax-like, but despite a few craters where acne had scarred her cheeks, she was pretty, good features and a shapely body. She was twenty-three and she'd been through this before. Raul looked back at the report.

"You were busted in Key West, I see. Sooner or later they're going to slam the door on you, Denise, and walk away." They wouldn't, of course, Jiminez knew, because there was no room in the jails in south Florida. Still, it sometimes worked as a scare tactic, unless you were streetwise, and Denise obviously was.

"Who are you?" she said.

"Raul Jiminez. Key West police chief." He looked at her and smiled.

Denise popped her gum. "Yeah," she said. "What do you want with me?"

"We talked to your friend Carol the other day, the one who was in jail. She got worried about you. You took off with her clothes."

"I don't have that fuckin' whore's clothes. I left 'em with one of her tricks."

"She says you took off because you were scared."

"Scared of what?" Denise took the gum from her mouth and stuck it to the underside of the table where they sat.

"Maybe murder," Jiminez said.

She squirmed, pushed her hair back and looked down at the table. "I don't know what you're talking about."

"I'm talking about Hamilton Wade."

She shrugged.

166

"We've got voice prints, Denise. We can identify you."

"That fat mouth," Denise said.

He supposed she was referring to Carol.

"You were there when he was killed, weren't you?"

A long pause. "I didn't kill him," she said.

"I didn't think you did. Otherwise you wouldn't have called the cops. But I think you saw who did kill him."

She slid forward in her chair, put her elbows on the table and rested her head in her hands.

"We're not talking about some petty-ass drug thing now, Denise." Raul got an edge to his voice. "This is murder. You understand?"

After a while she raised her head. Her eyes glistened; they had lost their anger. She shook her head. "I was on stuff," she said.

"What stuff?"

She opened her hands. "PCP, coke, some dope, I don't know what all. And I'd been drinking."

"But you were there when he was killed."

She nodded.

"Tell me what you saw."

She shook her head. "Someone came in the room. I remember—"

"What?"

Denise looked at her hands. "I remember thinking that Hamilton had got somebody to double-team with."

"Double-team?"

167

"You know, sex with two other people. He liked that."

"You had double-teamed with him before."

"Yeah."

"With men or women?"

"Always just two women."

"So if you thought you were going to double-team, it must have been a woman who came in."

"I don't know," she said. "I can't be sure."

"Then what happened?"

"Hamilton went away. I think I passed out. I heard some noise. When I came to, he was lying on the floor, blood all over the place."

"Nobody else was there."

Denise shook her head.

"You didn't see a gun, any kind of a weapon?"

She shook her head again. "But I didn't look. I just got out."

"Where'd you make your call?"

"A pay phone on White Street."

"And Carol was with you?"

Denise stared at him, a look of hatred in her eyes. Jiminez smiled. "Why'd you bother to call the cops?" he asked.

Denise pushed her hands through her hair again. "Look-it," she said. "I didn't know the guy was fuckin' dead. I wanted to get help to him, that's all."

Raul took an envelope from his shirt pocket. He took out a photograph and held it out to Denise. "You recognize her?"

She looked at the photo of Lee Bowman and shook her head.

168

"No," she said. "I don't think so."

"You want to be sure. You may have to testify in court."

"I told you, I was out of it. I can't remember."

19

Two weeks. At the most, two weeks, Lee had said. He had looked forward to her getting back. He missed her, but more than that, there seemed to be some juncture in their life, some impending crisis that needed to be dealt with, and the physical distance between them only made it worse.

Then she had called to say she needed more time. Her agent had lined up a couple of smaller jobs for her while she was in the city. "The city." The phrase irritated him, the same sort of irritation he experienced whenever he heard California referred to as "the coast."

In this case his irritation went deeper because it was Lee and because he knew that she was lying. She was using work as an excuse; she wasn't ready to return and face whatever perceived crisis they had to face. She was stalling.

When? Patrick wanted to know, trying to keep the irritation from his voice.

She wasn't sure. Not to worry. She would let him know.

Not to worry. In the city, and on the coast, people talked funny.

And beautiful women always got away with lying.

Patrick went back to his charts, studying the names, looking for something to jump out at him, the way things did in puzzles if you studied the clues long enough. He studied them, read the police reports over and over again. But nothing jumped at him.

The phone rang. He looked at his watch. Eleven P.M. It had been a half hour since he'd talked to Lee. She was probably calling back to apologize, say she'd be on the first flight to Miami in the morning.

He picked up the phone. Bill Peachy said, "Didn't wake you, did I?"

"No," Patrick said. "I was going over some papers."

"The word is out Raul Jiminez went to Miami the other day and interviewed the chick who was with Wade when he was killed," Bill Peachy said.

"No kidding. Where'd you hear that?" Patrick asked.

"There's no such thing as being upwind of a fart in this town," Bill said. "You catch every smell in town on this island. The problem sometimes is identifying them."

Patrick wasn't quite sure what Peachy meant. He remembered Lee's anxiety after she'd been questioned by Raul Jiminez. Shortly before she went to New York. The city. "So who killed Wade?" Patrick asked.

"That hasn't filtered down yet. Probably because the chick couldn't make a positive ID. But you can bet Jiminez is working on her."

"What else do you hear?" It was true, then, Jiminez wasn't going to share information.

"The chief would like to make Hamilton Wade for the killer of the three girls. If he can't get that to stick, any fisherman will do. He wants this over. What about you? Coming up with anything? The word is out you've been conducting your own investigation."

Raul Jiminez already knew that, but he would not be happy, Patrick thought, to know that the general public was getting wind of it, whether it was upwind or down.

"I'm trying to cover a few bases," Patrick said. "Without getting in Raul's way."

He sensed Bill Peachy smile. "Wise man. Can I be of any help?"

In fact it had crossed his mind to ask Peachy to help with some of the legwork. He was trying to get photos of the nine people who were on his list, while he waited to hear from the FBI and IRS.

"You out of work?"

"Another front coming through. Day after tomorrow, the fleet'll be tied to the dock for a week."

"Anything yet on Paco?"

"I'm working on it."

"You ever think about a wife?" Patrick said.

"No," Peachy said, "I've got a boat."

Wystan Lewis was having a party. Informal. A few people in for cocktails. Wondering if Lee was back, if they could come around. Patrick explained that Lee wasn't back. Not to worry, come along anyway, old man. You'll know everyone.

Patrick surprised himself by saying that he would be happy to. To what? Not to worry, old man, he thought. Wade's murder seemed to have dampened the social spirits of the literary community. Since he and Lee had entertained, this was the only other full-blown party since New Year's that he knew about.

It was as if the mourning period were over. Everyone was there, pockets of people huddled on Lewis's deck, their laughter erupting and wafting out over the water like fog.

Standing at the deck, a glass of rum in hand, Patrick watched a thin layer of clouds drift across and partially obscure the moon. The front Bill Peachy had predicted was moving in.

"What do you hear from your wife?"

Patrick turned. Raul Jiminez stood leaning against the dock rail. Cops were in high demand these days at social events. Jiminez had even attracted a small crowd that seemed to have followed in his wake, trying to be unobtrusive in its eavesdropping. Patrick gave his standard response—that Lee had some extra work to take care of. He wasn't sure when she'd be back.

"Pity," Raul Jiminez said. "I was hoping to catch up with her."

"I'll let her know, the next time I talk to her," Patrick said.

A woman squeezed past Patrick, her breasts, unrestrained in a loose blouse, grazing his arm. He thought of Lee. In the city. Working. Avoiding coming home. The woman said, "How's the case going, Chief?" Patrick thought he detected mockery in her tone. Perhaps she'd just had too much to drink.

Jiminez offered a smile and lifted his own drink. "Making progress," he said. "Making progress."

Wystan had joined the group. It occurred to Patrick that this party had been staged for just such a confrontation.

As if to confirm it, a mincing voice said, "Really? Then you must be close to making an arrest."

Patrick looked into the crowd, recognizing the speaker, another writer, a man who he'd always described to Lee as "swishy."

173

Raul said, "I can't comment on that."

The woman in the loose blouse had fitted herself neatly between Raul and Patrick at the dock rail.

"Why not?" Wystan Lewis asked. "It's been over two weeks since Hamilton Wade was killed."

"Because I'm in charge of an investigation," Raul Jiminez said. "And it's the way I do things."

Patrick could see the chief was annoyed, unaccustomed to not being in control.

The woman between them said, "Is Lieutenant Bowman . . ." She smiled up at Patrick. "Is Patrick helping with your investigation?"

Raul cast an accusatory glance at Patrick, as if this were somehow his doing. "He's helping with the other investigation," Raul said. It sounded weak.

"And how's that going?"

Raul finished his drink. Half a dozen people stood nearby. The rest of the crowd were scattered around the deck, laughing, drinking, not part of this. Raul said, "I think I got
the wrong party," left his glass on the deck rail and walked to the door.

The woman shifted a little and her body brushed against him once more. Patrick moved away from her and followed Jiminez out to his car.

"I don't have to put up with that shit," Jiminez said.

"The natives're getting restless," Patrick replied. "Wade may have been a creep, but he was one of their own." Jiminez was one of his own, Patrick reflected, but he could summon little sympathy for him. He said, "You could have told them about the witness."

Jiminez didn't change expressions. The cool, macho Latin. "What witness?"

"The one you went to Miami to interview. It's all over town, except with this crowd. They live in a different world."

"Not Hamilton Wade. He got around."

Was Jiminez smiling? Knowingly? It was a small town, a safe bet that others must have known about Lee's affair with Wade. If that was what Jiminez was getting at. Patrick thought of the woman back at the party. "You got something?" he asked.

"I got a man shot in the groin while some chick he's having sex with is in the room."

"The witness."

"And guess what?"

Patrick waited.

"The shooter was a woman," Raul said.

Lee had said: He thinks I killed Hamilton.

"Makes a neat package, doesn't it? One of his other lovers walks in, Wade's balling another chick, she shoots him in the *cojones.* Make him stop and think. Except it kills him before he's got time to think."

Patrick thought about it. "Why would she be carrying a gun?"

Jiminez shrugged. "Maybe she knew what she'd be walking into. Premeditated."

"You've got all of that, and you've got a witness. "

"The chick was out of her head on drugs. Wade was something. Those little fairies in there"—Jiminez tilted his head toward the house they'd just come from—"they've got no idea."

"Don't bet on that," Patrick said.

Jiminez opened his car door. "I'm not betting on anything. Just doing my job, if I can get some breathing room." He climbed into the car, a Camaro. A money car.

Patrick considered going back to the party.

As he started the car, Jiminez leaned his head out the open window. "Wade was shot with a nine-millimeter," he said. "Now you know as much as I do." He got that smile on his face again.

Patrick decided to go home. He was troubled by the information Jiminez had just imparted. There were undoubtedly many nine-millimeter automatics floating around Key West. But that didn't do much to ease his anxiety, knowing that there was one in his bedroom and that Raul Jiminez continued to focus attention on Lee's involvement with Hamilton Wade.

20

Darling glanced around the attic apartment. She had found the place by accident one evening while she was wandering around the streets. A For Rent sign tacked on the porch column of a dilapidated three-story house on Elizabeth had caught her attention. A phone number had been handwritten below the bold red FOR RENT. She had copied it down, made a call from her motel, and set up an appointment the following day.

The owner of the house was an elderly woman who seemed to live alone on the ground floor of the house, renting out the second floor, which she'd divided into rooms. And the third-floor attic.

The attic was one large, undivided room with mansard ceilings of bare rafters. Hastily painted plywood was tacked to most of the floor joists. The window frames were open and without glass. Thin squares of plywood had been cut to be wedged into the openings in case of rain. In the center of the floor was a bed, a huge floor fan ten feet away aimed at the center of the bed, a frayed electrical cord stretching to a bare outlet on the wall.

There was a sink, a small refrigerator, and a two-burner hot plate on a table along one wall that served as the kitchen. Next to it was the bathroom containing a shower stall, sink, and toilet. A nearby closet with a wooden rod behind a burlap cover served as the closet.

A scarred chest of drawers, a table, and one chair made up the remainder of the furnishings. It was perfect.

Darling would have her own entrance, there was no lease

agreement and no realty agency to go through. By Key West standards the place was also cheap; she was able to rent on a $75 weekly basis, with a two-week deposit paid in advance.

The landlady wore a hearing aid and made out the rent receipt in a book of numbered and faded receipts, adjusting the carbon beneath the thin paper. She asked Darling's name, but could not hear, or did not understand it, and asked Darling to write it out on the receipt.

Darling had written in a firm hand above the old lady's shaky scrawl: Gina Rigland.

Now Darling stood in one of the open window frames and watched the filtered moonlight through a layer of thick, fast-moving clouds.

When the fisherman's names that he had faxed to Chicago to be checked were returned, Patrick short-listed them and gave the list to Bill Peachy. It was a simple enough task; Peachy, who was on familiar turf around the fish houses, would find out what he could about the men on the list as quietly as possible: specifically, where they were on the nights the three women had been murdered.

Patrick, meanwhile, was running down his own list of names—some of which now had accompanying photos—that he'd gathered from the various lodging establishments around town.

He went down the list of names in the same alphabetical order in which he had previously written them.

The photo of Anthony Clemente, the convicted felon from Miami who'd come to Key West a month after he was released from jail, was a mug shot, full face and profile that showed a Latin male in his early thirties, with sleek, dark, thick hair, and a glowering countenance.

Patrick carried it and the other photos with him as he rode his bicycle to the motels where the people on his list had stayed. He tried to get some positive ID's by talking to bartenders in the area, maids, and people working the registration desks.

Almost everyone said the same thing: they couldn't remember, it had been too long ago. Or they vaguely remembered the face, but nothing else.

However, a bartender in a gay bar across the street from the motel where Clemente stayed remembered him. Clemente came in New Year's Eve around midnight, alone, and drunk; in the course of the next couple hours, Clemente had gotten belligerent, insulting some of the clients, calling them names, until the bartender was forced to ask him to leave. Clemente refused, and the bouncer was called and escorted Clemente outside, where he continued to hurl insults back into the bar. The bartender called the police, and that was the end of Clemente—the bartender didn't know if he was arrested or told to leave the premises.

"What time when all this occurred?" Patrick asked.

The bartender thought. "He was here at midnight, I know that. Maybe one, two o'clock when I called the cops. They must have a record."

Patrick said he'd check, then offered the other photos to the bartender. Tom Johnston, Daniel Leigh, Virginia Power, Steve Ross, and Nancy Thurman. The bartender said he didn't recognize any of them.

Patrick thanked him, went outside and continued biking around the area, going into stores, motels, bars, showing the pictures and asking the same questions. He had been unable to obtain photos of Ricky Garlind, Mike Priest, or Karen Wilcox.

It was tedious work, but Patrick didn't mind; in fact, he enjoyed it. He was learning, getting familiar with the territory, the killer's terrain, and by a process of elimination, weeding out suspects; even though he had no reason to believe that any one of the nine people on his list was the killer. On the other hand, he had no reason to believe the killer wasn't there. It was a place to begin. You got answers to a few questions, and raised more questions.

He would check with Jiminez about Clemente, but it appeared that the times were out of sync, since the last girl was killed while Clemente was being rousted. He had given Jiminez the list of names in a spirit of cooperation, but the chief didn't seem to put much faith in them, pointing out that it was unlikely, assuming that the killer was on the list, that he'd be using his own name—a fact Patrick was all too aware of. Which was why the photos were so important. Somehow he needed to identify quickly the three people whose whereabouts were unknown.

What he needed, Patrick thought, was a miracle.

Raul Jiminez worried about Rafe. The boy was seldom home and had taken to wandering the streets during the day in some female getup that would have been a total embarrassment if not for the fact that it also worked to disguise him. But word was out in the department, and Raul had come out of his office more than once to hear whispered conversations suddenly halted in mid-sentence as he passed by. The chief had no doubt as to what was being said; once he'd even heard Rafe's name mentioned.

Raul had tried to talk to Mercedes about it. Couldn't she encourage him to return to Miami? He'd been here, what, nearly two weeks? Shouldn't he get back up there if he was going to keep his job?

Mercedes wouldn't hear of it. Rafael was having problems. He needed to be home where his mother could look after him. But he wasn't home. He was out on the streets prancing around in women's clothes!

Mercedes wouldn't be swayed. Rafael was her youngest, her last child, and she blamed Raul for Rafe's condition, saying he had always been too hard on the boy, too macho. Rafe was sensitive, an artist.

Mother of God!

And on top of everything else, Raul was being hounded by the social elite, a bunch of *maricons* who thought he wasn't doing enough to solve the Wade murder. Raul turned down party invitations. He spent more time in the office, and the lunches with Maloney had now become daily occurrences.

Patrick Bowman was becoming a pain in the ass that he would have to deal with sooner rather than later, Jiminez thought. Bowman had his charter fishing captain helping with the investigation of a murder case!

Then there was the list of names Bowman was pursuing. The Chicago cop had brought them to him one day as if they were some trophy he'd acquired. Raul felt trapped into giving more attention to them than he thought they deserved, but he couldn't afford to have it look like he had neglected an aspect of the case if something ever came from Bowman's efforts. So he had taken the precaution of providing the names to the Monroe County sheriff's office, who were, as it turned out, already holding Virginia Power, wanted in Cleveland for embezzlement, in jail at the Marathon substation.

Power would be questioned about the beach murders.

In the meantime he was trying to think of a way to get inside Patrick Bowman's house. If Bowman had a gun there, like the one he'd glimpsed in a drawer, Raul was prepared to give better than even odds that it was a nine- millimeter. If so, he'd like to find some way to run a ballistics check on it. Maybe even get lucky and find a set of prints belonging to Lee Bowman—not that it would prove much, but it was a start. It occurred to him that she could have thrown the gun away if she'd used it to kill Wade. But maybe not. She would have no reason to believe that she would ever be a suspect; explaining the disappearance of the gun to her husband could be more trouble than keeping it.

Raul buzzed his secretary and asked her to ring Patrick Bowman. He might as well get this over with now.

***

From her window Darling had a view of the harbor and downtown Key West. She could see the exhaust stacks of a cruise ship docked at Mallory Square. For the past three days she'd been holed up in here, restless, looking out the window, feeling the pull, like some invisible cord was attached to her, steadily drawing her out.

Caution, she thought. Control. The old patterns were no longer acceptable. She needed a sign. The arrival this morning of the cruise ship, and the dire sound its horn made as the ship entered the harbor, seemed as good a sign as any.

She felt nothing, not even the cold. She read the stories about the Key West killings, and it was like reading a book in which she was caught up in the story, could relate even to the characters; but on another level it seemed to be all fiction, happening to someone else.

It was her sister Roberta's fault. Everything happened to Roberta. She had adventures, got into trouble and then got all the attention while Rachel looked on. Watched and listened.

Roberta had to be punished.

Darling shivered as the cold north air raised goose bumps on her forearms. She looked out at the street scene below her awhile longer, then went into the bathroom to begin her preparations.

21

The Full Moon Saloon. Six-thirty. Patrick sat at the bar drinking a beer and waiting for Bill Peachy. He shuffled through the photos as if they were cards, studying the faces, the eyes, the lines around the mouth and the furrows of the forehead, the set of the jaw. Speculating, trying to read something from a face even though he knew it was next to impossible.

Appearances were so mutable. Cosmetics, surgery, could transform anyone. Who hadn't been startled by the sight of a woman whose features had been transformed through the clever use of makeup? It happened all the time.

Was one of these people a killer? From a photograph he could do nothing more than speculate.

Take Tom Johnston, for example. A rapist. Black, with smooth, unblemished skin. A boyishly deceptive face, nothing unusual about it, except for the eyes. The eyes were different; flat, expressionless, they seemed to reflect nothing. He had seen eyes that were similar. Were they a killer's eyes? They belonged to a rapist, but were they common to all rapists? Hardly.

Still, he continued to look, trying to guess at the character that peered out from the glossy prints.

"You brought along the family album," Bill Peachy said, taking the empty seat at the bar next to Patrick.

Patrick smiled and handed Peachy the photo of Tom Johnston. "What do you see?"

Bill studied the photo. "No family resemblance."

"Care to make any assessment about his character?"

Bill grinned. "What is this, some kind of game?"

The bartender brought Peachy a beer.

"A game. Exactly," Patrick said. "Like pin the tail on the donkey. Except we're still hunting for the tail."

"He supposed to be a killer?"

"At least a rapist."

"You're kidding." Peachy stared at the photo once more. "I'd never have guessed."

Patrick handed him the other photos. "They've all got records," he said.

"Jesus. They look like ordinary people to me. I'll stick to fishing."

"You learn anything out at the fish houses?"

"Yeah, Jiminez has had men crawling all over the place. About as subtle as a nail in the bottom of your foot. They're not exactly bubbling over with information."

"That's why I thought a fisherman and not another cop might be a good move."

"Put my head on the chopping block, right?"

"You look like you came through okay. What'd you find out?"

Peachy shrugged. "The usual. A couple guys been inside for attempted murder, the same old stuff, jealousy, drug informants, that kind of thing. Some stabbings."

"Anyone we should take a closer look at?"

185

"There's a shrimper who's a nasty piece of work. He wasn't on the boat during the time of the killings. Everybody else has a pretty good alibi."

"Jiminez talked to the shrimper?"

"He seemed to have missed him."

"You got a name?"

Peachy smiled. "Paco," he said.

It was dark. Patrick pushed his bike in through the front gate of the house when a movement on the porch caught his attention. He propped the bike against the Spanish lime tree and walked toward the porch. Raul Jiminez came down the front steps. Patrick said, "I hope we didn't have an appointment."

Jiminez moved the cigarette he was smoking from one side of his mouth to the other without touching it with his hands. "No," he said. "I been trying to reach you all day. I thought I'd stop by, see if everything was all right."

"It is," Patrick said.

They stood facing one another, Jiminez two steps above him on the porch, bringing his height to the eye level of Patrick, who stood on the walk.

"I wanted to tell you. One of the people on your list, Virginia Power, the sheriffs got her locked up in the substation up in Marathon. They're gonna extradite her back to Ohio."

"Anybody question her about where she was over the holidays?"

"She was in Marathon, working in the Marine Bank there. People were with her on the nights of the beach killings."

The process of elimination.

"I thought you'd want to know," Jiminez said.

"Thanks," Patrick said.

Jiminez made no move to leave. He took the cigarette from his mouth and held it up, looking at the lit end. He said, "What sort a guns do cops carry in Chicago?"

Patrick stared at him. He said, "It varies. I've got a Browning nine-millimeter. It's my own, not standard issue."

Jiminez nodded, and flicked his cigarette into the bushes. He stepped down from the porch. "I suppose you brought it down here."

Patrick hesitated, knowing what Jiminez was getting at, angered by yet another suggestive comment from the chief. "Yeah," he said, deciding to hold himself in check, not to be rattled by this crap. "I did."

Jiminez nodded again and walked to the front gate. He stepped out onto the sidewalk, turned back to Patrick. "Any word from your wife, when she's coming home?"

"I'll be the first to let you know," Patrick said.

Jiminez waved and walked off. Patrick went inside, took the photos out of his pocket, eliminated Anthony Clemente's and Virginia Power's before going upstairs to look in his dresser.

The gun was there, in his holster beneath a sweater. He checked the clip and found it full. He could take it down, put it on Jiminez's desk tomorrow and tell him to run a ballistics check, since he seemed so interested in this particular weapon.

No, Patrick thought, he wasn't going to let himself be pressured by Jiminez. As he put the gun back in the drawer, he hoped he was being truthful with himself, that deep inside him there weren't other reasons for not delivering the gun to Jiminez.

22

Ten A.M. Mallory Square. Although the sun was shining, the wind gusted at fifteen to twenty knots, bringing the cold from the north. The sea, the color of dry cement, seemed to be torn between the opposing forces of wind and current.

Darling stood on the dock at the stern of the cruise ship, which offered some protection from the wind. She held her thin jacket together at the throat, the way she might have clutched a kitten by the nape of its neck, and surveyed the activity around Mallory Square.

People came on and off the ship via the ramp that connected it to the dock. They wandered in small groups, uncertain, unhurried even in the cold as they set out on foot to explore the town before the ship departed on the next leg of its cruise.

Darling searched for a face, a lone figure on the fringes of the crowd.

Someone out to make a couple of dollars off one of the disembarking tourists. A ripoff artist; a hustler. Someone hanging out, trying to get attention, waiting for someone to give her something, to make her happy.

A slut like her sister Roberta.

Darling saw her sitting on a park bench, legs crossed, her short, tight skirt hiked up to mid-thigh, a bulky cable-knit sweater protecting her from the knife-edged wind. She had a purse on a shoulder strap, similar to Darling's. She had more class than the street hustlers; but, Darling thought, there was no mistaking that pose.

Darling watched and waited. No one approached the girl or seemed to pay her any attention. It was too cold, and too early to buy sex.

The girl preened, took out a pocket mirror from her purse and applied makeup, arched an eyebrow with the tip of one finger. After ten minutes she stood up, wrapped her arms across her body, hugging herself against the cold, and walked from the square with an exaggerated hip-swaying motion.

Darling followed.

"Your wife's on line one," his secretary said.

Raul Jiminez sighed.

He had worked late last night and then had a couple drinks and dinner with a county judge before going home. He'd asked the judge about a court order to search a house. The judge, Julio Hernandez—Rafe had gone to school with his son—wanted to know what the search was about. Raul told him he was looking for evidence in a murder case.

"You can show sufficient cause?" Julio asked.

"Once I get in the house, I'm betting I'll produce a murder weapon."

Judge Hernandez smiled. "Raul," he said, "you know better than that. The courts don't work on gambling systems."

Jiminez did know that. He had been counting on another system, the "bubba" system, to bend the rules a little, two men with last names ending in E-Z could sometimes make things work where their counterparts got lost in bureaucracy and paperwork.

The judge wasn't buying it and quickly changed the subject.

Mercedes had still been up when he came in at ten-thirty, depressed. She was cold and distant. Sitting in the Barcalounger, her feet up, clad in pink terry-cloth house slippers. She was watching television.

Raul had tried to diffuse the situation before she could attack him, even though he'd called earlier to say that he wouldn't be home for dinner.

"I'm sorry. I had to work late. Where's Rafe?"

"Out," Mercedes said.

Raul didn't bother to ask what he was wearing. Around the house Rafe wore shorts—short cutoffs—and a shirt that was two sizes too big for him, the loose tail striking him just above the knees. With the one gold earring he now wore, and the shaved legs, it would have been impossible for a stranger to know whether he was a boy or a girl. Lately, Raul had begun to think that maybe Rafe should have surgery and be done with it. At least he'd have some identity then.

"It might help if you spent more time with him," Mercedes said.

Raul couldn't explain how uncomfortable he was around Rafe. It was more than just embarrassment—he didn't know what to say, how to talk to his son, this person, whoever he (or she) was anymore.

He mumbled something about when this case was over, went to the bar and poured himself a small glass of rum, then went up to his study. When he went to bed at eleven- thirty, he could still hear the TV downstairs, tuned to a Spanish-language program. He didn't hear Mercedes come up, and she was still asleep when he left this morning.

He lifted the receiver and said, "Ola."

"Rafe isn't home," Mercedes said.

Raul looked at his watch. "Mercedes, it's eleven o'clock in the morning. Rafe's an adult."

"He didn't come home last night," Mercedes said. "I haven't seen him since yesterday evening."

Raul felt the beginning of the tension that each day built up, until by the end of the day every muscle in his body was taut as a bowstring. He reached for a cigarette. "Maybe he got laid," Raul said. He said it without thinking. The idea of Rafe getting laid was too complex to contemplate.

"Please," Mercedes said.

"What do you want me to do?"

"I'm worried."

"You want me to put out a BOLO for my son? What should I tell the city police, the sheriff's department, and the state cops he was wearing—a dress?"

"A short black skirt and a bulky sweater," Mercedes said.

"Where did we go wrong?" Raul asked. It was a rhetorical question. He hung up before Mercedes could answer, even if she had an answer.

He would wait before putting out a BOLO on Rafe, He had

192

enough problems with two unsolved murder cases and the stalled investigation by internal affairs without being the laughingstock of the state.

There was something about the way she walked that triggered a slight unease in Darling, some momentary awkwardness in the way the girl moved—almost too exaggerated, as though she were learning to walk. At one point she stumbled slightly stepping down from the curb as she crossed Greene Street on Duval. Paused, and poised herself while she glanced over a rack of curios on an open-air stand. Then continued on up Duval Street.

Morning strollers were out, and the pre-lunch shoppers as well as a handful of people still living off the night's empty promise. Hangovers lingered in the eyes of a few of those she passed, and someone began to tune an amplified guitar in Sloppy Joe's.

Darling took it all in without losing her concentration on the girl ahead of her. Who was now crossing Caroline Street. Darling closed the distance until she was merely half a dozen paces behind. A blue and white patrol car eased along Duval, the one cop inside surveying the sidewalks without, as far as Darling could tell, paying any obvious attention to her.

The girl ahead walked as if she had no particular destination, ambled, pausing to look in shop windows, always aware of her looks, checking her profile, her windswept hair. Darling tried to will her onto a side street. It wasn't necessary; three-quarters of the way down the block before Fleming Street, the girl again twisted her ankle, and again Darling felt the apprehension.

But she was right behind her now, ready with a steadying hand, to help.

"You okay?" Darling asked.

"These shoes," the girl said, trying to smile, obviously in pain. They were in front of La Concha Hotel, the doors of the bar opening onto the street.

"I know," Darling said. "Heels on these sidewalks can be a pain."

The girl adjusted her shoe and took a step, wincing.

"I was about ready to stop for something, anyway," Darling said. "Why not join me?"

The girl smiled again, as though relieved. "I think I will," she said.

Darling held her arm as they stepped into the bar and took a table right by the sidewalk.

"Better?" Darling said as they sat down.

The girl nodded. "Thanks," she said. "What's your name?"

Darling told her, and the girl smiled. "What a great name."

They drank a beer, and Darling offered to walk along with her if she wanted company. Sure, that would be great. Darling suggested going up Fleming Street, past the antique stores.

The churchyard behind St. Paul's was empty. Darling noticed the park bench, the shrubs and trees that virtually hid it from the street, a quiet secluded spot right in the heart of downtown. Perfect.

The girl, Rafaella, was still limping. She seemed to be taken with

194

Darling. An instant bonding had formed that was more than Darling could have hoped for.

Darling said, "Look, let's go sit in there. It looks peaceful."

Rafaella wasn't really a slut, but she was lost, hopeless; she was like a child discovering the adult world, trying to figure out who she wanted to be, how she wanted to dress. Almost as though she were in the process of learning, absorbing styles, other people's manners. But in the end Darling could see she was doomed. Another few months and Rafaella would be picking up men on the street, just like the other sluts.

They entered the churchyard, Darling with one hand over her shoulder bag, the other guiding Rafaella. They sat down on the park bench. "This is nice," Darling said. "A perfect spot. We can talk."

Jiminez was eating the usual lunch at El Siboney with Neil Maloney. Piccadillo, beans, and rice. "I want you to call Patrick Bowman, have him come down to the office," Jiminez said. "When he's coming in, let me know. Then I want you to keep him for at least forty-five minutes." Maloney stared at him blankly.

"What am I supposed to talk to him about?"

"Anything, as long as you keep him busy for forty-five minutes. You might try talking to him about the Wade murder, about his wife's involvement with Wade. You say you've got a neighbor saw her going into Wade's place more than once, using a key to get in the back. Talk to him about that."

"Jesus."

"Talk about him, too, if you want."

"You want to tell me what's going on?"

"Nope." Raul mashed some plantain into his beans. If the judge wouldn't give him a court order to search Bowman's house, then he'd find another way to do it. All he needed was one fired round from Bowman's gun. He was taking a chance, his mind weighing the consequences. He was in deep on different fronts: the internal affairs investigation, the three dead girls on the beach. He needed a payoff; that was going to entail some risk.

Raul was about to get an update from Maloney on the investigation when two uniformed cops came inside, one a rookie, the other a seasoned officer who had been around for a half-dozen years. They looked around and walked over to the table where Jiminez and Maloney sat.

"Chief, some bad news," the veteran said, his forearm resting on his holstered revolver, the fingers of the hand gripping his belt buckle.

Jiminez knew it, felt it on some level of awareness even as the two patrolmen had come in the door. "Rafe?" he said.

The officer nodded.

Raul felt his jaw tighten, his mind turning on so many things at once—guilt, Mercedes, why he hadn't done things differently. He said, "Dead?"

The officer said, "They've got him in intensive care at Flaky's. He was stabbed three times, once in the throat."

Two hospitals in Key West, both of whose ridiculous names

196

became absurd at a moment like this, Jiminez thought: Florida Keys Memorial—Flaky's, and the privately-owned DePoo. Jesus, the things that came into your head. Mercedes was going to kill him.

"Let's go," Raul said, and went out with the patrolmen who escorted him, sirens blaring, to Flaky's.

23

My God! Darling stood in the attic window of her apartment and listened to the sirens. She was sweating.

She had gone into the church, entering from a side door after hearing someone walking nearby, the crunch of leaves beneath his feet, and the sound of a deep, dry cough which had come from the street side of the church along the narrow pathway that was thick with shrubbery.

Everything had gone wrong. She had opened her purse and offered Rafaella a cigarette; she didn't smoke. They were sitting on the bench, quiet, peaceful, talking. Talking about boys. Rafaella saying she hated boys, and Darling had laughed in disbelief because here was this young chick dressed in her tight black skirt, in the process of discovering herself, and doing it with the oldest cliche in the world. Sex.

Rafaella flew into a rage, angry with Darling for laughing at her, angry with her father because he didn't understand her, with her mother—who had always been too passive, who would not stand up to her father. Rafaella had jumped up from the bench and said, "Don't laugh at me."

Darling grabbed her by the wrists, to calm her down, and Rafaella tried to pull away. Rafaella strong, stronger than she looked; and Darling, frightened now that they would be discovered, that someone would come by, see her with this young girl and question her, reached into her bag and took out the knife.

And made one quick, slashing motion with it, cutting Rafaella along the muscle between her neck and shoulder. Rafaella fell to the ground, started to crawl, the black skirt now hiked above her hips, and Darling brought the knife up and down (hearing the dry cough and crunch of leaves behind her) into Rafaella's back. Rafaella rolled over, and Darling, dropping the knife back into her bag, ran from the yard and into the church, where she found herself alone in front of the altar.

She knelt and tried to compose herself. She was breathing hard, sweat ruining her makeup. She forced herself to kneel there, even when she heard through the open windows a man call out for help. And moments later the sirens started, and people's voices as a crowd began forming.

She stood up then and tried to walk casually toward the front of the church, leaning against the church pews. And walked away from the crowd along the street, which was peering into the back of the churchyard.

When she got back to the attic, she collapsed. Finally, as more sirens sounded, she got up and went to the window.

My God! Again she saw in her mind Rafaella crawling across the yard on her stomach, and then, as she turned over, her underpants twisting and pulling down on her hips. And Darling saw the mistake that she had made, why Rafaella's walk had caused her apprehension. My God! she thought. A boy!

Raul recognized a doctor he knew talking to a couple of reporters from the *Citizen* and *Miami Herald* outside the doors of the intensive care unit. The doctor broke away when he saw Raul come in. They nodded, and Raul followed him into the ICU.

A team of nurses and another doctor worked over Rafe, who lay on a table beneath arc lights. Raul noticed that a couple of the nurses' green surgical gowns were splattered with blood.

I've got to call Mercedes, Raul thought. He looked down at Rafe, covered by a sheet from the waist down, his body bare except for a thick piece of blood-soaked gauze near his neck. His body looked thin, pale like a child's. His son. Rafe's eyes were closed. He was plugged into two IV's, one containing blood. The other dripped a clear liquid into his arm.

Raul stepped back. The doctor who had brought him in joined him.

Raul said, "He going to make it?"

The doctor said, "Fifty-fifty. An artery was cut. He lost a lot of blood. Just lucky they got him here when they did."

"He conscious?"

"When they brought him in he was. He's under an anesthetic right now."

"He say anything?"

"One word," the doctor said. "Darling."

Jiminez went out in the hall and talked to the cop who had brought him here and was waiting.

"Who found him?" Raul demanded.

"A dirtbag, some bum who was sleeping in the weeds along the

200

side of the church."

"Anyone question him?"

"Yeah, the dirtbag heard some shouting, thought he was being rousted. Then decided he'd better move on. He walked back into the churchyard and found Rafe on the ground."

"He see anything, anyone else?"

"He says not. He heard two people talking—arguing, it sounded like."

"He recognize the voice of the other person."

"Chief, he's a dirtbag."

"I want him held," Jiminez said.

"He's down at the station now. Lieutenant Maloney's questioning him."

Raul nodded.

The two reporters walked over.

"Can we get a statement?" the *Herald* reporter asked. "Is the victim your son?"

"Yes," he said, thinking again that he had to call Mercedes. He started to walk toward the pay phones.

"Is he going to live?"

"He's got a fifty-fifty chance."

"Any idea who attacked him?"

"No," Raul said. He picked up the phone and dug in his pocket for a quarter.

"Could it be the beach killer?"

Raul couldn't find a quarter. The question had been in the back of his mind on the drive out to the hospital. "I don't know," he said. "You got a quarter?"

The *Citizen* reporter took a coin from his pocket, handed it to Raul and said, "The doctor said the last thing your son said was 'darling.' Any idea what he was talking about?"

Raul felt his face redden. "No," he said, "none." He dialed Mercedes.

The dirtbag's name was Joe Ott. Jiminez looked across the table at him; scraggly beard, dull eyes stabbed with nothing more than a little fear, what teeth he had were yellow, and a stink that would croak a maggot. Part of the winter migration. You took the paying guests, and put up with the freeloaders because panhandling wasn't a crime.

"Tell me again, Joe," Raul Jiminez repeated, looking at his watch. "Where's the knife?"

"And man," Joe Ott said, speaking fast, his words running together, "I tell you again I tell you many times as you ask I don't have no knife. I don't own no knife. Knife's messy, man. I never owned no knife."

It was one o'clock. He'd been in here for more than an hour now while Mercedes was at the hospital.

"Who knifed him, then?" Raul repeated.

"I tell you like I tell the other chief, I don't see nobody."

"But you heard somebody."

"Yeah, I heard voices. I'm sleepin', man, they woke me up. I don't know what's comin' down."

"What did you hear?"

"I hear one of them gettin' mad, cursin' Daddy, Mama, and mad at the other one for laughing."

Raul looked away from the dirtbag, wondering if he'd told Maloney this.

Raul went on. "What about the other one? Was it a man or a woman?"

"Man, I don't know, talkin' soft, you know, and I'm just comin' awake."

Raul stood up, stretched. He'd stay here all night if he had to, because the dirtbag was going to tell him something. He was going to make him tell him something.

"Let's start over," Raul said. "Where you from?"

"St. Louis."

The phone on the table rang. Jiminez picked it up. Mercedes's choked voice said, "He's gone."

CHIEF'S SON'S LAST WORD: 'DARLING.' There was a picture of the dirtbag who had found the body. Patrick clipped the story from the *Citizen*. He had heard about the attack on Jiminez's son, it was all over town, but did not know that Rafael had died. The *Citizen* obviously had gotten word at the last minute, allowing them time to change their headline; the rest of the front-page story had little new information.

Patrick Bowman read the story over three times, then tacked it up on the bulletin board that contained all the other information he was collecting about Wade's murder and the beach killings. Order. It was a way of viewing the world, of maintaining sanity. There were no dirty dishes in the sink, the bed was made, the house clean and tidy. He wanted something, he knew where to find it. Everything was in perspective, and sooner or later, he knew, it would yield significant results.

Lee had been away nearly three weeks. He missed her, spoke to her daily, but without probing into when she would return. They talked about the weather, her work, how the investigation was going. She never mentioned Hamilton Wade.

Darling. Lovers called each other darling, married couples, too, although he'd never called Lee darling, or honey, or sweetheart. Or baby. She had too much of an identity for that—he called her by name. Lee.

The phone rang. He picked it up and said, "Lee?"

Bill Peachy said, "Sorry, only me. I called to say that most of the shrimp boats are in. You might want to talk to one of the shrimpers who can usually be found in the Coral Reef Bar on Stock Island."

"Paco?"

"The one and only. He's got a thing for young girls. Keeps them in a good supply of drugs, I hear."

"Thanks, Bill. Maybe that explains why the girl I talked to was so reluctant to talk about him. I'll look him up first thing," Patrick said.

"You see the paper?"

"Just now. I thought the chief's son was a transvestite?" "He was. They kept it out of the paper. The kid was in drag when he was attacked."

"Was he gay?"

"He dressed up like a woman. What do you think?" "Doesn't mean he's homosexual," Patrick said. "A lot of them aren't." He'd encountered this more than once in Chicago. The guy, for example, forty-five, married, two kids in their teens, who got dressed up in women's clothes and went out selling Avon products door to door. Beaten to death and robbed one afternoon. When he was found and identified, the wife said she didn't know. He was a good husband.

"I don't know," Bill Peachy said. "He was scared to death of strange men, though. He ran like hell from me the night I saw him on the beach. I was going to warn him . . . her."

"That's your story."

"And I'm sticking to it."

Patrick thought about that. "Then you don't think a guy could've picked him up?"

"I don't know."

"But you couldn't have."

"No."

"You know any girls around here interested in men who dress up in women's clothes?"

"I don't know any, but if they exist, you can be sure a percentage of them live in Key West."

"So who the hell was he talking to?" Patrick asked.

"Pardon?"

"Darling. Who was darling?"

Peachy thought a minute. "Yeah," he said. "I see what you mean."

24

Paco was small, compact, with sinewy, muscular arms which, when flexed, rippled faded tattoos. Long, bony fingers with ragged, dirty nails gripped a can of beer. His skin held the deep tan of a fisherman, but the surface skin was dry and scaly, while his greasy hair was combed up in front in a 1950s-style wave.

Paco sat in the dingy fishermen's bar on Stock Island, nursing his beer.

When Patrick introduced himself, Paco, with the kind of stare that could only come from a glass eye that strayed, said, "Chicago. Never been there." It was a statement of firm denial, rather than conversation, the ready defense of an habitual detainee, a man who'd been through his share of police interrogations.

Patrick sat at the bar and ordered a soft drink, Coca- Cola. "I was wondering about two weeks around Christmas and New Year's," he said when the bartender, a fat slattern with burnt-orange hair, waddled off to get the Coke. "You around then?"

Paco turned back to his beer. "You're kinda outta your territory, aren't you? Is this official?"

"It can be," Patrick said. "Or we can keep it informal, enjoy the morning in these pleasant surroundings."

"Bullshit," Paco said.

The slattern brought a lukewarm can of Coke, pulled the tab on it and set it on the bar with just enough emphasis to spill some of the brown, foaming liquid down the sides of the can. Patrick asked for some ice. She sighed, but dipped a scarred plastic glass into a tub and slammed the glass on the bar with more emphasis than she'd used with the Coke can.

"Texas," Paco said. "Galveston."

"Doing what?"

Paco fixed him with the sidelong stare again. "Visitin' my family," he said.

"How do I know that?"

"Look, I got an eight-year-old girl I ain't seen in two years. Her mama's dyin' a cancer and I went out to find her a place to live. Check it out, all right?"

Patrick poured enough of the Coke in the glass to prevent it from being resold, and put a dollar bill on the bar. "I will," he said. He thought about mentioning Carol to see the shrimper's reaction, but decided against it. If Paco came down on Carol for talking to the cops, then Patrick would lose her. He could check out Paco's story without compromising a good connection.

He stood up and walked out. He heard Paco mutter, "Fuckin' cops."

As he got into the Buick he considered himself lucky to have tangled with the shrimper rather than the slattern.

When he got home, there were messages on the answering machine to call Lt. Neil Maloney. And Lee had called. She was coming back, she said, but she would call later and let him know just when. She sounded tired, not enthusiastic.

Patrick picked up the phone, called the police department and asked for Raul Jiminez.

Jiminez. What did you say to the guy? He'd been living inside a pressure cooker for the past three months, then his son is knifed and killed downtown in the middle of the day. Jiminez was a cop; Patrick was a cop. They'd seen this stuff all their lives, but it didn't make any difference when it hit close to home. You were never prepared. And there weren't any words, at least not anything special for a cop. When Jiminez answered, Patrick said, "I'm sorry."

"My wife called me a couple hours before Rafe was attacked. He didn't come home the night before. She wanted me to do something. I sat on it. I got two other kids coming home tonight. What do I tell them?"

How many times had he heard this kind of thing? How many times had he said, "Don't blame yourself." Words.

"Yeah," Jiminez said. "That's what I tell myself. You know what? It doesn't do any good. I'm working to keep from thinking about it."

A point Patrick well understood. "You got anything to go on?"

"No."

"What about a connection between this and the other killings?"

Jiminez sounded distant, distracted. "We're looking at everything," he said.

Patrick said, "I know how tough this is for you right now—"

"Listen, it's no secret. My boy, Rafe, liked to dress up like a girl. I got two daughters, they're coming in for the funeral tonight. Two daughters. And I get a son who wants to put on girl's clothes."

209

"At least the papers spared you. There was no mention of Rafael's . . . problem."

"He shaved his legs. They took him to the hospital wearing a tight black dress. He even had on girl's underpants."

"I know," Patrick said, "but look, if the person who killed him didn't know him, didn't know who he was, then in all probability they thought he was a girl."

"I know that," Jiminez said. "What's your point?"

"Your son's last words."

There was a pause. "I could've killed the fuckin' doctor gave that to the reporters," Raul said.

"I don't blame you, but does it give us something?"

"What?"

"Darling."

Another pause. Then, "Listen, Rafe always said he wasn't gay. I may be from a different generation, but still I find it hard to believe. You spend all that time dressing up like a woman, there isn't something—you know what I mean."

"Yeah," Patrick said. "But he was scared of strange men. You know that from Bill Peachy."

"Peachy? What's he got to do with it?"

"Rafe ran from him, remember? Bill was trying to warn him that night on the beach."

"I don't see the connection."

"Somebody got Rafe back into that churchyard in broad daylight. Pretty hard to do, I'd think, with people wandering all over the place.

Unless he went voluntarily."

"So maybe Rafe knew him."

"Okay, but who's he going to call darling?"

Patrick waited. Jiminez seemed to be thinking, and it wasn't a happy thought.

"Look," Raul said. "I don't know what you're getting at, and I don't know what Rafe was talking about. Maybe he was playing, you hear those people calling each other darling all the time."

Those people. Jiminez would never be able to accept Rafe's problems, even dead.

"Maybe. But I think we ought to look at all the possibilities."

"Such as?"

"It's just a thought," Patrick said, "but maybe Darling was the name of the person Rafe was with." And, in the back of his mind, a question that was gaining more prominence: could Darling be a woman?

When Jiminez hung up, Patrick held the phone to his ear and pressed the disconnect button with his forefinger. Then he redialed the police and asked for Lt. Neil Maloney. While waiting to get through, he thought it was as close as he and Jiminez had ever come to having a real conversation. Grief could do that, tear down some of the defenses.

"Maloney."

"Patrick Bowman returning your call," Patrick said. Jiminez had introduced him to Maloney once, but they had not spoken since then.

"Oh, yeah. Can we meet?"

"What's up?"

"I've got some information for you on those names you gave the chief."

"Sure," Patrick said. "When's convenient?"

"Tomorrow at ten? My office."

"I'll be there," Patrick said, and hung up.

He wrote out the word DARLING in block capitals, took it over and tacked it onto the bulletin board with the other names.

Darling stayed in, sat at the attic window, watched the traffic go by, and went out at night for a takeout meal which she brought back to the attic.

Rafael. The son of the chief of police. In drag. A boy. Who called her Darling, her name on his lips when he died. She had made a mistake, her first mistake, and it would have to be her last.

Was the cop, Patrick Bowman, smart enough to figure it out? She sat and thought about it, and knew that she had no way of knowing and perhaps no way of finding out. Therefore, she had to assume that, yes, the cops now knew her name.

Did it matter?

No, she thought, it just meant more and more caution. Bowman was good, but not that good.

25

Raul Jiminez drove his unmarked car—courtesy of the city— down
William Street past the white, trim, little eyebrow house with its dark
green shutters. On the yard side of the white picket fence was a
cobblestone walkway shaded by an old Spanish lime tree. A swing
on the front porch, everything immaculate, nothing out of place.
Like a playhouse, Jiminez thought, for people who had no worries.

Yet.

He still couldn't believe it; Rafe was dead. Mercedes wanted
him, begged him to take some time off, but Raul refused. He
couldn't sit home and mourn. Things were piling up on him, and he
had to act, to keep busy in order to keep control of events. It was his
nature. Even if he made mistakes.

Raul drove to the comer, turned and parked on Fleming, got out
of the car and walked back to the house. It was a quiet, residential
street, no one on the sidewalk. Raul opened the gate, walked up the
cobblestones to the front porch and knocked. No answer. He looked
at his watch. Ten-ten.

Patrick was downtown with Maloney. Raul figured he had half
an hour at the very most to get inside the house,
find the gun, and get back out. It was a small house; he figured he
would need fifteen minutes once he got inside, in case Bowman had
moved the gun.

Raul stepped off the porch and followed the cobblestones along
the side yard to the back of the house, which was completely fenced

213

in with a high canopy of palms and flowering hibiscus along the perimeter of the neatly trimmed yard. He walked up the steps of the wooden deck that led to the back door.

He knocked, then tried the door. Locked.

He hesitated a moment before slipping off his shoe and using its heel to break a pane of glass in the French door, slipped his hand inside the opening, turned the doorknob from the inside—and the door opened.

Breaking and entering. A felony. "Judge, you wouldn't give me a court order to search the place, I knew there was a murder weapon inside that house."

He could picture Judge Hernandez (both their names ending in E-Z counted for shit) sitting up there on the bench in his black robe. Rafe and the judge's son were school friends. "My own son was killed, Judge." Hernandez: "You can't gamble with the criminal justice system." Imposing sentence. Eighteen months, two years? Time off for good behavior?

There was another scenario, the one he had in mind. Bowman reports a robbery, someone broke in his home, stole his nine-millimeter handgun. The police recover it, and in doing so accidentally discharge it. Since it's a nine- millimeter, like the one used to kill Hamilton Wade, they run a ballistics test. And guess what?

Stepping inside the kitchen, that was the way he saw it going down. He decided to leave the kitchen till last, and moved through the rooms.

The dining room, one wall covered with a bulletin board covered with a bunch of names: DARLING, on the newspaper clipping, tacked up there among them.

Jiminez paused, regretting everything he'd told Patrick Bowman about Rafe. DARLING.

He walked straight upstairs to the bureau and opened the top drawer. Bingo! There it was, holstered, underneath a sweater just where he'd seen it the night of the party.

Raul picked it up, looked at his watch. It had taken him all of five minutes. He tucked the gun in his waistband, walked downstairs and out the back door, leaving the door ajar.

Following the cobblestone around to the front, he got to the gate at exactly the same time as the mailman. Mother of God, of all the fucking luck!

"Morning, Chief," the mailman said. "Sorry to hear about your son. A real tragedy." He held the gate, waiting for Raul to come out.

"Johnston, Tom," Lt. Neil Maloney was saying, reading from a report. "Black male, six feet, 182 pounds, from the borough of Queens in New York. Worked, when he worked, at a variety of jobs; mechanic, drove a delivery truck for a liquor company. Convicted of raping a thirty-three-year-old secretary on her way home from a convenience store the night of April third, 1985. Served eleven months, sixteen days." Maloney looked up as if to make sure that Patrick was following all this.

Patrick nodded.

"Johnston arrived in Key West on December twenty- first, last year. Stayed at the Pier House in a two-hundred-dollar-a-day penthouse suite. Departed Key West January fourth, 1989." Maloney looked up again and smiled. "Guess how he got to Key West?"

"He fell in love," Patrick Bowman said.

Maloney's face fell. "You already saw the report?"

"I was guessing."

"Oh. You want to guess who he fell in love with?"

Patrick smiled. "You're setting me up. You want me to say the woman he raped, but that isn't right, is it? The chances of that happening would be what, one in a million?"

Maloney drummed a pencil against the report on his desk. "Yeah, but almost as good," he said. "The guy goes to jail. A woman reads about it in the paper, sees his picture, and starts writing to him. Pen pals. A year later he gets out and they're all over each other. And it turns out she's rich as Croesus. A fairy tale with a happy ending for a rapist. A guy whose life was going down the drain faster than the last bathtub water."

"Ironic," Patrick said. "But what do we know about him while he was in Key West?"

"They were together night and day. He's walking around town in five-hundred-dollar linen suits and a panama hat. The dude. They're blowing money like Saudi Arabian royalty on their first trip out of the desert. He isn't out butchering street girls on the beach. He's got it made, a new lease on life, and it only cost him a year in jail. Put yourself in his shoes."

"Stranger things have happened."

"Johnston isn't the killer. People all over town remember him, a big tipper. He and the lady had a New Year's Eve party in their room, a private affair, a caterer running back and forth with champagne. The last time, one o'clock in the morning, right about the time of the murder, the rapist and his lady are in the big sunken bathtub together."

It crossed Patrick's mind that Maloney had gone through quite a detailed explanation of Tom Johnston just to get to this point. Why? Why couldn't Jiminez have told him this over the phone. After all, he'd made a trip to his house to tell him about Virginia Power.

"That seems to take care of Johnston," Patrick said. Maloney shook his head and began rolling the pencil back and forth in his hands like it was a cigar.

"Then there's Daniel Leigh."

Patrick saw his list of suspects being knocked down like kingpins. "What have you got on Leigh?"

"Living in a trailer on Big Coppitt ten minutes up the road from here. He's doing roofing, drives into town every day. He's got a girlfriend living out there with him who he likes to knock around once in a while, usually when he's drinking. The way he was New Year's Eve."

"New Year's is turning into a memorable night."

"It usually is," Maloney said. "Leigh beat the shit out of his girlfriend. Then took her to the hospital, where she had three stitches put in her lip. I gather he's got a history of finding women who'll

217

take his abuse."

Patrick nodded.

"Guess what time they were at the hospital?"

"About the time a girl was getting her throat cut on the beach."

"You got it, Toyota."

Patrick looked at his watch. He was supposed to be at the airport to pick up Lee at eleven. It was ten-thirty. He said, "Anything else?"

"When's your wife due back?"

"I'm on my way to the airport to pick her up. Why?" Maloney seemed relieved. He put the pencil down. "Just wondering," he said. "I think the chief wants to talk to her more about Wade."

"How's that going?"

Maloney shrugged.

Patrick stood up. "You ever hear of anyone by the name of Darling in Key West?"

Maloney seemed to consider it. "No," he said, "I haven't."

"No one in the phone book by that name, either. I checked."

"Rafael? You think he was using someone's name?"

"It seems possible," Patrick said. "Worth checking."

"The kid was kinky, but he wasn't gay, according to Raul and everybody who knew him."

"Which is why Darling may be a name and not a term of endearment."

"I see. You mention this to the chief?"

"I did. I'm not sure he bought it. And there's something else. When he was dressed up, Rafe was known to be terrified of men."

218

"So I heard."

"So maybe we're looking for a woman, somebody who another woman would trust."

"A woman named Darling?"

"It's just an idea," Patrick said. Maloney was scribbling on a notepad. Patrick went to the door. Maloney looked at his watch, smiled, and said, "Thanks for dropping by."

How many times over the years had they met each other at airport terminals? he wondered. A hundred? Five hundred? From that first late Delta flight when she'd flown in from New York to meet him, it seemed they had spent half their lives in airports. Quietly eating breakfast, or drinking coffee prior to departure; celebrating with Bloody Marys in the airport lounge on arrival.

Except when she'd come back from Europe and the celebrating was delayed.

She seemed different this time. They hugged. He kissed her briefly on the lips. She'd been away little more than three weeks. Her hair was shorter, and she had the anxious air of New York about her, pale skin, a sort of frantic look in her eyes.

They picked up her bags from the claim area and walked out to the Buick parked in front of the terminal. She breathed deeply, turned her face, eyes closed, to the sun. He opened the passenger door for her, and when she got in, walked around to the driver's side.

"Glad to be home?" he said.

She tossed her head, looked at him and grinned. For a moment he saw Miss Wisconsin Dairy Maid, 1963.

"It's warm," she said.

"It's been cold." As they drove he launched into a discussion of the weather, which had always amused her, but now she did not tease him.

Subdued.

She said, "How's the investigation going?"

He had told her on the phone about Rafael Jiminez. Now he described his meeting earlier with Neil Maloney.

"No leads, then, on Wade."

"I don't think so," he said.

They drove for a while in silence. He asked about New York, her work. She talked about it without enthusiasm.

After parking in front of the house, Patrick got the bags out and carried them up on the porch, where he put them down while he got his keys. Lee came up beside him and took mail from the mailbox. They both glanced at it, a couple of advertising circulars and a flyer with the picture of a missing child with an 800 number to call on one side and an ad for Stanley Steamer carpet cleaning service on the opposite side—also with an 800 number.

Patrick put his arm around her. "Lee," he said, "welcome home."

"Thanks," she said. She went in. He picked up the bags, carried them upstairs and put them on the bed. He was coming down the stairs when Lee called from the kitchen, "Patrick, what happened?"

He walked into the kitchen. She was standing there, the back door open, glass from a broken pane all over the floor.

"The door was open," she said.

He was trying to think back. It was only a couple of hours ago. He looked at his watch. It was almost noon. "I left here at ten, to go see Maloney. Everything was fine," he said.

"Then somebody broke in."

They began looking around the house. Everything seemed to be in order. No drawers ripped open, the TV, the stereo, paintings and furnishings, everything of value was in place. He went upstairs again. Nothing suspicious. Lee joined him.

"Maybe we scared them off when we came in," Lee said. She seemed calm.

Patrick went downstairs and out the back. Whoever it was could have gone over the fence. But there was no evidence of that. He went back inside, thinking about calling the police, when Lee called him from the upstairs bedroom. He went up. She had the chest of drawers open. "Did you move your gun?" she asked.

He looked in the drawer, picked up a couple of sweaters. It was gone. "No," he said. He pictured Jiminez standing on the front porch the other night when he came in, the cigarette in his mouth while he talked. *What sort of guns do you carry in Chicago?* And then: *When's your wife get back?*

"I'll call and report it," Patrick said. He went to the phone beside the bed and dialed the city police.

Lee was standing there hip shot, staring into the drawer that contained sox, sweaters, and at one time, his Browning nine-millimeter.

26

Jiminez wasn't in his office, so he talked to Lieutenant Maloney. Maloney said, "I'll send someone over there right away. When'd you say it happened?"

"Between the time I was in your office," Patrick said, "and when I picked my wife up at the airport after I left you."

Maloney seemed to be writing, the ever-present pencil in his hand. "You're sure about the time?" he said.

"We had an appointment for ten o'clock," Patrick said. "I didn't leave the house until a few minutes before that. I locked up and got back here around noon."

"And as far as you know, the only thing missing's the gun."

"We've been through the house. Whoever came in here got what they came for."

Maloney was silent. Patrick waited. "I'll send someone over," Maloney said again.

Fred, the detective who came to the house an hour later, had blow-dried sandy-blond hair, a moustache the same color, and blue eyes. He had an expression that conveyed constant irritability, and without smiling asked questions while filling out a lengthy report. He took a couple of pictures of the door, the window busted out, and dusted for fingerprints. Fifty minutes later, when he left, Lee said, "I wonder if anyone ever thought of calling him Fred Friendly?"

They were eating lunch. Maloney said, "Patrick Bowman called to report that his house was broken into sometime this morning."

"No kidding," Raul Jiminez said. He ate with a voracious appetite, holding a fork in one hand, Cuban bread in the other. Tomorrow they were burying Rafe, and he was spending more and more time away from home, away from Mercedes—who was silently blaming him for Rafe's death— and the two girls who had arrived last night. Under other circumstances he would have taken a week off, but with five separate murder investigations under way, that was out of the question. "Anything taken?" he asked.

"His handgun, a nine-millimeter Browning. Nothing else."

"Who's investigating it?"

"Fred."

Jiminez nodded and took a large bite of bread.

"The thing is," Maloney said, not touching his own food, watching Jiminez eat, "it happened right around the time Bowman was in my office."

"So?"

Maloney leaned forward across the table, lowering his voice, "Jesus, you asked me to talk to him, to keep him occupied for forty-five minutes."

Jiminez looked up, stopped chewing. "You suggesting something? If you are, forget it. Fred's got the case. I'm sure he'll take care of it. Stop worrying. Eat your lunch."

Raul wished it were that simple, that somebody could tell *him* to stop worrying. And he would stop. Like that, bingo! Nothing to it.

***

"Nine people," Patrick said. "Four of them are in the clear. And out of the other five I can't trace three of them. Which means they made up a name when they registered. Who does that, uses an alias? A guy who's got a record, right?"

They were in bed, her first night back. They'd had dinner out, talked about the break-in, then Patrick brought her up to date on the investigation. She had listened intently, asking questions, and when they got home, he went through the names on the bulletin board with her. She read the article on Rafe Jiminez. Darling.

Now they lay in bed, Patrick on his side facing her, propped up on an elbow.

"And you think one of them killed the girls on the beach?" Lee said.

"I don't know," Patrick said. "It's information, that's all. Part of the process."

"And the Jiminez boy?"

"I don't think the chief sees a connection, doesn't want to see a connection," Patrick said. "And maybe there isn't one, but it was a full moon, a knife attack, and the kid was parading around in a short skirt. Unless it's a copycat, I think we're dealing with the same sicko."

"Why can't Jiminez see it?"

Patrick had thought about that, wasn't sure he could answer it. But the feeling he got from Jiminez was that the chief wanted to connect everything to Hamilton Wade, bring it all back to the jaded writer, a dead man. Lee's lover. Patrick didn't see any good reason to bring Wade up. Instead, he said, "I don't know."

"But you do know that this is going to continue, these killings, don't you?"

Yes, he knew that, and it worried him, because if it was the same sicko who killed Rafe, then there was a good possibility that he or she would kill again—soon. His theory about the moon, which was a week away from being full, no longer seemed to apply.

Rafe probably was an unintended victim; had the killer known Rafe was a male, Patrick thought, the odds were good the boy would be alive now. So Rafe was a mistake. In the sicko's mind mistakes had to be corrected.

One way to correct them was to return to the scenes of success— in this case, the beaches. Darling would go back to the beach, Patrick was sure of it.

"What are you thinking?"

"Huh?"

She had scooted across the bed and draped her legs over Patrick's. She wore a white cotton nightgown that rode up over her thighs. "What are you thinking?"

"We never called each other darling. Why?"

"Too soppy," she said.

He felt himself harden, and pushed forward slightly so that his stiff penis pressed between her thighs.

"Darling," he said, as he eased into her with a sigh.

Ricky Garlind, male or female? According to Chicago, the FBI had a Richard Garlund with a U wanted for mail fraud, but no Ricky Garlind with an I. Ricky Garlind had paid cash for his or her stay in Key West and there were no records of any credit transactions. Ricky was running from something. What? Why?

Karen Wilcox and Mike Priest. Wilcox and Priest, common enough last names; some were even wanted—none, however, registered Karen or Mike as first names.

What's in a name? A rose by any other name. Darling. Too soppy. Fax darling to Chicago, and call Wayne Higgs at the FBI.

Names. Postcoital thoughts on the verge of sleep. He would give it more thought in the morning.

In the morning the mailman came, regular as clockwork, you could set your watch by it, give or take fifteen, twenty minutes. Ten o'clock, ten-fifteen, the gate opened and there he would be, in blue, a blue mesh-bill cap with the Postal Service logo, his pushcart containing a sack of mail parked on the sidewalk as he came up the porch steps with the Bowmans' mail.

Patrick greeted him at the door. "Morning," he said.

"Morning." The mailman handed Patrick his mail.

"We were broken into yesterday," Patrick said. The mailman had handed over the mail and half turned to leave, all in one motion, the practiced rhythm that kept him to his schedule. All day he would look at the same houses, rain or shine, the same scenes, noticing, Patrick hoped, any irregularities. "It happened about this time of day. I was wondering if you noticed anything different."

The mailman put one foot on the first step down from the porch. "No," he said, "I didn't. More and more of that kind of stuff going on in Key West, though." He moved off down the steps and across the cobblestones to his pushcart.

"Thanks," Patrick said.

The mailman picked up a stack of mail bundled together with a rubber band. Then turned back to Patrick. "I'll tell you something, though." He smiled like he was about to offer up a joke. "You must have connections, because you got fast response from the law."

"How's that?"

"The chief himself was walking out of here when I came by yesterday."

"Jiminez?" What kind of a gun do you guys carry up in Chicago? Bring it down with you?

"Yeah."

"But not coming out of the house, was he?" Saying it without any real concern in his voice.

"Nah, from the side yard there."

"Oh, yeah," Patrick said. "That was before I got back. What, around the same time, ten-thirty?"

"Something like that." He tilted his pushcart and moved along.

When he was in with Maloney, Maloney going through each detail, stuff he could have given him over the phone, stuff Jiminez could have given him.

Patrick went inside and called Lieutenant Maloney.

Maloney said, "Your gun was found."

227

Patrick said, "Was it ever lost?"

"What's that supposed to mean? You reported it missing."

"Who found it?"

"The dirtbag who was in the churchyard, the guy reported Rafe's murder, had it in a sack he carried his stuff in, said he doesn't know how it got there."

"You questioned him, of course."

"Fred did. No fingerprints, and the dirtbag denies breaking into anybody's house. He claims somebody must've dropped it in the sack."

"And he's probably right," Patrick said.

"What do you want to do?"

"Come in and talk. To you."

"When?"

"Now."

"Okay. Oh, and by the way, the gun was fired."

The phone rang five minutes later, just before he was ready to leave the house. He heard Lee answer it upstairs, and delayed leaving until she finished talking. She came downstairs, looked at him and said, "That was Jiminez. He wants to talk to me."

Move, get out of this place, Darling told herself. She could imagine the landlady, whose deafness seemed to make her talk loudly and who, Darling had noticed, also talked aloud to herself, coming up the stairs to the attic with the police in tow. The chief of police. Rafaella's father. And Patrick Bowman.

Several people had seen her with Rafaella on the street, but would they recognize her, remember her, just two women walking down the street together, having a drink in a street-side bar? No one had reason to pay any attention to them.

Unless Rafaella was being watched. To make sure she didn't get into any trouble. But the cops had passed them, and wouldn't they have been there when the two of them walked into the churchyard?

And how were they going to find her in this place, in a town that rented to thousands of seasonal people by the day and by the week? Even if they knew her name now.

Questions. Too many questions. She was safe here; for now she was safe, and despite the voice of urgency suggesting she move, she felt safe. She sat at the window watching the traffic below her and daydreamed of the night, and the beach.

Patrick phoned FBI headquarters in Washington and asked to speak to Wayne Higgs, head of VICAP, with whom Patrick had shared information in the past.

"I need some information," Patrick said when Higgs came on the line. "A name I'd like you to run through your computer."

"Sure," Higgs said. "What is it?"

Over the years, he'd spoken to Higgs on the phone at least a dozen times. Not once had he ever heard the man display a sense of humor. He was always all business. "Darling," Patrick said.

Higgs waited. Finally, he said, "That's all? Just Darling?"

"That's all I've got, and it's a long shot."

Higgs sighed. "I'll do my best. Might be a day or two."

"I understand," Patrick said. "I'll be waiting."

27

"One of Wade's neighbors, a woman lived across the street, saw you going into his place on several occasions. Said you had a key and went in the back gate whenever you wanted."

Jiminez had taken her to another room, not his office, and Lee had the feeling she was being watched. A glass in the door reflected the room, and she was sure someone would be looking through from the other side, to identify her. The woman across the street from Wade? Or the girl he'd been making it with when she went to his house the last time? And then Patrick was with someone else in another part of the building.

"Hamilton and I were friends. I often used the pool when he was away," she said.

"And sometimes when he wasn't?"

"Sometimes."

Jiminez smelled of rum and the accumulated smoke from the endless cigarettes.

She should have stayed in New York. She had thought about it. Thought about telling Patrick that she had decided to more actively pursue her career. She was forty years old, with a face that under the right lighting and in the hands of a sympathetic photographer could pass for thirty. She could still get work, and like Lauren Hutton, with whom she had often been compared, there was work out there for models now who had turned the corner. Lee had managed her career well.

But unlike Lauren Hutton, she had shot and killed a man.

She had had to come back to Key West, not to confront her own crime, but to relieve her guilt (she hoped) by helping Patrick with his investigation. An act of redemption? She wasn't concerned what it was called, wanting only to protect her marriage—and her life.

Raul Jiminez wasn't any help. (Patrick had told her they'd found the gun.) A ballistics test could prove that it was the weapon used to kill Hamilton Wade—but without her prints on it, or an eyewitness, it could hardly convict her. Was the witness looking at her right now?

"We found your husband's gun," Jiminez said, as though he'd tuned into her thoughts.

She smiled coolly, relaxed, giving nothing away. "Patrick told me," she said.

"We want to run some tests," Jiminez said. "That won't bother you, will it?"

"Whether it does or doesn't, it's what you're paid to do."

"And I'm doing it." He smiled at her behind a cloud of smoke. "Mrs. Bowman, is there anything you can tell me that could help with our investigation into Hamilton Wade's murder?"

Lee returned his smile. "I'm sorry, I'm afraid there isn't."

"The photo of you in Wade's camera."

"I'm a model. There are hundreds of pictures of me around the world."

"Naked? In a man's bed?"

"Isn't that my business, Chief?"

"Yes, for now."

"May I go?"

"One last question?"

"Have I got a choice?"

Jiminez stubbed out his cigarette. "Were you having an affair with Hamilton Wade?"

"I don't see that that's any of your business." She stood up. "Now may I go?"

Jiminez held his hand out, palm up, and gestured toward the door. Lee walked out.

Patrick sat facing Lieutenant Maloney in his office and thought of Lee, who would be facing Jiminez in another office. Lee. His wife, the woman he'd lived with for fifteen years. How many times had they made love over those years, repeated expressions of love, talked and discussed countless intimate details of their life together?

Who was she? How well did he know her? How well did anyone really know anyone else? A question he had asked himself more than once. Perhaps life was nothing more than an accommodation, an acceptance of the *appearance* of knowing, while the sickos, the darlings of the world refused to be accommodated, accepted.

"Lieutenant Bowman . . ."

Patrick looked up from the desk where he'd been gazing distractedly at the back of a picture frame on Maloney's desk.

"Here's the investigating officer's report on the theft of your handgun. I made a copy for you."

Patrick picked it up, glanced at it casually, then replaced it on Maloney's desk.

"I've been thinking about the meeting we had the other day," Patrick said. "About the timing."

A look passed across Maloney's face, but he didn't say anything.

"Jiminez tell you to call me in?"

Maloney picked up the pencil and began twisting it. "He wanted you to have that information."

"I wonder why he didn't tell me himself."

Maloney shrugged. "I guess he was busy," he said.

"Yeah, he sure was. At ten-thirty the mailman arrived and met Jiminez coming from the back of my house—the back, Neil, where the break-in took place. While I was sitting right here in this office."

Maloney was fluttering the pencil between the index and middle fingers of his right hand.

"Mail carriers make good witnesses," Patrick went on. "They've got the authority of a uniform and the Postal Service behind them. They're reliable. They work the streets every day. They see things, and juries tend to believe what they see. Jiminez wasn't up on the front porch, which would have been natural if he was checking to see if anyone was home. He was around back. If I scour the neighborhood carefully, it may be possible to find some more witnesses who maybe saw him go in, who will verify that he was in or around my house for at least half an hour. Maybe somebody will even remember hearing the sound of breaking glass." Patrick picked up the report and crumpled it in his hand. "It's been a while since I worked a robbery detail, but I think I can get better results than Fred."

"Here's your gun," Maloney said lamely. He took a sealed manila envelope from a drawer and put it on top of his desk.

"Yeah," Patrick said. "Jiminez keeps asking about that gun. In fact, he showed up at the house late the other night asking about it."

Maloney forced a smile. "I guess he's checking all the nine-millimeter automatics he can find, in an effort to crack the Wade murder."

"Maybe," Patrick said. "But let me tell you something. Even if it was the murder weapon, it'll never be admitted as evidence in court, not when the police chief had to break and enter to come up with it. Jiminez is either dumb or he's desperate. Personally, I'd say desperate."

"A few unsolved murders could make him that way," Maloney said. "Especially when one of them's his own son."

Patrick nodded, watching Maloney toy with the pencil. "Tell me one thing. Did Jiminez ask you to brief me, have me come in the other day?"

Maloney stared at Patrick without saying anything.

Patrick waited. Then said, "I guess that's as good as an answer. You might want to think about it, if you get called to testify. I hear you're next in line for chief. Is this something you want to cover up, risk your career over? Give it some thought."

"Thanks for the advice."

"Don't mention it. By the way, the guy you said who had the

gun?"

"A dirtbag, Joe Ott."

Patrick grinned. "The same guy who found Rafe, you said." He stood up, picked up the brown envelope from Maloney's desk and walked to the door. "That should tell you something," he said. "A smart cop like you." Patrick walked out of the office.

There was a message on the answering machine to call his contact at the FBI. Lee was not home. Patrick went upstairs, dumped the Browning out of the manila envelope onto the bed; the clip had been removed and fell out alongside the gun.

Patrick picked it up and examined it. Two bullets were missing from the clip; he distinctly remembered having a full clip when he cleaned the gun. He jammed the clip back into the butt of the gun and placed the weapon back in his drawer.

He then called the number that had been left on the answering machine. Nearly a minute lapsed before Wayne Higgs at VICAP came on the line.

"I've come across something," Higgs said. "I don't know if it will be any use."

"On the Darling name, I hope," Patrick said.

"You know how many Darlings we've got outstanding warrants for?"

"Why do I get the feeling I'm going to be disappointed," Patrick said.

"Yeah, none, zip. But wait, there is something, and I don't have the details in front of me, but if you think it's worth it, I can do some more research on it."

"Shoot," Patrick said.

"We do have a Darling, one from our open-case files going back twenty-seven years ago. Roberta Darling." Patrick felt the first uneasy stirrings of hope. "What'd she do?"

"She didn't do anything," Higgs said. "She was a victim."

Jesus. "She's dead," Patrick said, trying to keep his frustration in check.

"Yeah, she's dead. Roberta Darling, fifteen years old, was killed January first, 1962, in Key West."

"And the murder was never solved," Patrick said wearily.

"Apparently not," Wayne Higgs replied. "You think it might tie in with the case you're on?"

"It might." Patrick wasn't sure how. A twenty-seven- year-old unsolved murder in which the victim's last name was Darling seemed like a flimsy link to the present murders, but other cases he had seen had ultimately gotten solved on flimsier links. It all had to be checked.

"How'd the FBI get involved with the old case?" Patrick asked.

"The victim's father was a federal judge from Philadelphia."

Influence, Patrick thought. He said, "What else can you give me?"

Wayne Higgs said, "Edward Darling retired from the bench five years ago. The family had money, although most of it was tied up in investments, and the old judge was an alcoholic. Just the two kids, both girls, Roberta and Rachel. Rachel was seven when her sister died. Roberta was rebellious, apparently quite a handful. Drugs mostly. A few minor scrapes with the law."

Patrick had picked up a notepad and pencil and was making notes. "Keep going," he said.

"They found her body in a clump of bushes near the beach in Key West. The family was there staying in a hotel. Roberta slipped away from the group in the evening, and the family went looking for her."

"And found her."

"Yeah, a couple hundred yards from the hotel in the weeds. Her throat was cut."

"Jesus."

"The cops had found her first. She'd been dead half an hour, and while the cops are investigating, the rest of the family comes trooping up, attracted by the flashing lights."

"With Rachel?"

"Yeah," Wayne Higgs said. "Seven years old. And guess what? A reporter from the local paper has heard about it and comes by with his camera and gets their picture."

"You've got that?"

"I Fed-Exed it to you this morning."

"Good man," Patrick said. "The killer was never caught and there were no leads, right?"

"That's about the size of it."

"What happened to the family?"

"Rachel went into counseling, and that's as far as we go."

"What are the chances of getting an update on the entire family?"

"It's still an open case. I can run it by our field agents in Philly and see what they have."

"Thanks, Wayne," Patrick said. "And if you can make it priority I'd—"

Wayne chuckled. "I'll see what I can do," he said. It was the nearest thing to a laugh Patrick had ever heard from him.

When Lee came in he was standing at the bulletin board comparing names—Darling with Ricky Garlind, Mike Priest, and Karen Wilcox, the three people for whom there were no known whereabouts or firm identities.

Was Ricky a man or a woman? Could he eliminate Mike Priest on the basis of gender? Not if Rachel Darling was posing as a man. Was that possible? Rachel and Rafe. Rafael. The female form of Rafael was Rafaella. Did the boy use that name when he was in drag? Something to find out.

Rachel. What was the male counterpart of Rachel, Richard? Something else to check out. A diminutive form of Richard was Ricky. A link, tenuous, but still a link.

But damn it, the boy Rafe, Rafael, Rafaella, whatever he called himself, would not have been persuaded into that churchyard by a man. The evidence was against it. He got his kicks by dressing up as a woman and being with other women; he was terrified of men— including, perhaps, his own father?

There was a built-in trust among women.

Assumption: Rachel Darling killed three girls on the beach, lured them to their deaths because of that trust. And Rafael Jiminez trusted women; he, too, was lured to his death in the churchyard by a woman.

Which eliminated Mike Priest. Leaving Ricky Garlind— still of indeterminate gender—and Karen Wilcox, as possible aliases for Rachel Darling. With Ricky as a stronger candidate because there was some appealing connection between Rachel and Ricky?

Jesus. It was too farfetched. It would take a task force to check every rental unit on the island for more Ricky Garlinds. Or Karen Wilcoxes. Suppose she was continously moving, changing names each time she moved. It would be impossible.

Not impossible. If Darling were here—and Wayne Higgs's report could help to verify that—then in all probability she was paying rent. Somebody had a record of her via a rent receipt, or a hookup with the gas company, or City Electric.

Not impossible. Just a lead that had to be worked.

He turned. Lee was standing, leaning against the doorway into the living room.

"Five minutes you've been staring at that board," she said. "I even said hello. You didn't move."

"Sorry," Patrick said. "I think I've got something here. How'd it go with Jiminez?"

"He's still hounding me about Hamilton."

"He thinks Wade killed those girls?"

"And I killed Wade."

240

Patrick held himself back from saying, Did you? He hadn't told her of his suspicion that Jiminez had stolen the gun. He said, "I think Jiminez is going to have to revise his thinking."

She walked over and put her arms around him, her hand massaging the back of his neck, her face resting against his. "What's going to happen?" she asked.

"I wish I knew," Patrick said.

He broke away from her, went to the phone and called Jiminez's office number. His secretary answered and said, "He's gone for the rest of the day. It's his son's funeral this afternoon."

Patrick had forgotten.

28

St. Mary's Star of the Sea was filled with family, friends, uniformed law enforcement and city hall employees, both the political elect and their appointees. The mayor was there, and three out of the four members of the city commission, the fourth having sent his regrets because he had to be out of town. All the county commissioners attended, as did the press, who came with cameras.

Jiminez had considered having a private service for members of the immediate family only. Given Rafe's perversion, Raul would have preferred that over this public spectacle, had it not been for an earlier realization that he might get some personal mileage from the public witness of his family's grief.

Funerals, like marriages, brought people together, focused their attention for an hour or so on the bereaved family while sympathy was passed among them like a collection plate. It made for good politics.

Raul sat in the roped-off front pew with Mercedes and their two daughters, both girls wearing solemn expressions on their well made-up faces, holding hands while Mercedes hid her grief behind a black veil.

The rest of the family, Rafe's grandparents, aunts and uncles, and numerous cousins, some of whom Raul hadn't seen in five years, shared the pew directly behind them.

When it was over and the organist struck the first notes of a dirge, people stood and started slowly filing out, mingling, talking, offering condolences, while waiting for the cortege to the cemetery where they would put Rafe's ashes to rest in a vault.

Raul was grateful everyone had agreed upon cremation, which conveniently avoided the question of how Rafe should be dressed had he been buried conventionally.

Raul caught sight of Patrick Bowman and Lee, who must have come in late; they were standing at the back of the church, near the front doors.

Raul looked for Neil Maloney, who had been seated in the third row, at the head of the police detachment. Raul caught his eye just as Maloney moved into the aisle. Neil came back and shook hands. "I don't want to see the Bowmans. They're standing in the back," Jiminez whispered. He gripped Maloney's elbow. "Get 'em out of here."

Maloney nodded and walked away. Raul took Mercedes's arm and held her at the edge of their pew while the throng cleared. Maloney had conveyed Bowman's accusations and threat after their meeting this morning. Raul didn't feel like a confrontation now, not here, anyway. It would be counterproductive. Bowman could wait.

Maloney said, "A word," and crooked his finger. Patrick followed him out the double-wide doors of the church. Lee walked beside him. They went to the comer of the church and stood under the shade of a large tree.

Maloney said, "The chief doesn't want to see you here. It's the wrong time."

Patrick watched the crowd assemble in front, groups forming, people pausing to chat, to smoke, and then move on. Patrick said, "I think we've got an ID on the beach killer."

Maloney, too, scanned the crowd. "A name?"

"A name," Patrick said. "Check your records from twenty-seven years ago and look for a homicide victim, Roberta Darling. Her body was discovered in the mangroves."

"Darling." Maloney said it softly, as though it were a deadly disease.

"She had a sister, Rachel. I've got the FBI running a background check on her. If she's here, I think it might be wise to find her."

"The chief doesn't buy your theory that a woman's behind these killings." Maloney looked at Lee. "He's got his own theory, and I think, under the circumstances, you're going to have a hard time selling him on this. What, a vindictive sister?"

"Maybe, maybe not," Patrick said. "But I don't think you can afford to overlook this one."

"What do you want to do, put an ad in the paper? Say, 'Rachel Darling, come to police headquarters and talk.'"

"A task force," Patrick said. "Comb every realty agency, the utility companies, all the rental apartments in town."

"Looking for Rachel Darling." Maloney smirked.

"She may be using another name, perhaps several, and she may be moving around."

"What names?"

"I'm working on that now."

Maloney shook his head. "The chief will never buy it."

Patrick said, "I don't think he's going to have much choice."

Maloney turned and walked away. Lee said, "What was that all about?"

Patrick watched Maloney move into the crowd. He didn't see Jiminez anywhere. The press was taking pictures. Patrick thought about getting one of the reporters over and giving him a story.

He said to Lee, "It was Raul Jiminez who broke into the house."

"And the mailman saw him leaving," Lee said.

"You overheard me question him?"

She nodded.

He should have known. Lee was not one to pry when he wasn't yet ready to divulge information. He had wanted to confront Maloney first for confirmation of his suspicions, and, more importantly, wanted Lee to see Jiminez without being forewarned of anything.

"Are you absolutely certain?" Lee asked.

"Judging from his actions today, yes."

"But what does it mean?"

"He's compromised himself," Patrick said.

"Meaning?"

"He can't act on anything he took out of the house."

"The gun."

"Yes." He looked at her, a husband conversing with his wife, but it was more than that, he was looking for a reaction, some sign, an answer to the question he couldn't bring himself to ask.

"What are you going to do?"

"Talk to the media," Patrick said.

They stood at graveside, beneath the shade of a canvas canopy, the sun beating down, reflecting off the white concrete tombs stacked three high, one of which now held his son's ashes. The crowd was dispersing, quietly ambling back to cars parked in the street outside the fenced-in cemetery.

Jiminez pulled Maloney aside, walked with him over to another gravesite, a crumbling old gravestone, the earth pushed up, mounded, as if to dispel its occupant, who had been dead a hundred years. Mercedes and the family stood or remained seated under the canopy.

"Well," Raul said, "what did Bowman want?"

"You remember an old case from years ago, a girl killed out in the mangroves by the airport?"

"Mother of God! What do we get, maybe three, four bodies a year floating up into the mangroves around here?" Maloney nodded.

"How many years ago?"

Maloney said, "Twenty-five, thirty."

Jiminez stared at him blankly. "Give me a break," he said.

"Her name was Roberta Darling," Maloney said.

Raul reached for his cigarettes, lit one and, exhaling, said, "Darling." In the same perplexed tone of voice Maloney had used with Patrick Bowman moments earlier.

"Bowman is trying to make a connection between that case

and—" Maloney gestured toward Rafe's burial tomb.

"One word," Raul scoffed, "from a—" He stopped himself short of referring to his dead son as a *maricon.*

"The girl had a sister," Maloney went on. "Bowman thinks she could be in town."

Jiminez shook his head. "Killing people. This guy's supposed to be the professional, the expert, and he wants to blame it on a woman for a crime commited thirty years ago."

"He wants to set up a task force to find her," Maloney said.

Jiminez ground his cigarette into the swollen earth of the hundred-year-old grave. "Forget it," he said, and walked back to where Mercedes and the girls waited.

The photograph of Rachel Darling taken twenty-seven years ago in Key West standing wide-eyed over the body of her murdered sister arrived Fed Ex as Wayne Higgs had promised. And Higgs called, coincidentally, while Patrick was examining it. He said, "Rachel Darling is an actress who had been living in New York for the past ten years. Her father, the judge, was killed in a car accident four years ago, and her mother died eighteen months later. That came in from the Philly bureau office moments ago. Fast enough to suit you?"

"I'd like to find out everything I can about Rachel Darling," Patrick said.

"I rather suspected you would," Wayne replied. "I've asked the New York bureau to run a further background check. They may prove a little slower than our guys in Philly, though."

"I could get the NYPD involved," Patrick said.

"I'm beginning to take a personal interest in this case," Higgs said. "I'll push them."

"I think," Bill Peachy said over the phone with more irony than Patrick was accustomed to hearing from him, "Raul Jiminez is getting ready to put the screws to you."

"You think, or you know?" Patrick asked. "I'm interested in what you know."

Since the cold front, Peachy had been out daily with charters. Nearly a week had gone by since Patrick had talked to the guide.

"The chief's not buying your link between his son's death and the other murders."

"I'd hoped you were going to tell me something I didn't already know."

"He's working the angle that the writer, Wade, killed those girls. He's trying to build on that theory. He thinks if he can find out who killed Wade, he may be able to prove that Wade was behind the beach murders."

"How?"

"He's got an idea that whoever shot Wade did it because he, or she, knew Wade was the killer you're looking for."

"Why didn't whoever it was just turn Wade in to the police?"

"Because, according to Jiminez, there may have been a personal link between them, something Wade was holding over the person's head."

Patrick felt like he'd just been given news of the sudden and unexpected loss of a family member. He changed the subject. "What about Jiminez's son?"

"A separate case. Jiminez is under pressure. He's got to come up with something fast."

"I don't buy it," Patrick said. "The heat's going to take its toll. He'll be lucky to get off with anything less than third-degree burns. Bill, there's a killer sitting out there who is driven. She's going to strike again, and we've got a chance to stop her, but we need some manpower to do it."

"She?"

"I'm not a hundred percent yet, but it looks more and more like a woman."

"What kind of manpower are you talking?"

"The kind that can get utility companies to open up their records, check rental agencies for new tenants, and canvas the town with rental apartments not listed with any agency."

"You don't want much. I think I'd rather try to find that barracuda you lost your first day fishing."

"I just need a little cooperation," Patrick said.

"From Jiminez."

"That would help."

"Let me see what I can do," Peachy said.

"Soon."

"Tonight. I've got a charter tomorrow."

Lee was reading. Patrick stepped out onto the upstairs deck and looked up at the sky. The moon was only a day away from being full. He was working against the odds, against everything he had learned about serial killers, who were white, usually male, and above average in intelligence. In his experience, they appeared normal, often conventionally charming and sane. And more often than not, as children they had been victims of abuse themselves, suffering either physical or psychological abuse at the hands of family members who had criminal histories.

Women who killed often did so from passion, driven to some extreme edge of violence they may not even have been aware existed, the result of being pushed too far for too long. Vengeance.

Who was Rachel Darling? Where was the pattern, the stamp, life's fingerprint that would explain everything?

He was moving too quickly. First things first. Where was Rachel Darling?

He turned and could see Lee, who had come upstairs. She was in the bathroom, the door ajar, and he could see her reflection in the mirror as she began removing her clothes.

Who was Lee Bowman? The time she'd flown to him from New York, the first time they slept together, she lived in his apartment for two weeks before returning to New York. A month later she was back again. When they weren't together, they talked on the phone each night, planning their next visits. They couldn't get enough of each other. But six months later, when the idea of merging their lives came up, he remembered what she said: "I love you, I know you're probably good for me, but I don't know if I can be faithful, or even if I want to."

He tried to make light of it while admiring her truthfulness, and at the same time feeling troubled, disturbed by the prospect of their future together. Still, he had smiled and said, what? Something lame like, let's cross that bridge when we get to it.

He guessed they were crossing it now for real for the first time.

29

The Key's section of the morning *Herald* had the story of the funeral, but the feature story was devoted to Patrick Bowman. It expressed the Chicago lawman's belief that the Rafael Jiminez murder was linked to the recent savage attacks against women, and his belief that they were all perpetrated by the same killer, who would undoubtedly strike again, perhaps in future random attacks, unless caught.

For the first time since the killings began in late November, Patrick Bowman said, they had a solid lead, evidence that would hopefully bring about an arrest very soon. He would not elaborate on what that evidence was for fear of jeopardizing the case.

It went on to list again Bowman's credentials. Then quoted the president of the Chamber of Commerce, who said he had every confidence in the police, who he felt had the situation in hand, and that the community as a whole was in no danger.

Near the end of the article the chief of police stated that the so-called beach killer was no longer a threat to the community and that he would soon be able to provide the evidence necessary to confirm this remarkable assertion.

Jiminez offered no comment on Bowman's claim nor would he confirm or deny that there was an open rift between the two of them.

Patrick picked up his coffee, the mug leaving a damp round stain on the paper. He could call the reporter who had written the story and say, hey, you want to know about the rift, I can tell you. The

Key West chief of police broke into my home, stole a gun, and now wants to use it as evidence to blame a dead man for the murder of three young women on the beach.

He sipped his coffee while he tried to think of other ways to broadcast Raul Jiminez's criminal conduct.

Why was he worrying about this? To protect Lee?

Protect her from something he couldn't even bring himself to talk to her about. A sense, a feeling, an instinct. Dread. The kind that preceded some crisis after which you knew life would never be the same again.

The phone rang. Lee was not up yet. He went into the living room and got it in the middle of the second ring. It was the mayor.

"I just saw the paper," he said.

"Titillating stuff," Patrick said.

"How serious is the conflict between you two?"

Patrick laughed. "Let's put it this way. I don't think I'll continue to be retained by the chief as a consultant on this case."

"But you do have strong evidence to support your claims in the paper?"

"Evidence," Patrick said. "Enough to warrant a stepped- up investigation. I won't know just how strong it is until the next couple of days. But I don't recommend waiting until then to begin a manhunt."

"What are the odds that he will kill again?"

Patrick didn't bother to quibble over the pronoun. If the mayor thought the killer was a male, it was probably best left that way.

"I'm not a bookmaker," he said. "But in my experience, serial killers don't stop until they're caught."

There was silence from the mayor.

Peachy had called back last night after midnight. He'd talked to the mayor, he said. And to the commissioners. He'd lobbied them one by one, as he was accustomed to doing over the years. He thought they had listened and were sympathetic, Bill said. More so than when he lobbied them over an environmental issue.

The mayor said, "It's possible to override Jiminez, but I wouldn't want to do so without good reason."

Patrick thought for a minute. Then he said, "Give me fifteen minutes of your time and I think I can show you the reason."

Mayor Sheldon said, "Raul, it's been a rough time. We don't want to fight over this."

Jiminez spread his hands out in front of him, looked at them, then began to clean his fingernails with the index nail of his right hand. "No," he said. "What is this, Eric, politics?" The mayor was up for reelection this year.

"I'm not going to make a speech about the common good, interests of the city, that sort of thing," Sheldon said.

"Good," Jiminez said. He finished with his left hand and began cleaning the right.

"But I'd like you to reconsider. I'm asking you, as a favor, to reconsider your decision."

"And if I won't?"

The mayor sighed, the sort of sissy sound that seemed to irritate Jiminez more these days since Rafe was killed. A self-proclaimed gay, the mayor had drawn national attention to himself, part of the outsiders who'd come in to change the politics of Key West. Twenty years ago such a thing would have been unthinkable.

"I suppose, then," the mayor said, "you'd leave me with no option."

What was this bullshit? He was being threatened. Jiminez knew the mayor understood the workings of city government. The police chief worked for the city manager; the mayor and the commissioners had no say over how the chief of police ran his department. For that matter, neither did the city manager. Jiminez established policy within the department. So what was this bullshit?

"You know you can't fire me."

The mayor smiled. "No, of course not," he said. "There is, however, the internal affairs investigation."

Jiminez smiled and said, "It's my understanding that with the workload we've got right now, and the fact we are undermanned as usual, the internal affairs investigation isn't a high priority."

They were in the mayor's office, approximately twice the size of the chief's. The mayor's desk was clean, some pretty pictures hung on the walls, and everything about it annoyed Jiminez.

The mayor sighed again. "Patrick Bowman is thinking of bringing charges," he said. "Against you. In legal terms, the commission of a felony. Specifically, breaking and entering."

"Fuck him," Jiminez said. And stood up.

"Think about it," the mayor said. "A simple task force, two or three men on special duty assignment. The commission and the city manager are behind this. They'd like to see it in place. It would save a lot of embarrassment for everyone."

Raul had thought about it. It wasn't so much that he considered it a waste of time; more that it appeared that Bowman was running the investigation. "Is that all?" he asked.

"I hope so," the mayor said.

Raul turned and strode out of the room.

"As you know, I've got two men working these cases exclusively," Neil Maloney said. "If you include your son's murder as part of the same investigation."

Jiminez didn't say anything. He was still feeling the sting of the mayor's efforts to interfere with his job. And he could feel his health slipping; he was smoking more, drinking more, and sleeping less.

"One of the detectives is dividing his time between the Wade killing and the beach murders. He has been questioning downtown businesses, anyone who might have seen Rafe that day."

"Anything?"

"Maybe," Maloney said. "We've got a waitress in the La Concha sidewalk caffe who thinks she might have served him." Maloney looked down at his desk. "She can't be sure—they've got hundreds of tourists in and out of there every day—but we showed her a picture of Rafe. She thinks it was him. She remembers someone dressed the way he was coming in, having a cold drink. He was lame. The waitress thought he was a woman."

"The La Concha's a block from the church," Jiminez said.

"If it was Rafe, he wasn't alone."

Raul lit a fresh cigarette from the butt of the one he had been smoking, before stubbing out the butt in his ashtray. "The waitress describe who he was with?"

"No," Maloney said. "Except it was a woman."

"Mother of God," Jiminez said.

"The waitress remembers two women sitting at one of the street-side tables, and she wouldn't have remembered that, she says, except for the one having twisted her ankle. There was nothing unusual about the other one."

"They leave together? She see which way they went?"

Maloney shook his head.

"You check for footprints back in the churchyard?"

"It's mostly grass back there. We haven't had much rain for a while, but the area remains sealed off."

"You get a print, we can try to match it with the partial we got from the Martello, where the girl was killed over Christmas."

"That was from a sneaker. We're looking at that," Maloney said.

Jiminez sat back in his chair, stared up at the ceiling while he smoked. When he finished the cigarette, he leaned forward again, looked at Maloney and said, "In forty-eight hours I want a list of every new meter connection, gas hookup, and telephone installed in the last three months."

A smile appeared on Maloney's face. Jiminez cut him off before he could interrupt. "I want a list of new tenants for the same period from every real estate agency in the city that handles rental property."

"What about the independent places that advertise in the paper, or just hang out a For Rent sign?"

"Check with the tax assessor's office, get a list of houses that are taxed on multiple-dwelling units. Then find out from the owners who's living in them."

"In forty-eight hours."

"Starting now," Jiminez said, "and that's continuous hours, not working hours."

"What about Bowman?"

"What about him?"

"Do we use him?"

"Fuck him," Jiminez said.

Darling was sick. A miserable cold and flu combined; every muscle and joint in her body seemed to ache, and she was running a fever. She lay in the bed, one minute shivering with cold, the next so hot she was unable to keep the covers on. Her collection of clippings along with the morning newspaper lay on the bed; Patrick Bowman's picture, the Chicago cop who said he had evidence pointing to the identity of the killer.

Darling. It had to be the name, but so what? They couldn't search every apartment.

Still, it was not a convenient time to be sick. She should be up, paying closer attention, perhaps even moving, although it occurred to her that taking a new place could bring more attention to her than simply staying where she was.

The old lady downstairs had seen her once, maybe twice, and had never looked at her beyond a passing glance. She doubted the woman would recognize an old picture of Darling even if they had one.

She had purchased a portable radio, and she listened to the news every hour. She would like to have sat in the
window, watching the street, but right now she couldn't move. She took aspirin, drank lots of hot tea that she made on the two-burner hot plate.

Rest, sleep, she had to throw this off, get back on her feet; and before she dozed off, thinking: still so much to do.

30

Wayne Higgs said, "Rachel Darling gave up her apartment in the West Village six months ago. Somebody in the theater where she worked said she had told people she was going to be traveling. Going out to the West Coast to look for movie work. Nobody's heard from her. But they aren't surprised; she was a loner."

"What about credit cards, other names she might have used? Ricky Garlind, for example. Or Karen Wilcox."

"She got a sizable inheritance when her mother died, so she's probably paying cash if she's on the run. I don't know anything about other names. We haven't been after her, and she has no previous record on our files, as you know."

Patrick thanked Higgs and asked him to stay in touch if anything developed.

From her home she could time herself as she walked around the block. It took a little over seven and a half minutes. Call it ten. Which meant she could cover six square blocks in an hour. Without telling Patrick what she was doing, Lee set out the next morning at eight with a notebook and pen. She would take the blocks between William Street and downtown's Duval, working toward the Gulf, two to three hours' work. Wherever there were signs indicating apartments for rent she stopped and inquired, asked questions in as unobtrusive a way as possible about the tenants, in some cases even getting names.

She felt good walking the streets, well-aware that it had almost nothing to do with either exercise or fresh air, and everything to do with the almost religious sense of relief that it gave her to be doing something to help Patrick find this killer.

Crime and punishment. Redemption. I should have converted to Catholicism, she thought.

She knocked on the door of a large two-story frame house with several rusting appliances sitting on the front porch and a tattered For Rent sign attached to one porch column.

"I saw the sign," she said when a shirtless man in shorts and flip-flops came to the screen door, one edge of screening tom from the frame.

The man was unshaven, carrying the slightly sour smell of overnight sweat. "I've got one apartment. It's six hundred dollars," he said. Adding, "A month."

She looked down at the floor of the rotting porch.

"Two bedrooms," he said, as if to justify the rent he was asking.

"How many tenants do you have?"

He looked at her and said, "Three."

She smiled, trying to disarm him. "Are any of your tenants women?"

He grinned back at her. "There's a few guest houses in town that are for women only, if that's what you're looking for. This isn't one of them. I'm renting apartments. What you do in them is up to you, as long as you don't break up the furniture."

"I wasn't—"

"Men," he said.

"What?"

"The other three apartments are rented to men. You interested?"

Turning to go, she said, "I'll think about it."

Patrick Bowman tried to think of one word that might best describe the photograph of Rachel Darling. The photograph that Paul the busboy now stood looking at.

"Tough," Paul said. "She a dyke?"

As a description, "tough" wasn't bad, although Patrick had received no information on whether she was attracted to other women. Paul handed the photo back.

"She seem familiar, you recognize her?" They were standing in Key Lime Square just before noon, outside the restaurant where Paul was currently washing dishes. Patrick had found him by checking City Hall records, since all service employees were required to register with the police.

"No," Paul said. "Am I supposed to?"

"I thought you might have seen her on the beach sometime."

Paul shook his head. "I don't hang out over there much anymore."

"I was thinking about before, when those girls were killed."

"Man, I told you, I never saw her before in my life."

Patrick nodded and watched as Paul walked back to the restaurant. Patrick stood staring at the photograph. It was true, the picture suggested a certain masculine quality; but despite the long, slender shape of the face with its deep-set eyes, high prominent cheekbones, and a mouth that was too wide, Rachel Darling would not be considered unattractive. Of course, it was hard to tell exactly when the photo was taken, as Wayne Higgs had pointed out.

Rachel Darling apparently didn't care to spend much time posing for a camera.

Her face was determined. That was the word. More in the expression than anything conveyed by her features. The dark eyes staring straight ahead at the camera were unwavering. The lips set, without hint of a smile or the suggestion of shyness. Straightforward. What you see is what you get.

Determined.

Was he looking at the face of a killer?

No one except Rachel Darling knew the answer to that question.

Lieutenant Maloney said, "We've got a list of names from the gas company and City Electric. We're still waiting on the aqueduct authority for requests for new water service, and info from the realty offices concerning rentals."

"What changed the chief's mind?" Patrick asked. From Key Lime Square it was a short walk to City Hall. He brought the photograph of Rachel Darling to Maloney so he could make a copy of it.

"The mayor." Maloney smiled.

"Is Jiminez still pissed at me?"

Maloney lifted a stub of pencil from behind his ear and said, "I don't think he's spending a lot of time thinking about you right now. A waitress at La Concha remembers Rafe being in there with a woman just before he was killed."

Patrick said, "Maybe she should look at this photo."

"I was going to take it over there myself," Maloney said.

"Mind if I tag along?"

"Be my guest."

"And by the way, unless you're pissed, too, I'd like a look at those names."

"No problem," Maloney said. "Just don't tell Jiminez I gave them to you."

The waitress at La Concha, like Paul the busboy, was unable to identify Rachel Darling from her photo as the woman who had accompanied Rafael Jiminez sometime before he was stabbed in the churchyard.

The girl studied the photograph a long time. Then she said, "I don't know, I can't be sure."

"You think you could be sure if you saw her, if she walked in here again?"

"I don't know. Like I already explained, I remember the other one more because she was hurt. You wait on as many tables as I do, you get so you don't even see faces unless there's something unusual."

Patrick nodded. He left Maloney, crossed the street and walked down to the church in search of Carol, to show her the photo. He didn't find her until that evening; she didn't recognize the picture, either.

Rachel Darling's luck continued to hold.

It was the large frame house with the door that led nowhere. The porcelain doorknob that she had photographed at night several weeks ago, four blocks from her own home. It wasn't the last of the old mansions in Key West, but it was one of the few that hadn't been restored and turned into an expensive guest house or hotel.

The weathered siding had gone a decade or more without paint. There was no fancy gingerbread trim, no exotic landscaping, just the stark, bare house with it's widow's walk atop the open, windowless attic.

Frequently, an older woman could be seen cleaning the street or sweeping up the sidewalk with a homemade broom fashioned from a palm frond. A curious eccentric figure, a holdover from the days when Key West existed as a community and less as a tourist haven.

Lee remembered seeing a For Rent sign on numerous occasions when she passed the place. It was not there today.

The old woman was. She scooped leaves from the curb into an old-fashioned long-handled dustpan with her makeshift broom.

"Excuse me," Lee said.

The woman paused in her sweeping, looked up, then continued to sweep.

Lee said, "Is this your house?"

The woman looked up again, wagged a finger toward downtown and said, "Duval Street."

Lee decided she was deaf rather than rude—rudeness that could often boil over in locals constantly assaulted by the demands of tourists.

Lee raised her voice, "I'm looking for a room, an apartment."

The woman looked up from her sweeping again, this time with a slight smile. "I hear you," she said, "no need to shout. If I have an apartment to rent, I'll put a sign up."

"I know. I've seen the sign before," Lee said.

"So why did you ask?"

"Perhaps you have something coming up."

"Perhaps, but not that I know of."

"How many apartments do you have?"

"Five, and they're all rented. Including the attic."

"I'd like to leave my name, a phone number where I can be reached."

The woman sighed irritably, mumbled something to herself, then continued sweeping. Lee turned, started to walk away. "Here," the woman said, pointing to the porch. Lee turned and, smiling, began walking back toward the house, when a sudden reflection of light, probably off the tin roof, caused her to look up. When she did, she caught a brief glimpse of a woman's face ducking back from the attic window overlooking the street.

Lee followed the old woman into the house, where she was told to wait in the hall. The woman disappeared through a door into the main body of the house, returning moments later with a book that she opened and handed to Lee, asking her to write her name and number.

It was a small spiral notebook, dog-eared, torn, and stained. A list of names were above the line where she wrote her own. Three of them were women's names.

She wrote slowly while memorizing the women's names above her own.

Darling pulled herself from bed. Still feverish and aching, she went to the window and looked out onto the street where she'd heard voices. The deaf landlady and someone else, a woman who was asking about apartments. There were no apartments. The sign had been taken down soon after Darling had moved in. The place was full.

So why would someone come asking about a place that wasn't even advertised? Unless she had a reason to snoop around, a reason that had nothing to do with wanting an apartment.

Their eyes met briefly when the woman who had started to walk away from the house turned and looked up at the attic. Darling ducked away from the window. But she noticed the woman's clothes, her looks, and knew immediately the woman didn't belong in this dingy place.

They were coming inside, the old woman beckoning her in.

Darling went to the door and opened it so that she could hear them in the hall, the deaf old woman leaving the woman in the hall while she went to get something. A receipt book? With her name, Gina Rigland, in it?

31

City Electric showed over five hundred requests for electrical hookups for the month of January. Patrick went through the names and addresses. Sixty percent of them were in the Old Town area. At a quick glance he could find no connection to Rachel Darling, Karen Wilcox, or Ricky Garlind among the names.

Those names from City Electric that were not duplicated on the list from the local gas company, as many of them were, provided no more insight into a possible alias. Patrick paired each name from the utility companies with Darling, Wilcox and Garlind, pondering them for a couple of hours, trying to establish a link but failing.

And wondering for the umpteenth time if he was pursuing the wrong angle. It was possible, of course; his instincts were not infallible, but the Darling aspect was too strong to ignore.

He paused to fix himself a snack, and came back to the dining room table to eat it, staring at more names.

It was possible Rachel Darling wasn't living in Key West. Perhaps she was on a boat—she could afford it, according to Wayne Higgs. Or living up the Keys someplace, and driving into town when the murderous mood seized her, before escaping back up U.S. 1.

But he had already checked with the rental-car agencies and the airlines. Again, Rachel Darling, Karen Wilcox, and Ricky Garlind were absent from those records. He was up to his eyeballs in names. And none of them were leading anywhere.

So was he barking up the wrong tree?

Perhaps. But he was barking, and whatever tree Rachel Darling was living in, she was surely listening. Which left open the possibility that she might flee before they could drop a net around her. He worried about that even while clinging to the belief that she was still here.

The day passed quietly, the whir of the overhead fan and an occasional breeze through the open windows rustling his papers as he shifted and sorted names like they were color charts from the paint store.

Shortly after three o'clock in the afternoon, Lee returned. She walked to the dining room, kissed him and dropped her open notebook among his papers.

He looked and saw more names.

She said, "I did a little detective work." Running her hand down into his open shirt, massaging his chest. Jesus. It was the first time she'd initiated anything between them in what seemed like weeks.

He said, "And now you want to be paid."

She said, "That's corny."

He said, "Which rhymes with?"

She laughed, nibbling her lower lip between her teeth, and said, "Let's fuck."

When he got back to the names a couple hours later, it caught his attention with the startling clarity of a car backfiring on a quiet street. Garlind—Darling. All the letters were the same.

He said, "Jesus," and reached for the phone.

***

Fifteen years ago, maybe even ten, he would simply have gone to the mailman and had a quiet word. A word to the wise. And that would have been it. Sufficient, as they said. He would never have had to give it another thought. But that was then, this was now.

Times changed, too fast and not always for the good, Raul Jiminez thought. Never for the good. He sat there with the ballistics report on his desk and knew that he might as well burn it in his ashtray for all the good it was going to do him.

He could use it to make an arrest, but he knew from talking to Lee Bowman that he was never going to get a confession, so what they'd wind up with would be a trial in which he, Raul Jiminez, was both witness for the prosecution and a defendant. And whatever happened, he was finished. Whether he went to jail or not, he was out of a job, his name and reputation smeared.

So what did he do? He slipped the ballistics report into an envelope, wrote Patrick Bowman's name on it, and locked it in his drawer. There had to be another way to deal with this problem, but time was running out, Raul thought. If he was going to survive, he would have to move soon.

Nervousness seemed to be a constant part of Neil Maloney's personality, Patrick thought. The guy was always on the expectant edge of disaster. He had the air of a man never quite comfortable with his own body; he was ill at ease, awkward. Patrick had tried unsuccessfully to reach the lieutenant yesterday evening. He had asked a secretary to leave a message for Maloney that he needed to see him. Urgently. And would come by first thing in the morning.

Maloney said, "Rachel Darling. You're sure?"

Patrick tried to sound reassuring. He said, "I believe she's in an apartment over on Elizabeth Street. She has no reason to believe we know that."

Maloney squirmed in his seat. "But there's no guarantee that it's Rachel Darling who's living there," he said.

Patrick said, "You want a guarantee these days you pay for it. Everybody wants to be let off the hook." He smiled.

Maloney wasn't smiling. He fiddled with his eternal prop, a pencil, while studying the sheet of yellow paper Patrick had given him. "Two names," he said. "You're making an assumption on the basis of two names."

"Anagrams of Darling," Patrick said. "Garlind and Rigland."

"Still, you don't know. You're only assuming that they're one and the same person."

"An assumption that's worth looking into," Patrick said.

Ricky Garlind, Gina Rigland and Rachel Darling. Clever. He had come downstairs after making love with Lee, and looked at the names again, this time with a clear head. Feeding the dozen or so new names Lee had brought him into his pairing system, and after five minutes studying them, there they were: The connection he'd been looking for all along.

By mixing the letters of her last name Rachel Darling—if his assumption was true—had come up with at least two aliases, perhaps more. For her victims (at least Rafael anyway) she had used her real name. A deliberate choice? Patrick had pondered the thought that Rachel might be using her real name with her victims. Playing out a psychodrama as she tried to avenge her sister's death.

But if it was a psychic choice, it had to have backfired when she ran into Rafe Jiminez, twisted and terrified of men; whose last spoken word had identified a killer. Rafe, whose father, the chief of police, wouldn't believe him.

Forget the motive, Patrick told himself, and concentrate on finding her.

Neil Maloney said, "I'll have to okay it with the chief."

"You're in charge of the task force, aren't you?"

"That's different," Maloney said.

"Why? You're just going to check on one of the people whose name was on the list."

For a moment it looked like Maloney was going to snap the pencil that he held gripped in both fists. "You and me," he said.

"Just you and me," Patrick agreed. And of course the specter of Raul Jiminez, he thought.

Her name was Connie Pinder, nee Russell, which was about as close as you were going to get to pure native in this town, Neil Maloney told him on the drive to the Pinder house. Stories abounded about Mrs. Pinder, whose husband, a doctor, died six months after they were married. For the past forty years Connie had lived alone in the big house. Three years ago she began taking in boarders.

"She's a little crazy," Maloney said. "Eccentric."

They parked a block from the house. Lee had told him that she had glimpsed a woman looking out the window of the attic yesterday when she was there, so it seemed best to use some precaution, not drive up and get out of a car looking like a couple of cops.

The house was closed up. Except for the fact that the street and sidewalk were clean, from the outside the house looked as if it were unlived in. The downstairs windows were shuttered, the door closed.

They walked to the porch and Maloney rapped on the door. Waited a few seconds and knocked again, louder. "She's deaf," he said to Patrick as he beat on the door once more.

It opened and Connie Pinder stood glaring at them. Maloney showed her his ID.

Connie Pinder said, "I didn't call the police."

"We'd like to talk to you, Mrs. Pinder," Neil Maloney said, his tone of voice professional cop. "Just a few questions."

Connie Pinder stood staring at them, one hand resting on the door, the other jammed against her hip. Her head, Patrick noticed, was large for her body, slightly out of proportion, which gave her a stern appearance despite the unwrinkled skin and staring, childlike eyes. Hard to tell how old she was, Patrick thought. Sixty, eighty. She edged the door a little wider and Patrick followed Maloney inside.

They were in a narrow hall with a stairway along the outside wall and closed doors opposite it. Connie opened the first of the doors and they stepped into her living quarters. Dark, with the outside shutters closed against the window, it took his eyes some time to adjust from the bright light of the street. When they did, he saw the spartan Victorian furnishing, the dark wood walls containing what looked like ancestral portraits. A roll top desk littered with papers. Connie pulled a chain on a lamp on the desk and the dim glow of no more than a forty-watt bulb shaded by a green glass canopy offered some mottled light. Enough to see into the alcove beside the desk and a single sleeping cot. There was the lingering smell of perfumed talcum powder.

Connie turned to face them, her body bent slightly at the waist. "You came about the woman in the attic," she said. "I know it."

"What makes you say that?" Maloney asked.

Connie Pinder shook her head. "There was something about her when she first moved in. I said to myself, this one's trouble."

Patrick said, "What's her name?"

She turned toward him like it was the first time she'd seen him. Then turned back to Maloney and said, "I've got it here somewhere."

She rummaged through the papers on the desk and brought out a receipt book that she carried to Maloney. "There. Apartment seven. The attic."

Neil read the name aloud. "Gina Rigland."

"That's her," Connie Pinder said.

Patrick walked over to her and handed her the photograph of Rachel Darling. "Is this her?"

Connie took the photo without looking at Patrick. She held it up close to her eyes. "Could be," she said. Still talking to Maloney.

274

"We'd like to talk to her," Patrick said.

"That might be difficult," Connie replied. She actually looked at Patrick when she spoke. "I heard her come down the stairs about two this morning. She hasn't come back.

Connie Pinder showed them up to the attic and stood in the doorway while they looked around. Other than the huge floor fan which was blowing across the bed, there was nothing to indicate that anyone was living here. They walked around the open space, checked the bathroom, which contained nothing more personal than the fixtures. Patrick pushed the curtain away from the makeshift closet. Empty.

"She's gone," Connie Pinder said from the doorway.

"Her rent paid up?" Patrick asked.

"Through tomorrow," Connie said.

"She leave a deposit?" Maloney asked.

"I don't require it. She rented by the week and paid in advance."

"How long was she here?" Maloney asked. Patrick walked over to the bed.

"Thirteen days—two weeks, I think. It's on the receipt."

Patrick lifted the cover on the bed. The sheet was soiled. The odor of dried sweat rose from the bed. He got down on his knees and looked under the bed, pulling out a scrap of paper. It was newsprint, an old section of crime report clipped from the *Key West Citizen*. He turned it over and stared at his own picture together with Raul Jiminez, the front-page story from the news conference Jiminez had called to introduce Patrick to the press. He stood up and walked over to Maloney, showed him the clipping.

Maloney glanced at it and turned to Connie. "She still have a key to get in here?"

Connie said yes, unless she'd left it in the room. They hadn't come across a key.

Maloney said, "Mrs. Pinder, I'm going to have to put a man in here in case she comes back."

Connie nodded. "Just tell him I don't want any smoking, and if he's here after tomorrow, I'll want some rent."

Darling watched. She watched from the corner of Caroline Street, sitting on the stoop of an abandoned house that collected winos, street people—the homeless. Like herself. Homeless. She sat in a pair of jeans, a man's shirt, a floppy hat, its brim pulled low around her face. And still sick, she sweated. One of the bums tried to hand her a can of Budweiser. She said no, she wasn't well. Someone else said she should get a bottle of wine, that would cure her. She rocked on the stoop, hugging herself, and watched.

She saw the two men walking up the street and knew even before they were close enough to recognize that they were cops.

Patrick Bowman and another one. A guy in jeans and a loose shirt worn outside his jeans. The kind of clothes cops wore when they didn't want to be recognized, but always were. You could spot them a mile away. She would bet the shirt was hiding a holstered gun tucked into his waistband.

She watched them go up onto the porch of the house—her house until she was forced out in the early morning for fear something like this would happen.

It was the woman, the woman who had come yesterday afternoon nosing around, asking the old lady questions. A cop, too? Probably. These cops were in the house half an hour—going through the attic, she supposed, which she'd left less than eight hours ago. Clean. They would find nothing.

But she was homeless. She could get on a bus and be in Miami in five hours. Or take a plane. Unless they were watching, too, watching the terminals, checking everyone leaving Key West. Perhaps even a roadblock, easy enough when there was only one road in and out of here. Did they have a picture? If so it would be an old one; she hadn't had a picture taken in years.

No, she was safer for the moment staying here, hanging out with bums. One of them turned to her, a young man with rotten teeth, his face swollen. He grinned. "Your place or mine, baby?" he said. And laughed.

32

There was a memorial service in the Monroe County library exactly one month after Hamilton Wade's death. Monday morning at ten o'clock. The time usually set aside weekly by library officials for literary readings, talks, the occasional film, and, more and more frequently, memorial services.

If she hadn't stopped on her way out to look at the magazine rack where her picture peered out from the cover of the latest *Vanity Fair*.

But she did, and it was history.

Later, she would wonder about the timing of her actions. The coincidence. If she'd gone to the library one day earlier, or a day later, it might have been different.

Lee walked around the corner from her house to the pink stucco building and into the conference room in back where folding chairs had been assembled in rows, behind them a large coffee urn on a card table which also contained paper plates filled with pastry.

All the writers in town were there, even those who openly despised Wade. A sort of rally, a Who's Who and who's to be seen, Lee thought. Mortality. It struck everyone, even literary lions, and it never hurt to pay your respects. It could serve as a sort of preview for each other's send-off.

Wystan Lewis served as the official spokesman to introduce those who had been asked to remember Hamilton Wade. Wade, Lee knew, had not been particularly fond of Lewis, called him a pissy, little poet. Lewis had been in awe of Wade and had known him the longest, their literary careers overlapping.

Lee took a seat on the aisle. Lewis told a couple of anecdotes about Wade, which drew some chuckles. Then read a poem he had written especially for the occasion. A rather pissy, little poem, too, Lee thought. Then Lewis introduced the next speaker. A young novelist, trying to build his own career, who was often compared to Hamilton.

While the writer was being introduced, Lee glanced behind her and saw Raul Jiminez in the back row. Their eyes met. She turned back and listened to the young writer read from Hamilton Wade's unpublished, unfinished novel. The work in progress at the time of his death. In which she was a character. And Patrick was a character.

And a killer was on the loose in Key West.

She forced herself to keep her eyes on the speaker, to listen to his words, Hamilton's words. Words she'd seen and read many times since the day she'd gone to his house—and killed him. She held back the tears that brimmed in her eyes.

People coughed. Someone blew his nose. A wave of anxiety seemed to sweep through the room.

Were people staring at her?

Why was Raul Jiminez here?

The young novelist paused, like an actor building the tension, then read the final sentence of Hamilton's first chapter.

There was silence, utter, unbearable silence, and then Wystan rose and introduced the next speaker.

The service lasted forty-five minutes. When it was over, Lee got up, nodded, spoke to a few friends and tried to slip quietly away. She was at the door when Raul Jiminez touched her elbow. She turned. "Could we talk?" he said.

Darling sat in the reading room of the library, enjoying the comfort of a soft chair, and the air-conditioning after a night of sleeping on the ground huddled next to the backside of one of the bums who had passed out and snored fitfully most of the night. A rolled newspaper had served as her pillow.

She could have gone on her own, but she felt a greater sense of safety in numbers. Anonymity. She'd noticed that street people were mostly ignored when they were in groups; alone, they attracted attention. Passersby stared. She didn't need anyone staring at her right now.

She had stared at herself in the mirror of the women's room in the library where she'd come to wash up. Even after a day and a half her appearance was changing. Her hair was matted. There were bruises on her arms from sleeping on the ground, and her face was getting puffy.

You can hang out in the library, the bum she'd slept next to on the ground told her. Catch some z's, use the facilities. He was right. By nine-thirty half the seats there were taken by people like her who were living on the streets. She recognized most of them.

She was still sick; the fever persisted. She didn't have to live like this, she told herself.

Get out of town. Go.

Now.

No. First she had to be sure she wasn't going to be stopped. And there was something still keeping her here, some final thing she had to do. It crouched in her mind like a wedge of moonlight. Tomorrow was the full moon.

Raul Jiminez said, *"Moonkill.* A hell of a title. I keep rereading those chapters."

"We've had this conversation," Lee said.

Jiminez smiled distantly, looking over her shoulder at the crowd gathered around the coffee urn. "I know," he said. "But different things keep coming up to make it more interesting. I keep learning things."

"About what?"

"You." Lee thought about turning and walking away, joining her friends who were having coffee and pastry. Instead she tried to appear earnest, detached. "And what about me."

"Denise recognized you."

The cool detachment was fading. "Denise?"

"The girl Hamilton Wade was making it with shortly before he was killed."

It occurred to her that Jiminez could be lying. Patrick had said he was desperate. She tried to keep calm, but her voice sounded louder than she would have liked. "What is this? I don't know what you're talking about."

Jiminez smiled. "Your picture was all over the room where

Wade was killed. I think the killer took the pictures down."

Lee stood frozen to the spot, glaring at Jiminez.

"You know who might have done that?"

Someone touched her elbow. She turned and Wystan greeted her. "I think Hamilton would have liked it," he said. "Don't you?"

Lee looked at Raul Jiminez. "I suppose he would," she said.

Wystan reminded her of a cocktail party that evening at five, said he'd see her there, and moved away.

Jiminez took an envelope from his pocket. "Something in here might interest you," he said.

"What is it?"

"A ballistics report. Showing that a Browning nine-millimeter handgun registered to Patrick Bowman was used in a homicide."

Lee stared back at him. She said, "The gun was stolen."

"After the Wade murder."

Lee felt her knees weaken. "Has Patrick seen it?"

Jiminez smiled again. "No, not yet. I want you to think about it," he said. "And remember that I'm right behind you, all the time, and sooner or later you're going to have to tell me what I want to know."

He turned and walked out of the room. Lee looked around at the crowd to see if anyone had overheard them. Apparently not. She was trembling. She left and walked into the reading room, trying to get hold of herself.

Darling was cold. She had dozed. A uniformed guard came by and tapped her shoulder. She opened her eyes, saw the uniform and looked away. She had the floppy straw hat on, which covered her face. The guard said, "No sleeping in here." And walked away.

Across from her a woman was standing at the magazine rack, thumbing through a magazine. A woman she had seen before.

A woman glimpsed from the window of her attic before she became a homeless person. A woman snooping, asking questions. A woman who was followed a day later by the police.

Darling raised her own magazine to partially obscure her face while allowing her to watch the woman at the rack.

She was quite pretty; older, Darling guessed, than she looked, well taken care of. Money. She didn't look like a cop, and she didn't look like a woman in search of a rundown apartment. Of course, Darling thought with some irony, a few weeks ago neither did she.

The woman standing at the magazine rack was also nervous. She was constantly glancing around her as though she were expecting someone. And her hands holding the magazine trembled slightly. She was holding a copy of *Vanity Fair* and seemed to be looking at the pictures, not reading the text. She didn't stay long, but dropped the magazine, open at the last page she had looked at, on the solid top of a bookshelf next to the magazine rack and left.

Darling stood up and walked to the bookshelf. The *Vanity Fair* was open to a page filled with pictures of a woman modeling clothes. She recognized the model.

She remembered the newspaper clipping on Patrick Bowman, married to the model, Lee Bowman.

Darling walked through the library and out the front door.

Walking up the street was Lee Bowman.

Darling followed.

Patrick was standing at the kitchen sink eating a sandwich when Lee came in. He was thinking about the cat fight that had awakened him at three o'clock this morning. He had laid there and listened to the two cats stalk each other, steady tension-filled murmuring that had an almost human quality to it before the cats began shrieking with childlike terror as they finally lunged at each other. Then the murmuring would start again as they backed off and began the stalking process all over.

It was pathetic. He hated to hear it because it reminded him of violent death. He'd heard humans who were in a death struggle make similar sounds, and he did not want to be awake at three o'clock remembering it.

Staring out the window into the backyard, he wondered if it would help to put some more ammonia down, if the cats would stay away. Maybe the last batch he'd poured around the edges of the house had worn off.

Rachel Darling. What was the antidote to Rachel Darling?

He had told Neil Maloney after they'd left Connie Pinder's that Jiminez should consider putting out a decoy.

A female officer, a couple of them, wearing street clothes and wired with a transmitting device. Walking the beaches.

According to Maloney, Jiminez had considered the proposal and rejected it. They didn't have the manpower, and Jiminez still refused to believe they were in the grip of a serial killer. He was pursuing his own angle, the Hamilton Wade link.

According to Maloney. Maloney who had put a man in Connie Pinder's attic. But Rachel Darling never returned.

And Rafael?

A separate case, Maloney said, echoing Bill Peachy. Jiminez was still treating it as a separate case.

In a couple of weeks Patrick would have to return to Chicago. For the first time since he was shot, he was practically free of all pain. But the thought of leaving here with an unsolved case troubled him.

When Lee came in, she said, "Did you find her?"

"Rachel Darling? No," Patrick said.

"So what will you do?"

"Go looking for her," he said.

Lee nodded, obviously distracted. She said, "Have you seen Raul Jiminez recently?" She had come up beside him, staring over his shoulder, out the window.

"No," he said. "Not since before his son's funeral."

"I just left him."

He said, "Where?"

"At the memorial service."

"What was he doing there?" Patrick asked.

Lee turned her face to his, put her arms around him. "I think we'd better talk," she said.

33

Wayne Higgs said that, yes, Rachel Darling had a history, an interesting history. An institutional history, Wayne Higgs said. After her sister's death she was in counseling for several months, beginning when she was eight. As a teenager she saw a shrink for a couple of years, and five years ago she was in the psychiatric ward of New York Hospital for several weeks with a history of drug and alcohol abuse. She was withdrawn, worked hard, but didn't have close personal friends. She continued to see a psychiatrist briefly after her release from the hospital. No one knew much about her personal life. She seemed depressed and distant but didn't encourage personal relationships. It's like she lived in a vacuum.

Was there a medical diagnosis? Patrick wanted to know.

Narcissistic personality disorder, Wayne Higgs said.

Patrick wondered but didn't ask where the FBI might have obtained that information. A patient/doctor relationship was always privileged, the information exchanged between them safe even from law enforcement.

Instead, Patrick asked for the names of any of the people whom Rachel had seen professionally. At least he could check them out, even if he couldn't question them about Rachel.

Higgs gave him what he had.

"There's another thing," Wayne Higgs said.

"What's that?" Patrick asked.

"She adored her sister."

Patrick called the shrink in Chicago who had often been helpful in previous cases. One of the questions that had been nagging him was the time delay—from her sister's death until Rachel began her own nightmare odyssey. Was it possible that she could have lived with that murderous hatred for so many years? He was certain that it was, but he needed to hear professional confirmation.

"Of course," Dr. Rhine said. "Simply a delayed response to repressed trauma. It happens all the time. Probably, though, something triggered her response."

"Like what?" Patrick asked.

"God, anything. Not even necessarily violent. Something she saw under particular circumstances, such as a color or a sound associated with the original trauma."

"Can I ask you to speculate?" Patrick asked.

"Don't you always?"

"I've got a girl, seven years old," Patrick said slowly, thinking while he tried to put the whole thing into perspective. "Her older sister is killed, murdered brutally, and the young girl sees the body moments after it happened. What does the future look like for the child?"

"Hmmm, that's a tough one," Dr. Rhine said.

"Worst-case scenario," Patrick suggested.

"Well, a good possibility is that the girl would repress everything, she might not even remember her feelings or the death scene itself."

"Until something triggered it."

"Right."

"Would she be capable of killing?"

"Hypothetically, sure."

"Okay, stay with the hypothetical," Patrick said. "What would make her target young street girls, hookers?"

"Jesus," Dr. Rhine said, "I'd need to know a lot more about her family situation, but it's possible that there could have been some sibling rivalry, the girl may have even felt she caused her sister's death."

"She adored her sister," Patrick said.

"How do you know? Maybe that's what she believes today, but she could also have repressed the earlier hostility."

Patrick made notes.

"Competing for Daddy's attention, which she got more of once her sister was dead. The young girls could represent threats to her own favored status, the money they receive being symbolic of gratification. She has to keep killing her sister, making sure that she stays dead to ensure her own position."

"Suppose the girl had spent a lot of time in therapy. Wouldn't all this have come out?"

"Not necessarily. The psychiatrist or whoever was treating her might recognize certain symptoms, but without the willing cooperation of the patient, it would remain buried."

"Again, until it's triggered by something outside her control."

"Or not," Dr. Rhine said. "It could remain repressed forever."

"It didn't, Doctor," Patrick said.

"I want someone on her," Jiminez said. "Night and day. If he has to spend the night in his car sitting in front of the house, that's fine. I want her to see him there before she goes to bed at night and first thing when she wakes up in the morning. I want her looking over her shoulder, and there he is."

"Chief," Maloney said, "who are we going to get? You said it yourself, we don't have the manpower to spare somebody like that in a twenty-four-hour surveillance."

"You've gotta change duty assignments, do it. I want this to be priority."

Maloney shook his head. "What if she complains? Or her husband complains?"

"She won't complain, believe me."

Maloney paused, picked up his pencil. He said, "Chief, you going to be able to justify this?"

"Neil," Jiminez said, "I don't have to justify anything. I'm conducting an investigation. We should be clear on that."

Maloney sat there for a while letting it sink in, then nodded, got up and left the office.

Jiminez sat at his desk with its mound of paperwork, and emptied the overflowing ashtray into the trash can beside his desk. He seldom left the office anymore. He'd dragged himself out for the Wade memorial, a necessity, but otherwise he might as well have been chained here. No windows. Sometimes you had to wonder who was doing the hardship duty, him or the prisoners over at the county jail.

Faustos Food Palace. The advertising proclaimed: "Not just a grocery store, but a social center." And the one that had always drawn a laugh from Lee: "You can't beat our meat."

Lee, a woman whose sense of humor could swing from raw schoolboy stuff to the sophisticated. Like Lee herself, he thought. A woman who could swing. His wife of fifteen years. He had learned her sense of humor in fifteen years, but apparently little else.

Her words kept repeating in his mind like a continuous play recording.

"He was evil . . ."

"Girls, some of them still in their teens, were drugged and seduced."

"Everything was filmed. Everything. Secretly."

"All for material, something to write about."

"Debasing."

"The humiliation."

Patrick watched a dirt bag slip two flat cans of sardines into his soiled jeans while Lee's words continued their discord in his head.

"The pictures he had on the walls."

"The diaries."

"We were all in it, used."

"No one has that right."

"And then the novel, his secret life prowling the beach."

"He was mad."

Patrick had left the house, walked several blocks and finally gone into Faustos. The Food Palace. Where you can't beat our meat.

Was she confessing, trying to confess? He had left, realizing that if she was, he didn't want to hear it. He was a cop, not a priest. There was no confidentiality protected by a confessional. He had professional responsibilities, a job to do.

There was also the law. A spouse could not be forced to give incriminating evidence against his or her mate. Which came first, the spouse or the cop?

He wandered through the aisles, distracted, uncertain, pausing to stare blankly at shelves of bottled wine. When he looked up he saw the same dirtbag pocket a package of Kraft cheese slices. Patrick thought about buying a bottle of wine, taking it home, cooking dinner, having the wine, pretending nothing had happened.

He watched the dirt bag move down the aisle, something familiar in his demeanor. Patrick followed him, borne along out of habit. The habit of preventing crime, of pursuing criminals. In this case it proved unnecessary.

When the guy tried to go through the checkout line, paying with a five-dollar food stamp for a bag of candy he'd picked up, the store manager came up, asked him if he wanted to pay for what he was carrying in his pockets, too.

The dirt bag looked bewildered, then angry. He started mumbling something. Patrick said, "I'll take care of it." And took five dollars from his wallet. The dirt bag shrugged, lifted the sardines and cheese from his pockets.

Patrick got his change and went outside. The dirt bag was sitting on the sidewalk trying to open the cellophane cheese wrapper. "What would that have cost you, a couple weeks in jail?" Patrick asked.

The dirt bag tore at the wrapper with his brown teeth.

"I saved you some trouble," Patrick said. "You owe me one. We're going to take a walk down to the State Attorney's office."

The guy looked up at him like he was crazy. Probably the same look he gave the police when they found the Browning nine-millimeter automatic tucked among dirty clothing in a grocery bag he kept his stuff in, Patrick thought.

Lee was not at home when he returned around five- thirty, after more than an hour at the State Attorney's office.

The dirt bag, Joe Ott, had been around Key West for years, never in any real trouble except for the occasional shoplifting from Faustos, panhandling, and disorderly conduct on the rare occasions when he could afford to get drunk. He had spent time in jail.

The attorney who questioned him focused on his record, contained in a computer printout that lay on his desk. There was Ott's report of the Rafael Jiminez murder. And more recently, the discovery of a stolen gun among his possessions.

Joe had continually denied any knowledge of the gun.

The attorney kept asking where the gun came from, and Joe Ott would reply, "It came from the bag, man. That's where they found it."

"Who put it there?"

Joe Ott said, "I don't know who put it there."

"Did you steal it?"

"I never stole it."

They kept going over the same ground.

"According to the police chief you did," Patrick said.

Joe Ott had the same look of bewilderment he had in the grocery store when he was accused of stealing.

Joe Ott said, "Bullshit."

"Then how'd you get the gun, Joe?"

"Somebody put it there."

"Who?"

"I don't know who."

"Somebody dropped a gun in your bag and you don't know who or why?"

"How many times I gotta tell you? No, I don't know nothing about the gun."

"The cops question you about the gun, Joe?"

"Yeah, several times."

"Who did you talk to?"

"I told you, the cops."

"Which cop?"

Joe shrugged.

"Did the chief himself question you, Joe?"

Joe Ott nodded.

"What did he say?"

"He asked questions, just like you are."

"He scare you?"

"He tried."

"How'd he try to scare you?"

"The kid who got cut up behind the church the other day."

"Rafael Jiminez, the chief's son?"

"Yeah."

"What about it, Joe? Did the chief think you killed Rafael?"

"He said they were gonna put me away."

"For murder?"

Joe nodded again.

"What did he want you to do?"

"Cop a plea."

"Admit to stealing the gun?"

"Yeah."

Patrick looked from Joe to the attorney and back to Joe. "You refused?"

"I never killed nobody, and I didn't steal that gun."

"But the chief let you go."

"He said to keep my mouth shut or they'd bring me in and lock me up."

Half an hour later, when Patrick got home, Lee was gone. He went upstairs. Everything in the house was the same. Except the way it felt. It felt like it belonged to someone else. He was a stranger in his own home. He didn't relate to things that had been familiar for more than ten years.

Patrick took out his legal pad and sat at the dining room table with the picture of the seven-year-old Rachel Darling standing at her sister's death site. The girl's eyes showed nothing except the white light of the flash.

He looked through his notes he'd made while talking to Wayne Higgs from the FBI and to Dr. Rhine.

Wayne Higgs said Rachel Darling didn't like having her picture taken. She was shy, distant. There was the one picture of her as a seven-year-old caught in the trauma of her sister's death. Another showed her in a group photo, not posed, perhaps unaware that the picture was even being taken.

Patrick went to the kitchen and poured himself a shot of rum, then sat back down at the table, ruminating over the portrait of Rachel Darling, both the photographs and the one he was creating in his mind.

After half an hour, when Lee still hadn't returned, he went upstairs, opened the dresser drawer in the bedroom and took out the holstered Browning. It, at least, felt familiar. On the way out he noticed that Lee's camera bag was open on the bed. He looked inside and saw that her camera was gone. He went back downstairs, finished his rum, and called Bill Peachy.

34

Dusk. Eerie. A magical time. Mysterious. The light rapidly filtered away, leaving everything in a kind of milky suspension. Just like her life, Lee thought. In suspension. Since this afternoon when she had tried to confess to Patrick, and had failed. Father Patrick. Who wasn't able to absolve her. How many Hail Marys did you get as penance for murder?

She sat on the concrete retaining wall at the beach and looked at the water against the fading light.

Patrick had gone for a walk. Not angry. Just quietly said he wanted to get some air. Or had he said "needed"?

While she rambled. He didn't want to hear her because he couldn't forgive her. He was a cop before he was a husband. And he would be a cop long after he finished being a husband. That seemed clear to her, clearer than anything else, and she felt the misery of her depression.

He had forgiven her so many times in the past. He was a man she could talk to, explain herself, defend her actions, and he had always been there for her, regardless of the transgression.

He was a good man. But above all else, he was a good cop. And she had never committed murder before.

After two hours waiting for him to return, worrying about him, about the next move, she had finally gone upstairs, showered, put on the white robe, and stood looking at her face in the mirror. Her career face. The face that had stared back at her day after day while makeup was being applied for some photo assignment. A face that she'd cared for by not caring for it; once, on location in the mountains, she had cleaned her face with nothing but snow for a week, and it had never looked better. It was a face without vanity. A face with guilt.

The face of a murderer.

She had looked at the photograph of Rachel Darling, studied the face, the eyes, and wondered if Rachel ever looked in the mirror and thought: this is what a killer looks like.

No. There was a difference, wasn't there? Patrick would understand that, he would know that there was a difference.

Had she killed Hamilton Wade out of self-defense? She saw him again, the image that she lived with, his hands around her neck. Had he really been going to kill her, or had she just imagined it? And each time she had the same thought: he was choking me, he didn't know what he was doing. And a thousand times she heard again the sound of the gun when she pulled the trigger.

She had tried to confess.

Patrick went for a walk. And Lee, standing at the mirror, ran her fingers through her hair and walked to her closet in the bedroom and put on a skirt. A miniskirt and a cheap cotton blouse.

Then she left the house after grabbing her camera as an afterthought, and started walking. She walked to the beach. With one idea in mind. Maybe Patrick would forgive her if she found Rachel Darling. Or Rachel found her.

The water turned from gray to black and it was night. The sky was cloudless, the stars thick as confetti. And she walked along the beach carrying her shoes. When she got to the White Street pier, she put the shoes back on and crossed to Atlantic Boulevard and the deserted Rest Beach. She noticed the blue and white patrol car parked across the street at a public phone. The sight of a cop in the area should have relieved her, but it didn't.

A few guys had passed her without speaking, but no women. It was still early, just after eight now. She wondered if Patrick had come home, if he was wondering where she was.

She walked across Rest Beach down to the water's edge thinking she would go all the way to Smathers Beach, then turn back. She passed the back of a condo, a larger one looming in the distance. No one was on the beach. After she had walked for five minutes, she stopped and stared at the water, then turned and looked back from where she had come. A hundred yards away someone was walking toward her, too far away to tell if it was male or female.

But in this desolate part of the beach, she felt her pulse quicken. Of course, there were the condos there. If she screamed, would anyone be able to hear her?

She walked on, thinking about Patrick, about making a decision. Did she stay on the beach or walk over to the road?

She turned and looked back again. Whoever was behind her was rapidly catching up.

Don't look back, somebody once said. Something might be gaining on you.

Lee slowed her pace.

When the phone rang in his office, Raul Jiminez picked up the receiver and growled into it. Someone in the dispatcher's office said the call was for Lieutenant Maloney, who had left word that he would be in the chief's office. He was. Sitting across the desk from him, where he'd been for the past hour.

Maloney had come to inform him of some bad news. A rumor was circulating, started by someone in the internal affairs division, that Jiminez was the subject of an investigation by the State Attorney's office. Maloney had taken it upon himself to pass the word to the chief personally.

Jiminez handed the receiver to Maloney and shrank back in his chair, lighting a fresh cigarette from an unfinished old one. A habit that had increased his intake by nearly a pack. He was now smoking three and a half packs a day. And paying for it, he knew. He looked like hell. He avoided mirrors and avoided Mercedes, coming into the house at night after she'd gone to bed, and out before she got up in the morning. He practically lived in the office.

A prisoner.

He avoided the press. And had his secretary monitor his calls. She also controlled who went into his office. He refused to accept personal calls and seldom went out, in order to avoid confrontations. The lack of windows in his office had suddenly become a blessing. He had deliberately cut himself off. He ran the force by communicating solely with Maloney.

Who had come to him with the news that the State Attorney's

office was questioning Joe Ott in connection with the theft of Bowman's gun.

Bowman. He wished he'd never heard the name.

Raul had spent the past hour discussing his options with Maloney, who listened without offering advice.

When the phone rang, Raul had just stated, "I suppose I could take early retirement, cite the stress of my son's death."

Maloney held the receiver to his ear, listened for a moment, then asked with some urgency, "Where are you?"

Smoking, Raul waited.

Maloney finally said, "I'll be right there." And passed the receiver back.

Raul said, "Now what?"

"The Bowman woman is out on the beach."

"So?"

"It's almost nine o'clock."

Raul looked at his watch. In the windowless cell of his office he'd lost track of time.

Bill Peachy gave Patrick one of the two handheld radios he had brought with him; one he carried on the boat, the other he'd borrowed. He told Patrick, "Guard it with your life."

Patrick had convinced his skeptical friend to be a part of a private posse, a task force of two.

"You're going to deputize me?" Peachy asked. "You got a badge?"

"You don't need one," Patrick said. "Think of it as a citizen's crime watch."

Peachy laughed. "What makes you think this woman, what's her name?"

"Rachel Darling."

"Rachel Darling is going to parade down the beach looking for more victims if she knows you're closing in?"

Patrick couldn't answer that question, couldn't explain to anyone that it was simply a feeling, his professional instinct, based on previous experience and hundreds of crime statistics showing that killers invariably returned to the scene of the crime. Something compelled them, some inner force, some determination that they could beat the odds, flirt with their potential captors.

Ted Bundy. Who had told officers they might have caught him if they'd staked out the site after finding that first body.

You learned lessons from the perpetrators as well as their victims. Sometimes what you were left with was only circumstantial evidence, but you began to recognize the patterns, and there was always a pattern.

Rachel Darling had broken her pattern once, but Patrick was certain that she would return to it, unable, or unwilling, to go against the obvious risks that her patterns imposed.

The question was not if, but when, she would kill again.

He said to Peachy, "I think she'll go back there."

"What if she doesn't? What if she strikes in another part of town, another churchyard, for example?"

"She's on the move, she's homeless," Patrick said. "Her sister was killed near the beach. She'll keep going back there."

"Maybe she's left town."

"You're thinking too much," Patrick said. "I've already considered those possibilities and I've made my choice. I need some help."

"What about the police?"

"One man, not an army. Especially not that one. Can I count on you?"

They met at the airport across from Smathers Beach, parked their cars, and Peachy handed Patrick one of the radios.

"I'll be down at the County Beach," Patrick said. "Take your time coming up Smathers, and stay in contact. You see anyone at all, let me know."

"Aye, Captain," Peachy said.

Patrick got in his car, drove down to the County Beach, and parked in front of West Martello Tower.

At any other time the fact that Lee hadn't come home before he'd driven to the airport to meet Bill Peachy would have been no cause for alarm. But circumstances were different, and several things played on his mind as he got out of the car and walked across the beach to the rear of the Martello Tower where little more than a month ago he had first questioned Paul the busboy.

One, she had gone out without taking either her car or her bicycle. Which was strange since she had been gone so long. She could have taken a cab, he thought. Someone might have picked her up, but why, when she had transportation of her own?

Two, and the thing that plagued him most, was her unsolicited help in locating Rachel Darling. She'd gone out looking, on her own, without even telling him what she was going to do. Why?

Was it guilt? It now seemed obvious. She was trying to free herself of that guilt by bringing in Rachel Darling.

He looked up the beach. The thought occurred to him that she could be out here now, needing to do more. She was carrying her camera, which she often did at night, and the thought of the camera called to mind the frozen look of Rachel when she was seven, caught in the flash of a newspaper reporter's photo opportunity. Tragedy.

Patrick turned and looked back across the White Street pier as the lights of a car swept across the beach. A police car pulled up beside another one near the public phones on the comer of White Street and Atlantic Boulevard.

He saw Lieutenant Maloney get out of one of the cars and lean into the window, talking to the driver of the other car.

35

She had followed the woman, the model, the cop's wife from her trim, pastel home on William Street to the beach. County Beach. Martello Tower, where Darling had only a few weeks ago cut a girl's throat.

Lee, the cop's wife, in her tight skirt, her intentions so obvious that Darling at first couldn't believe it.

The cop, so smart, sending his own wife out, using her like a baited trap. Proving that he wasn't so smart after all.

From where she sat in a dark corner of the White Street pier, she could survey the entire County Beach all the way to the end of Rest Beach and the street where it ended and Smathers Beach began.

A few kids were on the pier, smoking dope, and some older people who were fishing from the end of the pier.

Darling went unnoticed.

She watched as Lee walked toward the pier, her shoes in her hand, stopping to put them on before crossing over to Rest Beach.

Darling watched and waited. The pier was closed to traffic. A few cars went by along the beach road, turning off White Street. She could see everything, the traffic, the people on foot, even boats anchored offshore.

The moon, full and pale, had broken free and seemed to hang suspended as if it had just been hoisted from the sea.

Lee was walking along the water's edge. Darling watched as a cop car drove slowly along the beach road from where Lee had come, then pulled up to the public phones by the little park across from the pier. The cop got out and made a phone call, then got back in the car and sat there.

Lee was wired, Darling thought. They had wired her, and now all they had to do was sit and wait for her to come to the bait. It was so amateurish.

Darling stood up. She had on dirty jeans and a floppy T-shirt. She had cut her hair, whacked it off short. Without her makeup, dirty from sleeping out, hanging out with the dirt bags, she knew in the dark she would be taken for a man.

The cops were looking for a woman. Rachel Darling. She felt a need to go home, back to Philadelphia, where she could see her father, who would look at her and tell her she was beautiful, who wouldn't get mad at her because she was wearing old, dirty clothes. She was more like her sister Roberta now, and she had slept on the ground with a man. Her father wouldn't like that; he would scold her, but reward Rachel.

Daddy was dead; Roberta continued to live.

Rachel wanted to go home, but Roberta was there. She thought; *I can take care of Roberta.*

She walked partway up the pier toward the beach, then sat down in the shadows again, unseen. No one paid any attention. She waited, then slipped over the side and into less than a foot of water, her sneakers squishing in the bottom muck. She kept to the side of the pier and walked up to the beach.

Australian pine trees grew along the beach above the high tide and concealed her as she came out of the water and looked across the road where the cop sat in his car, the burning tip of his cigarette glimpsed as he smoked.

She went back down to the water's edge and walked along the beach, following Lee, who was now at least a hundred yards away, parallel with the condos.

Lee paused, turned and looked out across the water. She could hear footsteps coming toward her, a kind of muffled, hesitant step over the coarse marl, weeds, and debris that made up the beach.

Whoever had been behind her was now close enough that she could also hear the labored breath, the kind of breathing brought on by heavy exercise, or illness.

She turned and looked. Feeling fear. The figure approaching her, maybe twenty yards away, appeared to be a man. By his appearance, a dirt bag, a beach bum, someone looking for a quiet place to hang out for the night, where he wouldn't be disturbed by the police.

She breathed deeply, realized she'd been holding her breath, and felt a little easing of the tension and fear.

She stepped back up the beach a ways, walked slowly toward the trees as though she were going back to the road. She wanted to let the man pass her. But she also wanted to see him, keep sight of him, so she paused again at the edge of the trees and turned back toward the water.

He was tall, loose-limbed, thin-faced, wearing a stretched, dirty T-shirt and soiled jeans. His hair disheveled, matted, as though it hadn't been washed in several days.

He wasn't looking at her, but staring down at the ground as he walked. Twenty feet separated them; he was now at the spot where she had stood staring out at the water, waiting and watching. He suddenly stopped, turned, looking right at her. And said, "Nice night."

It was a husky voice, but pleasant, nonthreatening, not what she would have expected, although she would have been more comfortable if he just kept walking.

Still, she said, "Yes, very nice." And started to turn, to walk away, not wanting to engage in conversation here on a deserted beach at night with a . . .

A what?

He said, "Lee." Politely, perfectly natural, like they'd known each other all their lives.

She turned back, puzzled.

A muted laugh. He moved a couple of steps toward her, then stopped. "It's all right." The husky voice confident, personal. "I'm on a stakeout."

Jesus, of course. A cop. Someone who knew Patrick, who had seen them together. There was no anonymity in a small town like Key West. She should have known there would be someone patrolling the beaches.

She said, "With the police?"

He nodded.

She thought: Ask to see some ID. Then thought: Why? The guy

wasn't going to hassle her. He seemed about to move on. And she turned again to go back to the road. If the cops were here, she was wasting time.

But the guy caught her off guard again. He said, "You with us?"

"What?"

"I thought maybe you were working with us."

She shook her head.

"We've got a mobile unit at the park. I thought maybe they had you wired."

Wired? Oh, right. For sound. A small microphone, a bug taped to the body, something Patrick had often used on stakeouts.

She said, "No."

The guy smiled, raised his fist with his thumb extended. "Be careful," he said. And turned to go.

She smiled and started back up through the pine trees toward the road again. Feeling easier now.

She followed a path through the trees and shrubs, approaching two condos, one of which was still under construction. She had gone perhaps fifty yards when she thought she heard footsteps behind her. She slowed down, thinking the plainclothes cop had changed his mind, perhaps, and was coming this way with her just to make sure she was all right.

Then she thought: Why am I trusting that guy? He could be anybody. But how would he know the cops were there if he wasn't with them? Fool. He could have seen them just like she had. She put her hand into her bag without even thinking, looking for a weapon, any weapon, to protect herself. The guy had looked sort of crazy. The idea of being raped right here, in these weeds, so close to safety. She began to tremble. She wanted to run. Her hand closed over her camera and she lifted it from the bag. Ahead of her she could see the fence sealing off the construction site from the street. Another fence blocked out the occupied condo next to it. Without going back or farther into the wilderness, she was trapped. With her thumb she flipped on the strobe flash attached to the camera, waited a couple of seconds, then turned with the camera up, with her finger pushed the shutter-release button, and in the instant of the flash saw the face of Rachel Darling.

Lee turned and ran.

The beach was strangely empty for so early in the evening. Patrick looked at his watch. Nine o'clock. No one was picnicking along the concrete tables and benches, and it was either too early for the arrival of the stray male cruisers who worked the beach or they had found other locations.

Patrick walked to the other end of the beach near the Casa Marina Hotel where equipment for renovation work on the dock lay idle, protected by a chain-link fence. Dick Dock. Queer Pier. Names that had stuck to the pier with the same adhesion as the bronzed, oiled bodies that for years had congregated along its boardwalk.

He wondered if the Darling family had stayed at the Casa Marina twenty-seven years ago, when their oldest daughter was murdered near here. Again he saw the photo of Rachel standing at the murder scene. He couldn't get the look in her eyes out of his mind.

For twenty-seven years she had repressed that awful scene, until something caused her to snap, the trigger mechanism that brought her down here on this murder mission. And he was as certain of Rachel Darling now as he was of the night and the full moon that hung in the sky to the east. He felt like he was close to understanding the whole thing, if only he could figure out what had triggered her response after all this time.

He turned and walked back to the Martello Tower, passing no one. Across the streets the tennis courts were empty, as was the kiddie playground.

He passed the alcove in the fort where the Canadian girl was killed. The two patrol cars were still parked near the public phones at the entrance to the park across White Street. Patrick went over there.

No one was in either car; both were locked. He went to the phones, picked up one, deposited a quarter and dialed his own number. After three rings the answering machine came on and he hung up.

He walked across the road to Rest Beach and began walking along that beach toward Smathers. Moonlight spread across the water and dappled the shoreline. He thought about checking with Peachy by radio, but decided to wait until there was something to report.

Where was Maloney and the cop he'd been talking to?

The beam of a flashlight suddenly arced across the beach several yards ahead of him. Moments later, as he continued walking in the direction of the light, he could hear the sound of two men talking.

Patrick stopped when he got to the section of beach below the two condos, one of which was still under construction; a worn path wound through the shrubbery.

Two men were examining the path by the light of the flashlight. One of the men was Lt. Neil Maloney.

Patrick said, "What's happened?"

Maloney looked up, turned the light on him. "You seen your wife?"

"Not since this afternoon, why?"

"Half an hour ago she was on the beach. We've lost her," Maloney said, lowering the light.

The other cop was Fred Friendly, the silent, unsmiling detective who had been sent to investigate the break-in at the Bowman's and the theft of the Browning which now rested securely against the hollow of Patrick's lower back.

"You know what she was doing out here?" Maloney asked.

"I didn't even know she was here," Patrick said. "How did you know?"

Maloney looked at Fred. "He'd been keeping an eye on her," the lieutenant said.

Patrick felt rage, like a sudden unexpected shock of current that coursed through his body. He started to react, checked himself and said, "He was following her?" A statement in search of verification.

Maloney provided it. "Chiefs orders," he said.

Patrick turned to Friendly. "How long?'"

311

"The past twenty-four hours," Fred said without looking at him.

"How'd she get out here?"

"A couple of hours ago she walked from your home."

"What was she wearing?"

Fred looked up; and came as close to smiling as he ever would, Patrick thought. "A short skirt, blouse, a pair of sneakers."

"Jesus."

Maloney said, "Yeah, we're thinking the same thing."

Was this guilt? Something Lee had seldom experienced in life. Didn't believe in, avoided at all costs. No apologies; no excuses. Never complain; never explain. It was her credo; she had always lived by it. Had she really been confessing this afternoon before he'd left? And now was trying to redeem herself?

Maloney flicked the light over the ground. "Fred saw somebody standing near here. As he walked along the beach in this direction, he thought he saw a flash of light up in the trees there." Maloney pointed up the path.

"What kind of a flash?" Patrick asked.

"Like a flashbulb going off," Fred said.

"Christ! Lee has her camera with her."

"She carries a camera around at night?" Maloney said.

"Yeah, she takes a lot of night pictures using the flash." Patrick reached for the handheld radio and called Bill Peachy.

"Where are you?" Patrick asked when Peachy responded.

"Coming down Atlantic Boulevard. I just passed one of the condos and was going to work my way back over to the beach."

"You see anyone?"

"Nothing out of the ordinary," he said.

"I think Lee's in trouble. I'm moving into the condo area, the one under construction."

"I'll be right there," Bill replied.

Maloney said, "I'll call in for some backup."

"Tell them to get here without making any noise," Patrick said.

Maloney instructed Fred to maintain a patrol of the beach while he went back to the car to phone in. Patrick walked up the path between the condos and waited for Bill Peachy.

Lee knelt behind a column on the top floor of the condo that was under construction, its unfinished surface gritty where it touched her bare legs. She had climbed the three flights of stairs, without guardrails, that wound up the outside of the building.

Apart from the floor and corner columns, they were totally exposed on three sides. From where she knelt she could see the access to the stairs she had climbed moments ago. However, she had noticed when she was climbing that there were another set of stairs at the other end of the building. But from where she was now, she could not see the access to those stairs.

It was dark.

Some light from the moon bathed the building. She could hear the sound of feet crunching against the loose concrete from another part of the building. She knew that someone had come up the stairs after her; she had heard them on the first floor. What she was hearing now, though, was hard to identify; whether the sound was made by a human, or perhaps rats scurrying across the floor.

She wondered if Patrick would come looking for her.

From where she crouched she could aim the camera up into the face of anyone coming up the stairs, blinding them with the flash and perhaps giving her time to get to another hiding place.

If they came up these stairs. She looked over her shoulder into the darkness of the building in the direction of the other set of stairs and listened. Nothing.

There were other columns spaced across the floor, behind which someone could hide. She waited and listened. And thought about screaming. But who was going to hear her? The cops had been parked a quarter of a mile away, and it was doubtful if anyone in the buildings beyond this one would hear her. By screaming she would give her position away, taking away whatever element of surprise she had.

She knew that someone else was in the building. She could feel their presence. Was it Rachel Darling? She wasn't sure. When she'd taken the picture back on the path and seen the face in the instant of the flash, there was something familiar in it, something different, something recognizable that wasn't there when she'd been talking to what she thought was a man on the beach and who now she knew was a woman. Rachel Darling?

She had come looking for Rachel, wanting to find her, hoping to draw her out. Now that she had, if she had, Lee was terrified.

She heard the crunch of loose gravel again and knelt there,

holding her breath.

Patrick watched Bill Peachy running along the side of the road toward where he stood in front of the condo under construction. The lanky, dancer like grace of movement that Patrick always admired when they were on the water showed now in the way Peachy ran.

When he stopped in front of him, Bill wasn't even breathing hard. "What's going on?" Peachy asked.

"I think Lee's in here. And Rachel."

They stood facing the twin condos, the occupied condo showing lights in the windows, barricaded from the construction site, the moonlight creating shadows over its darkened, unfinished twin.

"She came up the path. It's the only place she could be," Patrick whispered.

Bill nodded.

Patrick pointed out the two open stairways at either end of the building and an open shaft in the middle where an elevator would presumably be built.

He said, "You take the stairs on that end, I'll go up these. Take a floor at a time and work your way up."

Peachy stared up at the cavernous structure that looked like the cross section of a honeycomb. He started to say something, then seemed to change his mind.

Patrick said, "Just be careful, no heroics. Don't use the radio unless it's necessary."

Peachy nodded and started for the stairs.

Raul Jiminez arrived at the park in an unmarked car. Maloney was waiting for him. "Where is she?" Jiminez demanded, getting out of the car.

"She disappeared off the beach," Maloney said.

"I'm in no mood to listen to that crap," Jiminez said. The mayor had called him just when he was getting ready to leave the office. Word of the State Attorney's investigation had already reached the commission. The mayor was suggesting—and it was only a suggestion, he had no authority to demand it, he said—in that mincing, faggot way of talking, that Jiminez consider resigning. Retiring. It could save everyone a lot of embarrassment and a protracted legal battle. Jiminez said he was busy, he was hoping to make an arrest tonight, and hung up on the mayor.

They had no proof, Raul knew, and weren't likely to find any. The dirt bag who had been found with Bowman's gun didn't know anything. The mayor was just playing politics.

But to be safe, Raul had typed a letter of resignation and carried it in his pocket. If he was going out, he wanted it to be on an upbeat note, a successful finale. The capture of the killer responsible for terrorizing the city would help. Then, when he turned over the ballistics evidence from Bowman's gun, Raul was sure he would get a confession from Lee Bowman.

"Where is she?" Jiminez repeated.

Maloney explained.

Jiminez exploded, "Mother of God, who's running this show, us

316

or Patrick Bowman!"

36

The silence was torment. Her right leg began to cramp and the grit on the floor cut into her knees. She tried to shift her position; one shoe scraped lightly across the floor. To Lee it sounded like a rockslide. She froze. Then turned and looked behind her. The building was at least a hundred fifty yards long, and the far end was in blackness. She thought about moving to a more central location, then decided against it, reasoning that she at least had one of the stairways covered and anyone coming up behind her would have to make some noise.

She looked at the luminous dial of her watch. She had been crouched here less than ten minutes; it seemed like hours. Patrick would surely have missed her by now, if he had returned home. If not . . . she didn't want to think about it.

The camera was a weight in her hand; everything in her life now seemed to be pulling her down, but she knew it was her own doing, even though she had never thought of herself as being self-destructive. If she were going to die, she would be free of guilt, but she didn't want to die. She wasn't ready to die.

She stood up and leaned against the column, trying to rub the cramp from her leg with her free hand when she heard what sounded like someone whispering. She stopped, cradled the camera and listened.

It wasn't the wind, but a kind of rustling sound. She waited, the camera ready, pointing in the direction the sound came from—right at the top of the stairs.

Her breath was raspy. The run had winded her, leaving her unable to breathe properly. She felt a wet, hot pressure against her lungs. Darling crouched down, six steps before the stairs gave onto the top floor of the building. She looked into the blackness below her, straight down to the ground, with no railings to stop a fall.

Darling held the knife in her right hand, using her left to steady her on the stairs as she crawled up one more step. The woman was up here, she had heard her. Just like her sister Roberta, noisy, and asking for trouble in her short skirt.

It had been crazy thinking she could leave here, that she could just walk out of town and back to Philadelphia when Roberta was still here, still tormenting her.

The bitch had even snapped a picture, the flash lighting up the ground, bringing it all back. Darling felt the pressure on her lungs and the pressure against her head, and she couldn't stand it. She wanted to run up the stairs, find the slut and cut her heart out.

Instead, trying to control her breathing, she inched her way up the steps.

Raul Jiminez climbed up the steps to the first floor of the condo, having sent Maloney and Fred to the other end. He figured Bowman had maybe a fifteen-minute head start on them. Raul tried to move through the building as quickly and quietly as he could, sweeping the beam of a flashlight across the first floor without seeing anything except the arc of Maloney's light in the distance.

There was no guarantee that anybody was even in here. Bowman had continually jumped to conclusions in this investigation, successfully getting the focus of the case shifted to bring attention to himself. The letter of resignation Raul was carrying in his pocket was weighted by that shift in focus, and he was damned if he was going to let Bowman steal any more headlines from him.

Raul shut off the flashlight while he climbed up to the second floor.

Patrick paused just before the mid-landing where the stairs made a hundred eighty degree turn before ascending to the third floor. He heard something, a sound that made him think of the hiss and rattle of a snake. He listened intently, but whatever it was had stopped. Cautiously, he stepped up onto the landing and looked to the top of the steps. There was nothing there. He had come across nothing unusual on the floors below; if Lee was in the building, then she had to be up here. Rachel could be holding her hostage, hoping to bargain for her own escape. The other possibility he wasn't yet prepared to contemplate.

He had taken three steps up when there was a brief explosion of light from a strobe and someone screamed.

Patrick held the Browning automatic pointed skyward as he charged up the steps.

The whispered rustle was stronger now, although more

intermittent. Lee remained standing behind the column, waiting. There were now sounds, coming up from the floors below her it seemed, muted but distinct indications of something moving around down there. She remained frozen in place, hardly breathing.

And then she saw it.

Something crawling across the floor in her direction approximately thirty feet away, working its way toward another column. Pausing every few feet in its forward motion. Lee thought of some ancient sea creature that had worked its way onto land, knowing, however, that she was in fact watching the progress of a human; when the crawling shape moved forward more, she could identify the person who had confronted her on the beach less than half an hour ago. More certain than ever that she was staring at Rachel Darling.

She waited, wanting to be as close as possible in order to get the maximum blinding effect from the flash. Lee watched as Rachel, or whoever it was, stood up behind the column a few yards from the one she stood behind.

Lee thought about running, wondering if she could make it to the other end of the building and down the stairs. Someone was there, she could hear them more distinctly now. She took a step back from the column, but as she took a second step she felt her shoe slip on the loose grit that grated beneath her foot.

She heard footsteps then, coming fast across the floor in her direction, and realized that whisper she'd been hearing was her pursuer's labored breath.

Lee turned and waited, trying to judge the distance—then stepped from behind the column, camera up, and hit the shutter release.

In the sudden white flash of light she saw Rachel less than ten feet away, saw the knife in her raised hand and heard her scream.

Lee turned and ran.

Patrick understood. It was the flash; Rachel Darling was frozen in time, a seven-year-old, her mind stilled by the reporter's flash camera; and twenty-seven years later, somehow unlocked, perhaps by another flash. It explained a lot of things that he didn't have time to think about now.

As he came to the top of the stairs he heard two figures running across the floor, their shadows barely discernible.

He shouted: "Lee!" And brought the Browning down, cradling it in both hands, knowing he would get one shot, and only one shot, if he was lucky.

In the same instant he heard someone thundering up the stairs behind him as Lee tripped the flash again, framing Rachel for a second.

In the after second, he fired.

Jiminez reached the mid-stair landing and trapped Patrick, who turned in the beam of his flashlight. "What the hell?" Jiminez demanded.

He charged up the steps, pushing past Patrick, the arc of his light cutting across the floor. Patrick followed. From the opposite end of the building Peachy came running, with Maloney and Fred close behind.

Jiminez swung his light on Lee, who stood leaning against a column near the back edge of the building, staring down at the prone figure of Rachel Darling, whose blood puddled beneath her.

Jiminez approached, knelt down and shined his light into Darling's open, unblinking eyes.

Raul was leaning over her, his free hand touching her face.

Patrick went to Lee. "You all right?" he asked. She stood there nodding, staring up at him.

Bill Peachy, who had come up behind him, suddenly shouted: "Look out!"

Patrick turned. Leaning over Rachel, Jiminez had tipped the flashlight away from her and turned his head, about to speak to Patrick, when Rachel raised the knife, still gripped in her hand extending over her head when she fell.

Jiminez turned back just as the blade slashed across his throat and fell from her hand. Raul had a hand out reaching for the knife, turned once to look at Patrick, then fell beside Rachel Darling.

Patrick raised the Browning, moved in to pick up the knife. He checked Rachel's pulse. She was dead. So was Raul Jiminez.

37

"One of these days," Bill Peachy said, "they'll get this town so clean nobody'll be able to live in it." He paused, waiting, but Patrick didn't say anything. And Peachy said, "You going back to Chicago?"

"Tomorrow," Patrick said.

"And miss the tarpon."

"Leave one for me," Patrick said. He tried to smile, failed, and shook hands with Peachy, who stood on the dock at the marina where Patrick had just rented a boat. Lee was already on board. Patrick stepped aboard, let loose a dock line and eased the boat into the harbor.

They sat in the nineteen-foot boat with its one hundred and fifty horsepower outboard, drifting at the edge of deep water just east of the Marquesas. He wanted her to see the flats, the way the water changed color in the morning light, the raw beauty of these uninhabited islands where the rules were different. Where there were no rules.

He took the Browning from a small bag he'd brought along. Then reached in his pocket and took out the envelope that contained the ballistics report Lt. Neil Maloney had found in a desk drawer in Raul Jiminez's office. Maloney had been promoted to acting chief.

Lee watched him without speaking. Watched as he dropped the

gun into the water and it sank.

It was the first time in his life he had ever suppressed evidence. Patrick said, "It's beautiful out here, but it isn't real."

"No," she said. "I see why you like it."

Patrick handed her the ballistics report.

She took it, read it, then stared down at the water. When she looked up, her eyes were moist. "Why did she do it?"

"Rachel?"

Lee nodded.

"Who knows. Maybe love. I'd like to think so. Something so simple, yet complicated."

Lee was quiet, biting her lower lip. She said, "And you? What are you going to do?"

He took the paper from her and tore it up into small squares, then released them into the breeze.

"I'm going back to Chicago," Patrick said.

Except for the idle of the outboard, there was silence.

"Without me," Lee said.

Patrick didn't say anything.

On the horizon Key West seemed small and insignificant. He had always played by the rules, because all he was and all he could ever hope to be was a cop. Maybe, he thought, he could be a better cop.

The Gideon Lowry Key West Mysteries

Killing Me Softly
Night and Day
Love for Sale
Blue Moon

The Florida Keys Mysteries

Suckerfish
Bounty Hunter Blues
Damaged Goods
Havana Hustle

Also by John Leslie

Hail to the Chief (with Carey Winfrey)
Border Crossing

Made in the USA
Middletown, DE
10 May 2019